ACADEMY OF VAMPIRE HEIRS

DHAMPIRS 101: BOOK ONE

ACADEMY OF VAMPIRE HEIRS:

DHAMPIRS 101

~Book One~

by

GINNA MORAN

SUNNY PALMS PRESS

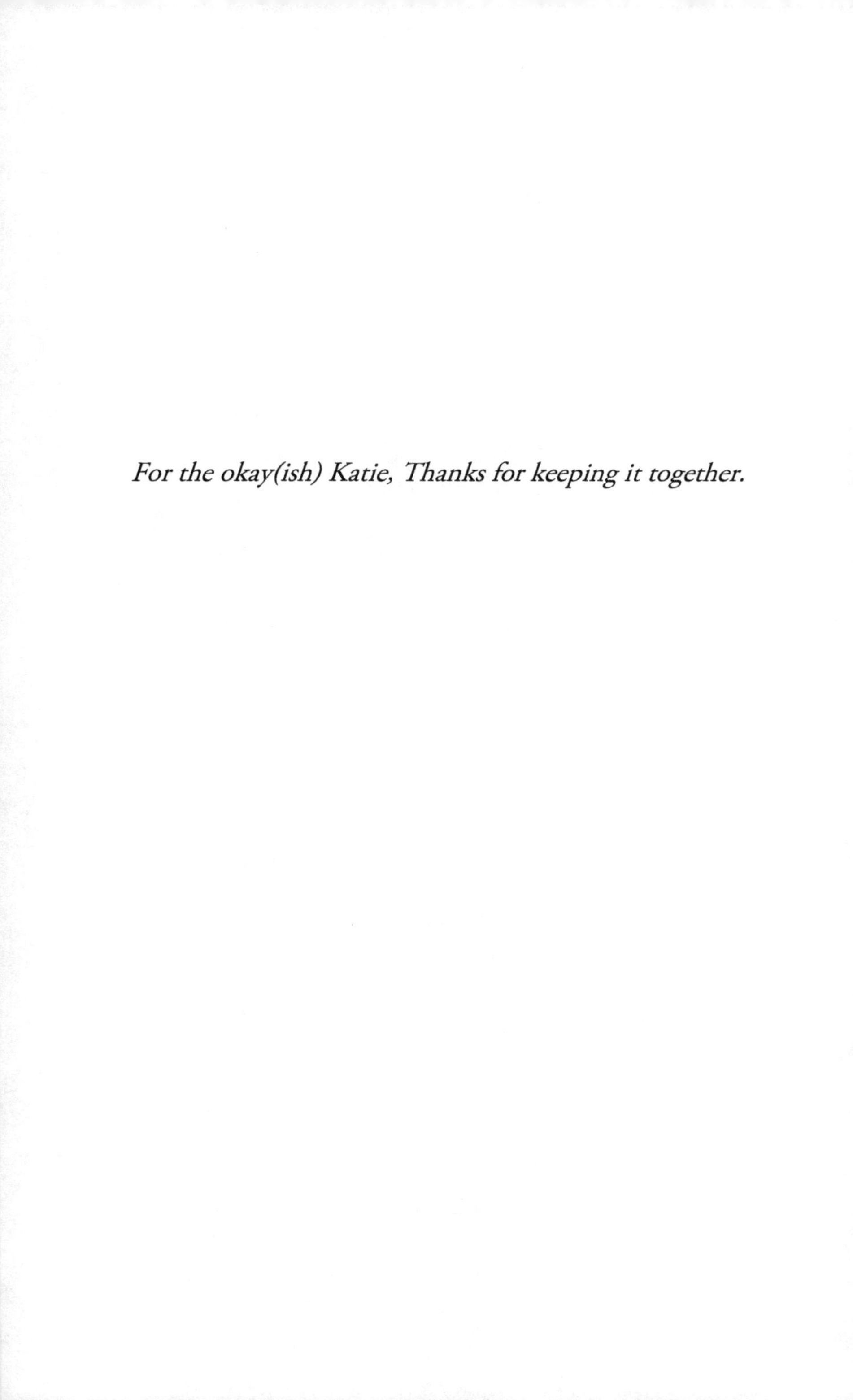

For the okay(ish) Katie, Thanks for keeping it together.

ONE

A DHAMPIR'S DUTY

"MY DUTY? *MY* DUTY? CAN you believe she said that?" I tap my fingers on the dashboard, bouncing my feet. The sun sets on the distant horizon as night descends on the desolate stretch of road that probably hasn't been driven on in years, maybe decades.

Rylie shifts her gaze from the road to look at me. "If my only duty for the next year was to get laid—" Tipping her head back, she releases a loud laugh that lights up the depths of her hazel eyes. "Shit, Fiona. Are you sure you really want to do this? You don't even know what's out there."

I fidget with the seatbelt, yanking and releasing the weathered fabric. "Don't care. What's out there can't be as bad as what's back there."

Frowning, Rylie drums her fingers on the steering wheel, her nerves not doing better than mine, and she's been out here twice before. But me? I have never left the protection of our community. The elders of Mount Light Haven wouldn't risk the life of the only dhampir to have survived to maturity in their care.

"It's worse. There are shadow dwellers everywhere," she says, tightening her mouth.

I flick my tongue across my lip. "Sounds perfect to me."

Rylie groans and shakes her head. "Come on, Fiona. This is serious. Night is coming, and once you open that door and get out, I can't stay. I can't come back."

I let silence fall between us as I think about her words.

"You're my best friend. You know that, right? I know you hate the idea of a union and procreating, but we'll still be together." Rylie's eyes glass over with her words. "I don't want you to die."

"If I go back, I will. You know what they expect of me."

"Things can change."

I unbuckle my seatbelt and swivel in my seat to stare out the window at the stretch of endless landscape, abandoned by humans and vampires during The Divide as everyone was corralled into walled-in cities. Blood Life Corp said it was to keep civility, but the humans who managed to escape knew it was much more than that. Someone has to protect the food source. And now, here I am wanting to enter one of the very cities I was taught to be afraid of. I'm joining the world that the elders say will eventually be the end of me. If a vampire were to find out about my bloodline, about the fact that as a dhampir, I survive on vampire blood, my life would be over. Done. Dead.

"They don't," I say, finally responding to Rylie. "Even leaving won't change things. But now, at least I have a chance. You know the moment I produce an heir, the elders will force me out. They'll expect me to fight back. I don't want that."

I've been told all my life that I'd die by the fangs of a vampire. A death of supposed honor. Fighting for humanity against the shadow dwellers who rule the general population of humans is the fate of a dhampir like me.

Elder Newberry called me a genetic anomaly—a symptomatic carrier of a mutation derived from the venom of a vampire—and the other Blood Rebels of the resistance against vampires declared me a gift to humanity. My great-great-great-grandmother was supposedly bitten while she was pregnant during the horrifying years of the Vampire Uprising that decimated the back-world. And up until my birth, the Flamme bloodline contained all male carriers. No one knows why or how, but the mutation chose to show symptoms in me.

"Fiona...if you can help, why wouldn't you want to? You can take Alder up on his proposal. I overheard him talking to Elder Newberry about training to be your handler."

I huff a breath. "That's exactly why I have to do this. Alder doesn't actually want a life with me. He wants to use me to gain status. I doubt that guy can even get me what I need. I asked him to bring me my blood source last week, and he didn't even step one foot into the bunker before saying he was late for training."

Her mouth drops open. "What? Seriously?"

I nod. "Like I said, he couldn't handle my needs."

"Too bad I couldn't be your handler." Rylie pouts her full bottom lip.

"I might've decided to stay if you—"

Something rams into the side of the SUV, shattering the rear window. Rylie screams, gripping the wheel, but the force of whatever hit us sends our SUV spinning across the uneven pavement. I fly out of my seat and onto Rylie, hitting my head hard on her window. Stars burst in my vision and my right eye blurs.

"Fuck. Fuck. Fuck," Rylie says, the world finally jerking to a halt. "The sun went down. I misjudged our timing."

She shoves me back into my seat and tries to stomp the

throttle. The tires spin, sending dirt through the air, but the SUV doesn't jolt forward. I twist in my seat and catch sight of two silver flashing eyes. A filthy, mud-covered vampire grips onto the rear, using his superhuman strength to stop our SUV from moving. Rylie doesn't give up, smacking her hands on the steering wheel, begging the SUV to go.

Taking a breath, I bend down and feel the floor for a silver stake, the only weapon I could find to take with me from home. No one leaves the guns unattended, and I thought the massive, sharp, dagger-like weapon would do better than one of the dull kitchen knives I use to help prep food in the dining hall. My hands comb through my small pile of clothes and toiletries until my fingers brush against cool metal.

Rylie doesn't have a chance to say anything as I fling the door open, praying the vampire doesn't suddenly let go of our vehicle. I blink through the haze created by the cloud of dirt and burning rubber and manage to stumble out of the SUV without eating shit on the ground.

I swing my arm out, slicing the air around me with the stake. Nothing attacks, but my fear instincts, born from the part of me that is human, want me to fight just to be safe.

No human can outmatch a vampire in strength and speed. The only thing that keeps rebels alive is the ability to predict moves and catch the assholes off guard. I've never fought a vampire in my life, and I just pray my training is enough to get Rylie and me out of this alive.

Covering my mouth with my shirt, I risk running around the hood of the SUV. I brace to get plowed down, but I can't sneak up on the vampire unless I go a way he won't expect. In this moment, I'm more brave than smart, going against my good sense.

Rylie jerks her attention to me, her wide eyes screaming at me to run without saying the words. It's in her training, and also in the rest of our colony's training, to protect me first. That's why the elders want to assign me a handler, especially for when they decide to kick me out into the world. I bet they never expected I'd leave by my own free will like this.

I motion for Rylie to honk the horn, something that goes against everything we know about surviving. Under Blood Life Corp law, humans are forbidden from driving. And back-world cars like the one Rylie stole from a soldier? They've been banned for decades. Our colony scavenged everything our vehicles need from abandoned cities. They've been passed down and taken care of for years. But they're loud as hell. Vampire magnets. Blaring the horn might bring dozens running toward us. But I need this. I need her to block out any noise I might make. It might also surprise the vampire and slow him down because of his super hearing.

Rylie doesn't listen to me right away, and I scowl and motion to her again. Squeezing her eyes shut, she pounds her hand into the steering wheel, honking the horn. The loud noise echoes through the night. The SUV barrels forward, speeding away without me. And hell. This was not what I wanted. Stupid vampire.

I rush toward the spot where a figure stands among the haze. The vampire sees me and disappears too fast for my eyes to follow. Dropping to the ground, I roll a few feet to lie on my back. I tighten my mouth to stop from gasping, clutching my stake until my fingers throb.

A heavy boot lands on my wrist before I have a chance to react. Pain swells up my arm, and I automatically release my weapon. A disgusting man, covered in grime, stands over me. He releases a low growl that stiffens every muscle on my body.

"If you don't fight, I won't kill you," the vampire says.

I stare at his mouth in confusion. The vampire only has one visible fang peeking out from beneath his lips. I've never seen such a sight. The three blood sources that live in Mount Light Haven never even show theirs except to me and not in a threatening way. I've been sneaking extra blood from them for two years now because the allotted amount the elders enforce isn't enough anymore—so my blood for theirs is just how it is. Their willingness was one of the factors that pushed me into leaving. I know I can survive among vampires if I just give a little to get a little. At least I hope.

The vampire takes my silence as compliance. "Good."

I remain utterly still and quiet. I know if I don't fight

right away, he won't give me my final donation. He'll try to bite me and drink what he wants. If I'm lucky, he'll try to take me to wherever the fuck he stays during the day—and from the looks of the dried mud, it must be somewhere outside. Probably in the shade. A vampire's light sensitivity gives them massive burns if they're in sunlight for more than a few seconds, but the shade does protect them somewhat. I hear it's hot as hell for them, though.

If that's the case, all I have to do is survive the night. There is no way this blood sucker will be able to keep me all day.

Grabbing my hand, the vampire launches me to my feet, tossing me a foot into the air so that I have to steady myself on him to get my footing. My skin crawls as I look into his eyes. The gesture goes against everything inside me, knowing that vampires can lock me in a gaze I can't escape to manipulate my mind—that is, if I hadn't just consumed way over my normal amount of vampire blood before leaving.

The biggest benefit of drinking vampire blood is that it stops the effect of mind manipulation while it's in the system, which lasts a few hours. Second, it offers some regenerative qualities to help a human heal. And of course for me, it helps me survive like human blood helps a vampire. It takes a special kind of vampire to give up that kind of power, so I know when I reach the city, it's the first thing I'll do, no matter what it takes.

"That's it, pretty donor. Don't look away." The vampire hooks his hand around my waist, holding me as I purposely slacken in his arms. I hope he can't tell that I'm faking it. I've practiced the technique of pretending to be mind manipulated a few times, but I didn't take it seriously. Now, I wish I had.

Bright lights flash in my eyes, engulfing us in the headlights of the SUV. Rylie honks the horn, and the vampire lifts me off my feet and spins me away.

"Don't move," he commands, dropping me to the ground.

The vampire disappears, leaving me in the dirt. I risk him noticing that he didn't actually manipulate my mind to do what he asked and prop up on my elbows. I spot Rylie turning the SUV around a few hundred feet away. I can't see the vampire yet, but I know that's exactly where he'll head.

Rylie honks the horn, the noise an incessant tune that steals any other sounds around. She navigates over the rough, compacted dirt in my direction. The closer she can get, the better off we'll be. Two humans against one vampire have a better chance to live.

The vampire materializes between me and the SUV, and he prepares to jump. Instead of rushing out of the way, he launches into the air and lands on the hood. Rylie slams the brakes, sending him falling in front of the SUV. She runs over the guy, and a loud noise rips through the air.

The SUV slows to a stop. I spot the vampire behind the vehicle holding what looks like a long metal tube. It's now that I realize Rylie didn't stop the SUV on purpose.

"Hey, asshole!" I yell, waving my hands in the air. "What are you doing? You can't expect me to wait around for you."

The vampire jerks his attention to me, his eyes flashing silver. He glances at Rylie in the SUV and to me, choosing to hunt the easier of the two of us. I brace to get my throat ripped out with no chance of defending myself, especially since the guy is now pissed the hell off. Instead of charging me, he strolls at a human's pace, taunting me, savoring the fear being stalked by a predator elicits inside me.

I lick my lips, suppressing my human rationale. Because even though my mind screams to run, a darker, more feral part awakens inside me. My dhampir half triggers me and usually takes over when I'm hungry or scared, and my deep-seated nature steels me in place. I might be the only person in existence who will bite back.

"Go on, pretty donor. Make a run for it. If you get at least twenty feet away, I might not kill you." The vampire flashes his single fang.

Tipping my head back, I can't control the nervous laugh bubbling from my throat. I know it's a terrible idea to comment on a vampire's appearance—I mean, I wouldn't be rude like this to anyone in Mount Light Haven, but stalker creeps do not deserve kindness.

"How am I supposed to take you seriously with one fucking fang?" My shoulders shake, my voice rising through the air.

Ah, hell. I really pissed him off now.

A deep, guttural growl escapes his throat, and he curls his fingers into fists. He picks up his speed a bit without moving so fast that I can't see him. He wants me to see him, to know that my possible death will come at any second. I dig my fingers into my palms, struggling to keep my shit together.

Movement behind the vampire catches my attention, and I try not to react to Rylie exiting the SUV. I do the only thing I can think of to muffle her footsteps and scream out as loud as I possibly can. The vampire's scowl shifts into annoyance like how dare I cause such a racket to ruin his hunt.

But it works.

Raising her gun, Rylie aims it at the vampire's back. I drop to the ground and cover my head with my hands as she opens fire. Loud pops pierce my ears, and I tilt my head up to watch the vampire startle. Bullets might not kill him, but if he's injured enough, it'll slow him down. Blood loss weakens a vampire and gives us an advantage. Unfortunately, it's the donor who shoots that ends up dead first.

Fuck if I'm going to let that happen. Rylie is only here because of me.

Launching to my feet, I charge the vampire. He directs

his full attention to Rylie as she unloads her gun on him until she runs out of bullets. He disappears from in front of me and materializes behind her, not giving her a chance to reload her gun.

"Rylie!" I yell, pushing my feet to get a move on it.

The vampire grabs Rylie from behind, and she thrashes, doing everything she can to break free. Bending her head, the vampire exposes Rylie's neck. She yells and jerks her head, managing to head-butt the asshole in the nose.

He roars, locking his fingers into her hair. Before I can reach her, the vampire pierces her neck, and she releases an angry yell, dropping a dozen F-bombs. The vampire drops her on my approach. I dive to the ground, spinning midair to land on my back, knowing he'll use the same move to get behind me. I kick my foot into his knee, buckling his leg long enough to sweep his feet out from under him. He hits the ground in surprise, and I don't give him a chance to get up.

I straddle his waist and lace my fingers around his throat. He doesn't even attempt to fight me. Any normal human without a weapon could never kill a vampire. But I'm not a normal human. I'm stronger, faster. My dhampir mutation gives me some vampiric traits without the annoyance of light sensitivity.

Grabbing the hem of his shirt, I surprise him by yanking it over his head. This vampire is scrawnier than the three blood sources back at the colony. He's probably so aggressive because he's hungry. I know the feeling. Blood hunger legitimately can drive me wild in a bad way. These are the kind of vampires I hate, but from what I know from growing up in Mount Light Haven is that they're far less dangerous than those who run the world—the ones who don't act like the starving monsters of the night.

Pushing my thoughts away, I search over his chest and stomach, ravaged from the bullets Rylie shot at him. I trace my finger around a hole a few inches below his ribs. It's not the ideal spot, but I don't know how else to do this. I don't think I can summon enough strength to shatter his sternum, so I'm going to have to literally get all up in him.

"What are you doing?" the vampire asks, not even fighting. He doesn't see me as a threat.

"What does it look like?" I ask, tightening my fingers together.

"If you think this will stop me from ripping out your throat...you might be right." His low voice creeps me the hell out.

"I know I'm right. I once had a blood source tell me I was irresistible. He could never tell me no."

"You've been claimed?" he asks, trying to tug the shirt off his head.

"No one claims me."

From my own experience, I know that blood hunger can also trigger blood lust. And I bet this guy hasn't been near a female in who knows how long. Males—both vampire and human—outnumber females by quite a lot. It's one of the reasons the elders protect women so fiercely. Also why we're so coveted in the city. Blood Life Corp can't expand the donor population without us. I'm nearly certain the only reason we're not all in cages is because humans still have a lot of fight. Giving the donors a sense of control and freedom keeps the peace. At least, that's what I've been taught.

"I'll claim you now—"

Jabbing my fingers into the bloody wound, I cringe as I feel the vampire's insides. I don't know exactly what I'm feeling for, so I twist and turn my hand, making him holler.

"Prop him up," Rylie commands, coming up to me.

"I thought you would've run. You need to run," I say while pulling him against me to hold him tight, his shirt over his face stopping him from biting.

The vampire suddenly stills in my arms, his dead weight knocking me on my back. Rylie groans at me from above, both her hands covered in blood. In one hand, she clutches a dagger. In the other, she squeezes the vampire's bloody heart. She releases it, and it splats in the dirt a couple of feet away. Removing a vampire's heart or cutting off its head is the only sure way to kill one. If not, they regenerate.

"Where exactly am I going to go?" Rylie asks me, wiping her hands on her pants, her question coming late. "The fucker ripped out the driveshaft. The SUV is done. It'll be safer to stay together and continue on to the city. Maybe I can find someone to help me get back to Mount Light Haven."

Pushing to my feet, I meet her gaze for a second before throwing my arms around her. "You saved my life, you know. I'll make sure you get home."

She releases a breath and pulls back. "You better. Look at my damn neck."

I shift her light brown hair away and cover my hand with my mouth. "Oh, shit. That's so—"

"Pathetic, right? One little hole. He barely even drank anything." She shakes her head and finally smiles at me, the whole shock of the situation making the both of us laugh.

I motion to the dead vampire on the ground. "I know how to make you better faster." Bending down, I jab my finger into his bloody stomach and then pop it in my mouth. I've tasted far better blood, but in times like these, a woman's gotta work with what she's got.

"Eff that shit," Rylie says, scrunching her nose. "He's all yours."

I hold out my hand to her. "Come on. Maybe there will be someone you might like in the city."

TWO

BITE BACK

THE CITY OF NOCTURNAL CROWN swallows the dark night unlike anything I've ever seen. A light haze glows from the towering wall, lit up to stop anyone from attempting to sneak in unnoticed. Digging in my backpack, I tug out the small ID tag I stole from a visiting soldier the elders thought I might be interested in. I turned him down like the other six who "happened" to stop by in the last week.

"Okay, so our story is that we were attacked and our mister was killed. You lost your tag in the fight," I say, reading over the name Blair Hughes etched into the metal plate to be worn around the neck.

Rylie inhales and exhales a few deep breaths. "They're never going to believe it."

I twist my lips. "Uh, let me do the talking then. You're in shock."

"I'm not in shock. I'm angry that a stupid shadow dweller broke the damn SUV and now I might die here." She closes her eyes, trying her best to stay in control. "I will not be a donor. I won't. I'd rather die."

I whack her in the arm. "Shut up and don't talk like that. I swear I'll get you home, so don't go rushing in with a death wish."

Heaving another breath, Rylie turns her gaze to me. "I'm sorry, Fiona. I trust you. I'm just...so not ready for this."

"It's a good thing I am." I lace my hand around her wrist and tug her arm. "Now, come on. Let me handle getting us in. I'll do what I have to so they don't register you. Promise."

"Even if it means letting the guard bite you?" she asks, raising her eyebrow.

I shrug. "Wouldn't be my first bite."

"Fiona." Her eyes widen at my revelation, and I blush like crazy.

Had the elders known I was sneaking to visit the blood sources, they'd have relocated them somewhere else. Because allowing a vampire to bite me is forbidden. They're not only charming as hell, but they're possessive. Give a little, and they'll keep wanting more. If they put a claim on someone, that's practically a death sentence. Even the heads of Blood Life Corp know that. It's why they have humans donate to a general pool that gets mixed and divided. Only the wealthiest, most powerful vampires can acquire a personal donor, according to one of the soldiers I denied.

I laugh off her concern. "What? It's not so bad."

"Not so bad?" Rylie's voice rises. "One-tooth hurt like hell."

"Because he didn't like you." I try to remain expressionless.

She groans. "You are something el—"

A bright light flashes over us, blinding me for a second while cutting Rylie's comment off. She automatically grips my hand, tugging me so close that our bodies touch. Our footsteps remain in sync, and we continue to stroll together with our heads bowed.

"It's past curfew," a deep, sultry voice says from somewhere behind the wall of light. "Show me your night passes."

A blip of fear trickles through me, and I tilt my head up and shield my eyes. The light clicks off. Darkness steals my vision, making me pause in my tracks. Rylie rubs her arm over her eyes, trying not to get dried blood on her face. We both look like hell. I'm surprised the guard asked for a pass instead of interrogating us about the vampire blood staining our skin and clothes. The dark ruby hue proves it's not human.

I clear my throat. "We don't have one."

My muscles stiffen at the approach of soft footsteps. A vampire in all black, carrying a huge gun unlike anything I've ever seen, steps from a guard house stationed outside an arched, gated tunnel that leads into the city. He stops a few feet away and drinks us in, probably looking for weapons. I left my stake behind because I know if I'm caught with it, they'll know we've come from rebel lands. If I were alone and clean, I'd have chanced sneaking it in. But now? No. Not worth it.

"Are you armed?" the vampire asks, crossing his arms over his broad chest.

I stare at him for a moment, trying to assess if he's the type that I can persuade. His flat brown eyes waver, trailing lower to check out my boobs. I try not to react to being obviously ogled and instead use it to my advantage and straighten my shoulders.

"We have a knife we took from our mister," I say, opening my bag for him to inspect.

The subtle click of the guard's fangs extending sounds in my ears.

My heartbeat picks up speed. "We didn't have a choice. We were attacked a few miles south. Our mister was lost—beheaded." I motion to Rylie. "She was bitten."

I pucker my lips in a pout and squint, trying to force

tears to fill my eyes. It doesn't work, so I tip my head down and whimper. "We were so scared. Had our mister not injured our attacker, we'd both be dead." I sniffle for good measure.

I peek up through my lashes and watch the vampire pull out an electronic device from his pocket. It's far superior to anything we had in Mount Light Haven, most of our stuff straight from the back-world when humans still controlled the world.

The vampire taps the screen with his finger, the glow lighting up his face and sharpening his narrow nose and thin lips even more. "Do you have your tags?"

Nodding, I hand over the metal chain. "Just me. The vampire ripped hers off her neck."

I shift on my feet, nerves getting the best of me as the guy enters in my information into his com device. Keeping my gaze trained on the wall, I watch him in my peripheral vision. He remains expressionless, not giving anything away.

One second the guy stands in front of me and in the next, he yanks me away from Rylie and presses my back into the wall. His eyes flash silver, and I realize that something must've gone wrong with the information. I glance at Rylie and shake my head so she doesn't do anything that could get the both of us killed.

"Look at me," the guard says, pinching my chin.

I do as he says and meet his dark gaze.

"You will not look away while I ask you some questions." He leans in a bit closer until we're sharing the same breathing air. Strangely, he smells of fruit. Oranges. His closeness does nothing good to my dhampir side as he attempts to manipulate my mind.

I force myself to slacken in his arms while he props me against the wall. I don't try to speak. He didn't ask me a question. If I even so much as breathe a word, he'll know I consumed blood. I made sure there wasn't any on my face when we abandoned the car.

"The tag you have states you're a male donor, twenty-nine, with blond hair and blue eyes," he says, answering my silent question about why he's doing this. "You are not Blair Hughes, are you now?"

"No." I keep my voice low.

"Who is Blair?" His eyes flash silver again.

"My brother." I pray with everything in me that whoever Blair was before the soldier stole his tag actually had a sister. It's highly unlikely, but maybe the universe will be in my favor for once.

The vampire growls. "Blair Hughes has no known siblings in the system. Why is that?"

Ah, hell. I remain placid, a dozen thoughts swirling through my mind. I need the perfect response or he'll know I'm not under his manipulation. He obviously thinks he's the shit at controlling humans if he doesn't suspect it already.

"My mister didn't want to register me." I brace myself

for his reaction, half expecting him to bite me.

"Because you're female," he responds, his eyes searching mine.

I don't respond.

"Does the same go for her?" he asks, referring to Rylie.

I've never been so relieved in someone's assumption of me. "Yes."

Breaking his stare, the vampire releases me from his attempt at mind manipulation. He combs his fingers through his short hair and taps a few things into his com device. I flick my gaze to Rylie, who looks ready to bolt at any second. It takes everything in me not to rush to her to grab her hand just in case.

The vampire's com device beeps and out shoots two slips of paper. He closes the space and hands them both to me. "Deliver these to the head of your daylight staff. They'll inform the Rockfords of the notice to register you two. If they fail to comply in seven days, you will be removed."

"What would happen then?" I know better than to ask, but I can't help myself. All of this is new to me. I don't know what a vampire's staff even does apart from providing blood. I'm also not familiar with the majority of Blood Life Corp law.

"You'll either be placed in the donor population or in another vampire household. But I doubt the Rockfords will let two females go so easily and will pay their fines." Wow. I can't believe he answered me or that he tries to reassure me that nothing will probably happen if I were actually to go to the house of whoever the Rockford Coven is.

It's enough to make me nod and grin. Because we're getting in. It's really happening. "Thank you," I say.

He nods and graces me with a smile. "You two should get going. Your temporary night passes expire in twenty minutes."

With a grin, I rush to Rylie and drag her through the open gate. Excitement pours through me, pushing away all of the fear and annoyance caused by Mr. One Fang. The second we exit the short tunnel, I freeze in my tracks and stare at a huge glowing map of the city. This place is a lot bigger than I thought. And holy shit. There are vampires everywhere.

Rylie smacks my shoulder, drawing my attention to her. "Stop smiling. You look too approachable."

I fake-glare at her. "I'm sorry if I'm happy we weren't drained upon arrival."

"The night's not over yet." Pulling me with her, Rylie approaches the huge map and studies it for a second. She taps her finger on the screen to bring up a directory that gives me information overload. I can't believe how easy they make it to find anything I can think of—from vampires to humans, stores, health centers, and even restricted, vampire-only zones.

Rylie touches a glowing square. "This will be our best option."

I read over the information that pops up on a bubble. "Tower B? You want to go to donor housing?"

"Where else will I find..." She lets her voice trail off and looks around. A dozen vampires watch and listen.

I shift nervously. "Yeah, okay. We'll head that way."

Staying together, we walk in the direction of a towering building we can see even from here. It glows with blue light like a beacon to attract every damn shadow dweller in the city to it. Of course, the fact that it's a human-only building is probably enough of a draw on its own that I'm sure hundreds of vampire stalk about in hopes to sneak a bite.

"This is so creepy," Rylie whispers, pressing her lips into a thin line. "Everything seems so normal."

I glance at her. "Right? I don't know what the elders are so—"

Blinding headlights flash over us, and I spin to see a sleek, silver car speed around the corner. It barrels right toward us. Rylie jerks my arm, yanking me out of the way. The driver wasn't even going to stop.

Anger bursts through me. "You asshole!"

The car screeches to a halt a block away. What the hell? The tires spin, sending smoke through the air as the driver puts the car in reverse and stomps the throttle. Rylie gawks at me with wide eyes. Helping her to her feet, I pull her with me to run down the nearest alley. I had no idea that a vampire could hear me call him an asshole from within a speeding car.

A car door slams, but I don't look behind me. I race deeper into the long alley with Rylie, my fear instincts screaming like crazy. The panic burns through me so intensely that it takes everything inside me not to shriek.

"Show me your fucking night passes," a deep, guttural voice says.

A hot as hell vampire materializes in front of us, blocking our way. I can't get my feet to slow as fast as Rylie does, and I let go of her hand and stumble right at the vampire. Like a true asshole, he steps out of my way. I hit the pavement hard, scraping my hands on the ground. Rylie covers her mouth to stop from making any noise.

I can't help it. "Damn it. Fuck. You ass. I'm going t—"

The world blurs and I hit my back on the wall, my string of profanity knocking from my mouth with the rest of the air in my lungs. The vampire glowers at me, tilting his head to the side. His bright blue eyes freeze my insides. I thought the guard's gaze was bad. It's nothing compared to whoever this guy is.

"Your night pass," he says, finally letting me go. "Now."

I drop to my feet and nearly fall again. Slowly shifting my hand, I reach into the front pocket of my jacket and withdraw the folded pieces of paper. I cringe at the sight of my trembling hand. My body needs to get its act together. I'm not even scared.

He hums under his breath. "You're unregistered."

"Not for long," I mutter, risking looking up at him. "The security guard says we have seven days for our household to file."

"Unless you never make it back. I find you quite...delectable, Ms. Rockford." The allure of his voice does something funny to my insides. I should be freaked out, but his words sound like the best idea ever. Because damn it, he's hot.

"Call me Fiona," I murmur, my voice softening.

For the first time since he abandoned his car does he smile. And holy shit does it make him even more attractive.

"Fiona," he says, stepping closer. "You don't actually want to return to a household who cares so little about you that they refused even to register you, now do you?"

"Nope." I release a breath at my response.

So does he. "Would you like to come with me?"

Hell yeah.

I don't get the chance to respond when I hear a car door slam. The vampire snarls and jerks his attention to the street behind us. I stare in shock as the guy's car zooms past the alley. Dread drips down my spine as I realize I'm alone with the guy. Rylie isn't here. And if Rylie's not here...

"Shit. Someone kidnapped my friend," I say, dashing toward the street.

Strong arms hook around my waist, lifting me up. The world blurs so quickly that I don't have the chance to orient myself. The guy shifts me onto his shoulder, carrying me like I weigh nothing.

"That bitch stole my car," he says, growling.

I tense at his words. "What?"

The world stops as headlights engulf us. The vampire roars and throws me forward. I screech, my body flying through the air. Tires squeal, and I brace for a helluva lot of pain. The ground flies at me at a speed I'm not sure I'll even survive. And if I do, I doubt I'll live through Rylie running me over with the vampire's car.

A figure materializes beneath me, catching me and darting out of the way of Rylie. I flail as a big hand presses into the back of my head, forcing my face into the hard chest of someone seemingly twice my size.

"Easy now, little bird. I got you," a sultry voice says.

"She's mine," the other vampire, the one who was driving the car, says. "Put her down before I gut you."

"Finders keepers, Culver. You have that one," the guy says, shifting me in his arms. "She seems more your type anyway. Probably O positive."

Rylie screams, and I jerk my neck and head-butt the vampire holding me. He drops me to the ground with a growl.

"Shit, I'm definitely keeping this one. AB negative for sure." The guy strolls around me. "Look at that hair. What color is it, love? Purple? You like attention, don't you? Want to stand out compared to the gen. pop.? Either way, I like it. You should wear it up, though."

This. Guy.

"Fiona, help!" Rylie says, struggling to break out of Culver's hold.

I hadn't realized I couldn't take my gaze off the even hotter vampire. His seriously muscular body flexes with his movements.

Rylie digs her fingers into Culver's wrists, scratching him hard enough that red lines appear on his arms. "Fiona, get it together!"

All Culver does is laugh. "Feisty, aren't they, Hudson?"

The guy, Hudson, continues to stand over me, drinking in every inch of my body. "What do you want to do with them?"

Fear grips my heart as Culver responds to Hudson with a smile, his fangs flashing dangerously close to Rylie's neck. She squeezes her eyes shut and braces for the bite she thinks will come. It's enough to push me to get my ass in gear, and I catapult to my feet. Hudson doesn't even try to stop me as I collide into Culver and Rylie. Culver releases her with a growl, and I bend down and sink my teeth hard into his throat.

"Whoa, shit," Hudson says, releasing a laugh. "Look at her go. How does it feel being her donor, brother?"

Culver locks his fingers into my hair, yanking me so hard that I accidentally rip his flesh. "Get her off me, you shithead."

I manage to spit in Culver's face before Hudson grabs

me from under the arms and drags me back. Culver rushes us and gets in my face. His eyes blink crazy silver with an expression I can only assume looks like murder on his mind, stealing away everything I thought was hot about him.

"Put her in the trunk," he says, snapping his teeth in my face. "We gotta go. Patrol is coming."

Hudson dangles me in front of him as he races to the car. Culver beats us there and pops the trunk open, forcing Rylie inside first. I yell, flailing, trying to fight the best I can.

But it's no use.

All I can do is shout one more time before the trunk clicks closed.

THREE

THE KINGS

"RYLIE, ARE YOU HURT?" I whisper as softly as I can into her ear.

Music blasts from inside the car loud enough to silence any noise we can make. These assholes plan to perform our final donations. I know it. If they wanted just to bite, they'd have done so in the alley.

"Rylie?" I ask louder at her lack of response.

She doesn't respond to me, her silence freaking me out. Licking my finger, I feel her face for her nose and hold my hand in front of her nostrils. My finger cools with her breath. Relief floods through me. I don't know what I'd have done if she weren't alive.

Propping up on my elbow, I shake her shoulder as hard as I can. "Snap out of it. Come on. You can do it."

I wish she'd have relented and drunk Mr. One Fang's blood when I suggested it. Had she just done it, Culver wouldn't have been able to silence her with mind manipulation.

"I'm so sorry," I say, deciding not to keep my voice low. What's the point if the vampires hear me? It's not like I'm going anywhere. "I don't know what else to do. This might hurt."

Pulling my arm back, I swing it at Rylie and punch her in the boob. She doesn't react to my attempt to break her mind manipulation with pain, so I try again. Harder this time. Something cracks under my hand, and Rylie screams out and slaps me across the face.

I touch my stinging cheek, tears welling in my eyes at the force. "Shit."

Rylie groans and flops back. "I think you broke my rib."

"I'm sorry." I reach to her, feeling for her hand.

Anger laces her voice, and she tugs her hand free of mine. "Don't. I'd rather have a broken rib than experience that mind manipulation hell again."

"I'm going to kill them, I swear," I say, shifting to prop myself up again.

"Doubt it," she mutters. "We're already dead, Fiona. There is no way they'll keep us alive. I stole the asshole's car. You bit him. It's over."

I puff a breath of air through my lips. I want to argue with her that it's not over until we're actually dead, but instead I ask, "Why did you steal his car, anyway? You were just going to abandon me like that?"

She doesn't respond right away, her heavy silence speaking volumes. She doesn't want to admit it, but that was her plan. Steal the car and haul ass while I was distracting Culver. I shouldn't be so hurt, because it's something she should've done. I'd deserve it. It's my fault we're in this mess. My desire to leave Mount Light Haven turned me into the shittiest friend ever.

"You know what? Don't answer that. I don't care," I say, lowering my voice. "I wish you had gotten away. I'd die if it means you get to escape."

A soft sob escapes Rylie's lips, and I reach out and try to take her hand again. This time she allows me, pulling me by the arm until I'm close enough for her to hug. She buries her face into my neck, doing her best to suppress the panic turning her into a mess. I've never seen her cry like this before. We were scolded all our lives if we dare cry over something. So it's so weird to see her like this now. I want to tell her to knock it off, but I don't.

"You're going to be fine." My words only make her cry harder.

She gasps a few short breaths. "I'm not. You're not. This is it."

Annoyance whips through me, and I flick her on the shoulder. "Knock that shit off. You can't give up already. What would the elders think? Or all of those soldiers vying for you to agree to pick one of them for a union so they can sex you the hell up?"

Releasing a squeal of a laugh, she whacks my arm, finally managing to get her crying to stop. "That's all you."

"Maybe they're coming after us." I try not to frown as I say the words. I mean, for Rylie's sake, I do hope they attempt to find us. I shouldn't be worried about if they do. But something inside me screams at even the idea of ever having to return to Mount Light Haven. Who knew that being in this trunk is far less a scary thought to me?

At least in here, I still have a fighting chance. If I were to go back to the rebel colony, they'd never allow me to leave my room again.

"Not us. You. They'd be coming after you." Her soft voice digs into me, and I can't stop the fury from awakening in my very being.

"Screw that. We're not going to die, nor am I going back to Mount Light Haven." I roll on my opposite side and bang my hands into the side of the trunk, trying to get it to pop open. "We're going to get out of here, and I'll find you a way home and me a place to live."

"Fiona," Rylie says softly.

"Don't *Fiona* me. Just believe me. I can do this."

She reaches out and digs her fingers into my leg. "No, I know. If anyone can, it's you. But listen." Cupping her hand over my lips, she silences me before I can open my mouth. "We stopped."

Shit. Shit. Shit.

She's right.

Closing my eyes, I try to listen past the blaring music. Muffled voices trickle through to me, and I bang my fists on the trunk again. They don't make cars like they used to in the back-world. This bullet-like vehicle is quiet as hell, odorless, and basically like a prison in the trunk with no levers to release the hatch. I can't even pull out the panel to try to shove my hand through the tail light, not like that will do me any good.

The music clicks off, leaving my ears ringing. Rylie tightens her hold on me, trying to roll me closer to her. If one of us gets taken out, we're both getting taken out. I don't think these vampires realize what the strength of desperation does. Rylie even hooks her legs around me to ensure it.

"Are you kidding me, Culver," an unfamiliar voice says loud enough for me to hear clearly. "You took two unregistered donors from Nocturnal Crown?"

"Headmistress Rasmussen will flip her shit and pull you from the running of region leader," another, softer, smoother masculine voice says. "You selfish bastard."

Culver growls, his scary predatory noise forever imprinted in my head. I'm sure I could pick him out from anywhere now. "Nocturnal Crown is ours. Unregistered donors are ours. And these two? They're mine. They broke Blood Life Corp law. It's in my right to do as I see fit, and I feel like performing a couple of final donations. If any of you has a problem, get the hell out of here. Just don't forget that I'll remember this when it comes time to fill the region's positions. As head of our coven, I'll cast you shitheads to the shadows."

Damn. For a second, I had hope.

A different growl cuts through the air, sending a chill through me. "That kind of attitude will get you challenged by another coven head, brother. If someone finds out that two unregistered donors got to you enough that you lost your cool to think about the general population, they'll consider you weak. Just think about it. Killing these donors isn't worth losing our good standing. Our coven is under the board's scrutiny. This isn't Stargazer Hills. We're training for power. A new region. We won't get an opportunity like this again."

"Not to mention the little bird is hot as fuck. Feisty. Look at that bite mark she gave you. Mmm. I wish it were me." Hudson releases a strange-ass noise from his throat.

My body decides it enjoys the hell out of the sexy sound, and I shiver, rubbing the goosebumps prickling over my arms. What is wrong with me? These assholes are debating whether or not we should live or die, and I'm lying here turned the hell on.

"It's going to be you next!" Rylie's voice startles me, her anger getting the best of her. "Fiona will devour all of you."

I don't get a chance to react before the trunk suddenly pops open. Without hesitating, I jump up and launch at the nearest vampire. He catches me in his arms with a surprised grunt but somehow manages not to drop me.

"Watch your neck, Aspen," the other unfamiliar vampire says.

The vampire, Aspen, shifts to dangle me out in front of him like a rabid animal. I snap my teeth and swing my legs. The other unfamiliar vampire takes me from Aspen and stretches his neck away, though he doesn't take his dark eyes off me. I tighten my legs around his waist, refusing to let him hold me away. Because he was right to warn Aspen. I'm now going to bite the hell out of this guy.

The vampire breathes a breath in my ear. "Please, miss. Don't bite me. If you bite me, I'm handing you right back to Culver, and I'd prefer not to."

His words are enough to stop me from ravaging the hell out of his throat. I don't think I've ever been asked anything so nicely.

"Fiona!" Rylie screams, her voice sending panic crashing through me. "Help! Do something!"

I twist in the guy's arms to peer behind me. Culver presses Rylie into the door of the car, forcing her neck to the side to expose her skin. I tense at the sight of his fangs extending longer than I thought possible. He's going to kill her. I know it. It'll be a kill bite.

None of the other vampires move, just standing by and watching this asshole.

"Please," I beg the vampire holding me. "You have to stop him. She doesn't deserve this. We weren't doing anything wrong when he cornered us."

The guy doesn't respond to me.

"Culver, stop! Stop! Kill me. Kill me instead. Please, I'll do anything. Just let her go." I smack the vampire's chest, resorting to getting Culver's attention to avert to me. "Let her go."

Culver releases Rylie without biting her and materializes behind the guy to look me in the eyes. He cocks his eyebrow, looking smug as hell, probably enjoying the fact that I plead for Rylie's life. Most donors wouldn't unless it was a parent protecting a child. Even Blood Rebels aren't known to play the martyr. But me? I don't want to spend the rest of my life, even if short, knowing that it was my actions that killed my best friend.

Licking his lips, Culver says, "Beg me again."

Oh, this fucker. Are you kidding me?

Just the way he demands me shows me how twisted he really is. And from what I heard, it sounds like he's up to run an entire region? If that happens, humanity is doomed. This is no longer about surviving or saving Rylie. Facing him now is so much more. Rylie realizes it too. Dashing toward us, she attempts to get close enough to back me up.

Hudson swipes her off her feet and tosses her over his shoulder. "Oh, no you fucking don't, O Positive."

The corner of Culver's lips pulls into a smile. "Give her to me, Torrance."

The vampire holding me hesitates, tightening his muscular arms around me. "I can't. Even if she broke Blood Life Corp law, we must hand her over to the proper authorities. As a female, she's protected, or did you forget that? You need to respect the law yourself if you plan to uphold it."

Culver growls, tightening his fingers into fists. "Last chance, brother. The laws aren't there for us. You'll see. This bitch is mine. Give her to me or I'll renounce you."

I tense, my body reacting to the fact that two vampires are about to fight over me with me directly in the middle of them. I suck in a few breaths, trying to get air to fill my lungs, but it seems impossible with Torrance's death grip on me.

"Knock it off, you two. You can settle this shit later. We gotta go," Aspen says, brushing his fingers through his blond hair. His blue eyes, an impossible shade lighter than Culver's icy ones, meet my gaze. "She's not worth jeopardizing our standing or our coven over."

A siren rings through the air, stealing my hearing. I cover my ears in an attempt to suppress the eardrum-bursting noise. Torrance cringes, but he doesn't drop to his knees like Hudson does. Aspen covers one of his ears and clutches the side of the car. Culver flashes his fangs and rushes us. I expect to get knocked onto the ground, but Torrance spins me again. Culver disappears, abandoning us and his car.

"Nobody move," a loud, commanding voice says, echoing through the night. "Put the donors down."

I fall onto my ass with a thud as Torrance drops me. I swing out my foot and kick him right in the balls. He falls to the ground next to me and flashes his fangs. I glower right back at him, not letting him intimidate me.

A light shines over us, stopping on each of the vampires. "Misters, my apologies. I hadn't expected the King Coven to be in the area."

The light clicks off as a bulky guard in all black, carrying a huge-ass gun on his shoulder, closes the space. He reaches out and offers a hand to Hudson first and helps him to his feet. Torrance gets up on his own and dusts off his dress pants. He steps closer and surprises the hell out of me by proffering his hand. My body reacts without my mind's consent, and I let him lift me to my feet.

The guard closes his space to me and tilts his head. "Where is your night pass?"

Digging into my pocket, I come up empty, realizing Culver either dropped it or had taken it when I showed it to him.

"Don't worry about them, Alfred. They're with us.

Donors from the academy," Hudson says, stepping closer. He puts his arm over my shoulder and smiles. "Right, love?"

I force my mouth to cooperate and fake a smile. "Right. We were just...having fun."

"Well, get the proper paperwork next time, Mr. King."

Hudson squares his shoulders and nods without a word.

The guard doesn't look like he believes it, but he turns away from me anyway. He gives Rylie a once-over and then shakes the three guys' hands. The second he vanishes, I charge toward Rylie. She gets my hint, and we both run from the vampires.

We don't get far. Torrance materializes in front of us while Aspen comes up from the side. A hand touches my shoulder from the back, and I twist and glower at Hudson. He pulls his hand back and holds it up in surrender.

"Come on now. You're going to leave without as much as a thanks for saving your life?" Hudson asks, tilting his head at me. "We could've let our brother kill you."

"Fuck off."

I attempt to push through the wall of muscle, not even caring that one of them could bite me. Since they haven't yet, I'm willing to risk my neck.

"Can't do...Fiona, is it?" Torrance asks, his dark eyes complementing the dark hue of his skin. He runs his fingers over the short, tight curls of his buzzed head. "It would be in your best interest to come with us."

"My best interest? I just want to go home. Point us in the direction of the Rockfords, and we'll be on our way. The security guard said that we have to inform them to register us in seven days."

Scrunching his face, Torrance looks at me like I've said the most ridiculous thing. "Impossible. The Rockfords don't have females on their staff."

I tighten my jaw to keep my voice even. "We were kept unregistered."

"Now that's a flat out lie," Aspen says, drawing my attention to his startling blue eyes. "We know all of the covens and their staffs in this city. We've been into all of their homes. You don't look like you're from Nocturnal Crown, especially how you blatantly disregard donor customs when speaking to the members of the future head coven of a region."

Torrance straightens his back. "It is our duty to see that you are run through the system and to figure this out."

"Like we told you. We belong to the Rockfords. You have never seen us because we hid," Rylie says. She sounds so convincing that if I didn't know any better, I'd believe her.

Hudson grabs her and locks her in a gaze. "Who are you?"

Hell. I guess she wasn't convincing enough.

Fear crashes through me as Hudson opens her mind. She can't resist his mind manipulation and says, "Rylie

Reynolds."

"Where are you from, Rylie?"

Her face turns red as she tries to resist, but it's no use. "Mount Light Haven."

"Shit," Torrance says, grabbing my wrist to stop me from running. "They're Blood Rebels."

Aspen growls. "Get them in the car."

FOUR

ACADEMY OF VAMPIRE HEIRS

I JIGGLE THE HANDLE ON the door for the tenth time, trying to get it to budge. I couldn't see much of the estate past the looming wrought iron gate Hudson drove us through. The assholes basically threw us at a guard and ran for it. Then that guy separated me from Rylie despite our pleas. Now, I've been locked in this tiny medical exam room with no response no matter how much I bang on the door.

Finally giving up, I shuffle back to the high bed covered in thin paper and sit down, regretting it immediately. I swear under my breath and stand, twisting to glance at my ass. I can already see some bruising peeking out from my jeans. Unbuttoning my pants, I tug them down a bit and shift to look at the damage in the stainless steel cabinetry.

"Damn."

I jump at the masculine voice, pulling my attention to the now open door. Heat floods my face at the sight of an attractive vampire just gawking at my bruised naked ass that I'm not quick enough to cover from him.

"Why didn't you knock? Get the hell out," I snap, trying to slide my pants back up. I cringe at the pain radiating through me. Now that my adrenaline has worn off, I hurt everywhere.

"May I take a look?" the vampire asks, coming into the room despite my demand for him to leave. "I'm a trained medical professional in human health. I promise you there isn't anything I haven't seen."

"Except my ass," I say, turning away from him.

He remains expressionless, though I swear his hazel eyes smirk at me. "Not true. I just saw it, and it could use some medical attention. Were you injured anywhere else?"

I shift on my feet and groan. "Do you not have a female practitioner on staff? Maybe someone...not so hot." My. Dumb. Mouth. But seriously. It makes a good point.

"I'm sorry, Miss..." He lets his voice trail off, waiting for me to fill in my name for him.

"Just call me Fiona," I mutter.

"Nice to meet you, Fiona. I'm Berkeley. I'm aware of

your current circumstance, so I must request you provide me your last name for proper documentation. I'm required by Blood Life Corp law to run you through the database to verify you're not a runaway." He glances up at me from his tablet. "And also, to answer your question, due to the short notice, I'm the only health keeper currently available. The nearest woman practitioner would not waste her time coming here to take care of something I'm qualified and plenty capable of handling."

"So not even like an old guy or something?" Damn it. This is awkward as hell.

"I'm also the old guy, if you're speaking of literal age and not the physical state of a donor."

Turning my attention from the tiles, I sneak a gaze at him again. Berkeley looks to be in his mid-twenties, boxy jaw, dark brown hair styled with some sort of product that keeps it neatly combed in place. His trimmed beard gives him a rugged edge along with his obvious muscles flexing against the tightness of his white dress shirt. And those hazel eyes of his. I can't help myself from peering into their depths. One second they're more green than brown and when he shifts his chin, the lighting catches in them, showing off a golden tint.

I purse my lips. "You know what? I'm good, really."

Berkeley shrugs at me and motions to the cot. "Then take a seat so I can go over your medical history before the exam."

"Standing is fine."

Waving his hand, he motions to the bed. "I must insist you sit."

This damn guy.

Clenching my jaw, I spin on my feet and drop my pants. Silence fills the room as I catch him off guard. I bet he was expecting me to fight more or to suffer, but there is no way I'm sitting, and he's obviously not going anywhere without the information he wants.

I shift and glare at him. "Uh, hello? You're making me extremely uncomfortable staring at my ass like that."

Berkeley snaps his attention to my face, and I swear blush crawls across his cheeks. Clearing his throat, he strolls to the cabinet and grabs what looks like a tiny gown from the stack folded neatly on the top shelf.

"My apologies, Fiona. I wasn't expecting you to be this injured. Would you please tell me if it was caused by one of the vampires who brought you in?" If I didn't know any better, I'd think he was concerned for me.

"Yeah."

His jaw twitches. "Were you struck?"

My eyes widen at his question, and I grimace. "I prom-ise you that if someone slapped my ass this hard, they would no longer be around. The guy was lucky I only kicked him in the nuts for dropping me."

A strange expression crosses his face, but Berkeley's fea-tures harden once again, not allowing me to read him. "I will take note of that. Now please, if you can undress completely and change into this gown, I'll treat your injuries and proceed with your health exam."

He doesn't give me a chance to respond and pulls a curtain to divide the room and to give me some privacy. I hesitate for only a moment and force myself to shimmy out of my clothes. I ease the gown around me, the back conveniently missing.

"While you finish changing, I'm going to ask you a few questions. Please answer truthfully. There is no point in lying. The headmistress of the academy will not hesitate to pull the answers out of you herself, and while it won't hurt you, I'm sure it'll be unpleasant."

I stare at his silhouette behind the curtain. "Headmistress? What's that? Where am I, anyway?"

Berkeley moves around the room, gathering stuff I can't see. "Headmistress Rasmussen is the woman in charge of the Academy of Vampire Heirs, which is where you are."

"Like a school? Why the hell am I at a school?" Education among the donor population was reformed to the bare minimum, focusing on trades unless deemed worthy of higher professions. In Mount Light Haven, the elders taught everything of the back-world, including basic education, so that we'd never forget the human history vampires want us to.

Berkeley's fingers grip the edge of the curtain. "Are you dressed?" he asks without answering my question.

"If you can even call this tiny gown clothing. It doesn't even cover my ass." I hug myself, watching him slide open the curtain.

He has the nerve to smile at me. "That's because you're wearing it backwards."

I gape at him. "Wait. That would mean...?" My cheeks burn like the gates of hell, and I cover my face with my hands. "Please don't tell me you want to see my vagina. I've had a health check recently."

His eyes flash silver, his face shifting from teasing to something else, something indecipherable. Tingles crawl over my skin at just the way he drinks me in without actually trailing his eyes down me. And damn. My body reacts, my lust clearly displaying itself as my nipples harden, and I rub my legs together. I lick my lips, and he drops his gaze lower to my mouth.

Catching himself, he smooths out his features and shakes his head at me. "That won't be necessary at the moment unless something abnormal comes up in your blood work or you have personal concerns. Even then, I'd recommend bringing in a specialist. So no, I don't *need* to see your reproductive organs."

The fact that he purposely says need instead of want doesn't go unnoticed by me. He knows it. I know it. And my body definitely knows it. I suppress my urge to make a joke—because really, the elders would deem me a traitor to humanity for even humoring such a fantasy—and straighten my shoulders.

"So only my ass," I say, playing with the short hem of my gown.

"I'll work as quickly and gently as possible," he says, again keeping his face expressionless except for his damn eyes.

I close my eyes and spin around. "Just hurry."

Berkeley helps me onto the cot, draping a sheet over my back and legs. I don't know if it makes it better or worse, so I keep my eyes closed and try to think of something else besides his cool fingers brushing across my skin.

"Try to relax," he says, his soft voice digging under my skin.

"You try to relax dropping your pants in front of me."

He chuckles. "Maybe if it weren't under these circumstances. Ask me any other time, and I'll prove that I can."

I giggle, and I mean full-on giggle, the thought way more amusing than it should be. Twisting my neck as far as I can, I glance at Berkeley, spotting the wide smile lighting his face. He doesn't look at me and concentrates on cleaning my skin before applying some sort of cream that numbs the pain of the bruising and scrapes from hitting the asphalt. Finally releasing a breath, I relax and turn around to rest my chin on my arms.

"See, this isn't so awkward now, is it?" he asks, draping a sheet over me to cover my skin. Rolling up a chair, he sits next to my head and removes his clear, nearly invisible gloves and tosses them in a bin.

I peek up at him. "It's still completely awkward."

"But at least you feel better, right?"

I don't want to agree with him. I'm annoyed that I do. Because whatever he did—he's far superior to the health keeper who tended to the wounds in our community. If I injured myself during training, the pain sometimes lasted for days.

"At least my ass does. As for the rest of me..." I groan and thunk my head on the cot. "What's going to happen to me?" Without the pain, I can think more clearly. "What about Rylie? Where is she? You didn't hurt her, did you?"

"Your friend is fine. She's already received her medical exam, answered everything she's needed to, and is now with the headmistress. As soon as we're through here, you'll see the headmistress as well," he says, touching my elbow.

I frown against my arm. "You sure you don't want to run away with me or something?"

Silence greets me, and I tilt my head up to look at him. His hazel eyes flash silver at the thought. My heart picks up speed, and I silently beg him—or maybe the universe—to give me a break. I don't know what exactly this academy is, but if it's full of vampires, it might not be good for donors. Right now, that's what they have to think me to be. If they find out about my dhampir mutation... I can't think about it.

"I can provide you blood, so you won't have to worry

about that," I add.

He blinks. "Fiona, please don't suggest such a thing."

I inhale a small breath. I don't have to ask him to know he considered the suggestion. "Why not? I don't want to be here. I didn't leave the safety of my colony for this. You seem nice enough. Nicer than any vampire I've encountered."

Leaning away, he tips his head toward the ceiling and scrubs his hands over his face. "I'm sorry. I'm training to oversee the Donor Division of my coven's pending region. I can't do anything to jeopardize our standing. My coven leader will shun me and outcast me."

Desperation twines around my chest, snaking tighter and tighter until I struggle to breathe. "Please, Berkeley," I beg, my voice only coming out as a whisper. "What if you just got my friend and me to the gate? We can handle ourselves from there."

His features sharpen as he masks any and all of his thoughts from me so that I can't use them against him. "I think it's best if we proceed with discussing your health history."

Like that, he shuts me down.

Anger rushes over me, and I manage to push myself up and ease off the cot without flashing my vagina at him. He jets to the door and blocks my way. Revealing his fangs, he releases a warning growl.

"Sit down. Now." He points back to the cot. "I will not

ask you again."

I ignore him, inching my way closer.

"Fiona, this is your last chance. Sit down or you'll leave me no choice but to inform the headmistress of your failure to comply."

Still, I ignore him.

He disappears, leaving me standing alone in the room. Fear trickles through me, and I stare at the open door. "Berkeley, wait. Wait!"

I guess I was wrong about convincing him to help me, and the last thing I want is to have someone break into my mind. With the right question, they'll discover my secret. I'll be dead or worse.

Berkeley materializes in front of me, meeting my gaze with a frown. "I don't have time for your games."

I step forward, twining my fingers together. "I'm sorry, okay. Can you blame me for trying?"

He shrugs. "I don't know much of anything about you, so I can't say."

"Then let me tell you."

Without a word, he motions me to sit on the cot. I ease myself down, relief flooding through me at the lack of pain from the gesture. I shift and cross my legs, pulling the sheet over me like it does much to hide me.

"My name is Fiona Flamme," I start, resting my hands on my lap.

"And how old are you Fiona?" he asks, pulling out his

small tablet.

I consider lying about my age and declaring myself to be a minor. People under the age of eighteen aren't required to donate blood, only people considered adults.

Berkeley tightens his jaw. "Before you lie, I want you to know that I'm usually ninety percent accurate in my educated guesses when it comes to donor ages. To me, you look between twenty and twenty-two."

Sighing, I say, "I turned twenty last month."

He nods and smirks like he's pumping his fist in his mind. "Have you ever donated blood?"

"Depends on who you ask."

"Been bitten?" His eyes study me with anticipation.

I hold his gaze. "Yes. But only during a blood exchange, not for donations."

While I can't see his fangs, I sure as hell can hear the click of them extending. I can't tell whether or not I like his response. Whether he now thinks I'm an easy target for a quick bite. But who am I kidding? I did beg the guy to run away with me in exchange for blood.

"Are you a virgin?"

"Are you?" It's my turn to smirk. "You know, I can tell if you lie. I'm eighty-five percent accurate in my guesses."

He flicks his gaze to mine like I've asked the most ridiculous question. "No, I'm not."

I open my mouth to tease him, suggesting that his hand doesn't count.

"And by your lack of admittance, I'm going to assume your answer is the same," he says, cutting off any chance to lighten the mood.

Swinging my arm out, I backhand him. "Hey, you can't just assume."

"I'm not assuming. I'm making an educated guess from what I know of Blood Rebels, the fact that you're female in a male-dominated territory, and you're twenty, which I know unregistered donors of the resistance believe to be a prime child-bearing age." He catches me off guard, his assessment pretty accurate of a lot of the women from my community.

"Maybe if I stayed longer," I say, looking at my hands. "I ignored six possible suitors in the last week. The elders were getting annoyed. According to Ms. Maggie, my standards were too high and I had a duty to our community."

He touches my knee. "Is that why you left and came to the city?"

"Yes." I peek up, catching him staring at me. "I don't agree with the purpose they pushed on me, but I'm also certain I won't agree with whatever the hell you want to do with me either."

He doesn't respond and taps away on his tablet. I shift nervously and lean forward, trying to get a glimpse of what he's writing, because it's obviously more than what I told him.

After a couple of quiet minutes, Berkeley sets his tablet

on a rolling tray and gets to his feet. "I think your responses will suffice. Let me take a quick look at the rest of you to make sure you don't have any more injuries. Then I'll draw your blood and you can get cleaned up and changed. Does that sound good?"

"Well, it doesn't sound bad." I slide off the cot and stand in front of him. "I honestly thought you'd ask a lot more medical questions."

"I'll get everything I need from your blood work."

"I guess that's something."

Berkeley offers me a smile, not one that quite lights up his face but a smile that makes this all seem far less troubling than it should be. It helps that I think he's hot as hell, and he reminds me of the blood sources back home—not as intimidating as the rest of the vampires I've met so far in the city.

He's quick to draw my blood and decides that I should take a shower to clean off the dirt and blood from my body before tending to the scrapes and cuts on my palms, arms, and knees.

Within the wall and behind a door I thought was a cabinet hides a small shower. Berkeley closes the curtain and waits on the other side for me.

I can't stop myself from standing under the steady stream of hot water long after I already washed myself.

"This won't be your last chance to bathe," Berkeley says, passively suggesting that I hurry my ass up without being rude. "I hate to interrupt what sounds like quite the enjoyable time, but I can hear someone coming to check on you."

Quickly shutting off the water, I grab the small towel from the hook and wrap it around my body. I peek out of the curtain and catch Berkeley messing on his com device. He puts it away and freezes at the sight of me. Starting from my dripping hair, he trails his gaze down my still glistening body all the way to my bare feet.

"What?" I ask, trying not to shift on my feet under the weight of his gaze.

He quickly composes himself. "Nothing. I had just expected your injuries to be a bit worse. Your friend was pretty beat up."

I swallow and lick my lips. "I consumed vampire blood recently."

His mouth forms an O.

"From the shadow dweller outside the city and then some other asshole who ran like a coward when the authorities arrived—Culver something," I continue.

"Culver King?"

I grimace. "Yeah, that's him. You know him?"

"Quite well. And the fact that you drank his blood complicates things just a bit. I need to make a note in your paperwork."

My brows pinch together. "Is it bad? Am I doomed? The guy totally deserved it."

Berkeley remains expressionless, but something shifts in his eyes. The warmth he had for me seconds ago turns cold, aloof almost.

After another minute of silence passes, he finally says, "I'm sure he did. Mr. King is known to have a temper, but he's also good at his job in maintaining order and why Blood Life Corp chose him as one of the new region heads and why he's here at the academy."

"Wait, he's here?" My heart beats wildly, sudden fear pouring through me. If that asshole is here, it can't be good for me. "Shit. You have to help me. He wanted to perform my final donation. He—"

A knock sounds on the door, startling me. I snatch the sheet from the cot to pull it around my towel, so I'm not standing in a tiny piece of fabric for whoever stands on the other side.

Berkeley shifts his gaze from me and to the door and motions for me to pull the curtain shut to hide me from view.

"I'm with a patient. Whatever it is you want will have to wait," Berkeley says, cracking the door open.

I can't stop myself from staring through a small gap.

"The only thing I need is for you to hurry up with my blood source." The familiar voice cuts through the room, stealing the air from my lungs. It's Culver. I can't believe it.

Anger rushes over me, and I yank the curtain back and glare. "What did you just call me?"

Culver flashes his fangs at me, his ice blue eyes penetrating me from over Berkeley's shoulder. "How much longer until she's released?" He ignores my question and instead talks to Berkeley. There's nothing more infuriating than being treated like I'm not even here, despite that Culver still hasn't taken his gaze from me.

"A couple more minutes. She has quite a few scrapes that need to be tended to. I'll be done shortly." Berkeley peers over his shoulder at me. "Maybe you can call the seamstress to bring her something clean to wear."

Culver's lips pull up more. "What she's wearing is fine."

I gawk at him, my mouth falling open. This lunatic can't be serious. There is no way in hell I'm stepping even a foot out of this curtained area in what I'm wearing.

Berkeley clenches his fingers at his side, releasing a soft growl. "I will not release her to you unless you bring her something appropriate."

Culver glowers, his eyes flashing silver. "Want to bet?"

Before I can react, Culver shoves Berkeley back, sending him crashing into the wall. I screech and scramble away, looking for anything I can use to protect myself. My fingers lock on a vial of my blood the second Culver closes the space to me. I smash it on his forehead, sending my blood splattering over the both of us.

He freezes, flaring his nostrils.

Berkeley hops to his feet and snarls, flying our way.

I never knew of anyone to survive being between two fighting vampires, especially if I'm the one they're fighting for.

I scream and brace for my death.

FIVE

CLAIMED

A HEAVY BODY CRASHES INTO me, knocking me out of the way of Culver and Berkeley. The world spins as Hudson flips me midair to take the brunt of our fall. We slide a foot on the floor, with me on top of him, but he manages to stop us from hitting the wall by stretching up his arm.

I gasp and clutch onto his shoulders. For the first time, I look at him. And I mean really look at him. His jade green eyes crinkle in the corners with his smirk complementing his messy, chestnut brown hair with streaks of copper as damp as mine like he just got out of the shower. Except he's dressed...and I realize I'm not. He realizes it too and drops his gaze from my eyes to my boobs pressed into his taut chest. I groan and tilt my head down, trying to figure out exactly how to get to my feet without exposing more than just the tops of my breasts. Stupid tiny towel. Damn sheet.

"Shit," a soft voice murmurs.

I jerk my attention to the door, spotting another familiar and unwanted visitor. Aspen's light blue eyes rove over me as I lie on Hudson, now frozen and afraid to move. Hudson relaxes under me, obviously not going anywhere either. He's enjoying this way too much, his smirk widening into a cocky-ass smile. He shares a look with Aspen, and the two of them have a silent conversation with their eyes.

"The threat is over, love," Hudson finally says to me. "You can get off me now. Or not. I'm rather quite comfortable."

"The only way I'm getting off is if someone gets me some clothes," I snap, trying to ignore the fact that the longer I remain in place, the more I notice all of Hudson's muscles beneath me.

Aspen disappears without a word, leaving me in Hudson's arms. He keeps his hands planted on the small of my back, and I shift a bit, my nerves and something else— something deep-seated, awakened by his closeness—getting the best of me. His scent engulfs me in a tantalizing sweet wave. I'm nearly certain my blood lust might control me if one of us doesn't move.

"Will you please stop squirming," Hudson says, his voice lowering. "You're turning what I thought was fun into complete torture considering my brother has annoyingly already claimed you."

I frown and meet his gaze again. The second I do, I realize exactly what he's talking about as his boner flexes against my pelvis. In normal circumstances, I might scramble away. I might even apologize. But right now? My body decides to go crazy, excited that he finds me as attractive as I find him.

I shift again. "Control yourself."

His smile vanishes, his eyes flashing silver. "Stop looking at me like that."

"Like what?" Ah, hell. Is he flirting? Am I?

"Like you hate the idea that someone other than me put a claim on you."

Goosebumps prickle over my skin, and we continue to stare at each other. He dares me with his eyes to look away, but I won't. I'm not afraid of him locking me in a gaze. He couldn't. Not yet at least.

Leaning closer, I hover a few inches away from his face, inhaling a breath of his sweet scent. "I don't know what you're talking about. And so you know, no one can claim me, especially not that asshole you just called your brother."

"Is that so?" he whispers, digging his fingers more firmly into my back.

"I'll prove it."

I don't know what comes over me, but I bow forward even more, pressing my weight into him, really feeling the extent of his desire. He tilts his head, his soft lips puckering, his eyes closing in preparation for my kiss.

A tap on the door jerks my attention away, and I whip my head to see Aspen standing in the doorway with a clothing bag dangling from his fingers. He releases a soft growl, his fangs peeking from beneath his lips. He glowers at Hudson, and Hudson scowls, his fingers tightening around my waist even more. My fear instincts go off like crazy, knocking some good sense into me.

With one hand, I cover Hudson's eyes. I push up with my other, scrambling to pull up my towel. I get to my feet and rush toward the small shower like it'll somehow protect me.

"My apologies, Ms. Flamme," Hudson says, now standing with his back to me. "I didn't mean to frighten you. If you could please get dressed, I'll escort you to Headmistress Rasmussen."

I don't respond to him and tug the curtain closed, realizing that he's not leaving the room. Aspen disappeared sometime during my scramble to get myself together, and I can't stop thinking about what he saw almost happen. How I almost kissed Hudson. And what the hell? Hudson was with Culver when he cornered me in the city. He helped him. How his gorgeous green eyes suddenly made me forget all those things freaks me the hell out.

Hugging myself for a moment, I gather my nerve to unzip the dress bag Aspen left for me. I gawk at the simple white button-down top, black pants...and a tie? Tonight was the first time I've seen someone wear one—Culver— and it's also the last thing I want to wear. Along with what appears to be the donor issued uniform are a matching set of lacy undergarments. Neither piece looks suitable for normal wear, but it's all that's in the bag. I just hope it was a mistake on Aspen's part—because it seems like something a guy wouldn't think about—and not actually part of the uniform.

"I never thought I'd offer to help someone get dressed, but do you need any? I expect you don't know how to tie the tie," Hudson says from the other side of the curtain.

I finish buttoning my shirt. "I'm fine."

"You're not going to wear the tie, are you?" The light-ness in his voice combats the sudden intensity that had blossomed between us.

"Nope."

Pulling the curtain open, I stand before him. He drinks me in from my head to my dirty boots that I put back on, because there is no way I'm walking around barefooted. If I somehow figure out how to escape, I'm not going to find myself on the run without shoes.

Hudson's lips tilt in a frown. "I don't like it. The towel was hotter."

This. Guy.

I whack him on the shoulder. "Don't expect that shit to happen again."

"What if it's me in the towel? While I technically have a private bathroom, I wouldn't mind using the coed showers in the donor dorms."

Pressing my lips together, I try my best not to react and stroll past him through the open door. I have no idea where I'm going, but I must be heading in the right direction because Hudson falls into step by my side.

He glances at me in his peripheral vision, managing to focus on the hall in front of us and me at the same time. We pass several doors to rooms identical to the medical exam room they locked me in. From what I gather, I'm in the Human Health Center of the academy. It's a good sign that none of the rooms are occupied. I half expected to find all the humans here with various injuries. I can't imagine this place being safe. Not if it is a training school for vampires. From what I know, too many gathered could cause major problems if they're not all in the same coven.

Hudson grazes my hand with his, getting me to look at him. "When we reach the lobby, you need to bow your head."

I scrunch my nose. "What the hell for?"

"It's common practice for the donors training for positions on vampire household staffs," he says nonchalantly.

I place my hands on my hips. "But I'm not."

His jaw twitches, his green eyes turning away from

mine to look ahead of us in the hallway. "Please, just do it. You'll garner less attention that way. It's already bad enough that you're female, claimed by Culver, and previously unregistered. Those things combined make you a target to get messed with. I'm not in the mood to fight for someone I don't even get to keep."

I open my mouth to ask him a target for what, but the second he opens the wooden door to the grand lobby, it would be like me asking the obvious. Dozens of vampires hang out in small clusters around the grand room. Marble floors glitter with flecks of gold that accent the shiny golden light fixtures glowing above various pieces of what I can only assume is back-world art.

A crystal chandelier scatters fractals of rainbow light across the floor. A couple of different seating areas contain couches and chairs with coffee tables. Vases of different white flowers fragrance the air in such a way that I can't help inhaling a breath through my nose.

"Head down, Ms. Flamme," Hudson says, keeping his voice as low as the others in the room.

I want so badly to ignore him and strut through the room like I would back at home when dozens of gazes train on me. But there is something far different and worse being under the scrutiny of a bunch of male vampires, with the exception of one female. A room full of soldiers who want to devote their life to me rather than expect me to devote my life to them boosts my confidence. These guys? Their hungry eyes consume every inch of me, making me feel more like food.

"This area is dedicated to vampire residents only. You can pass through, but do not stop." Hudson closes the foot of space between us and touches his hand to the small of my back. I can't help feeling like he's protecting me. Who knows? Maybe he really is despite his previous comment. But not for my benefit. Probably for his brother's.

"Whatever you say," I mutter under my breath. "I wouldn't want to stop and socialize anyway..." My voice trails off as I spot three familiar faces sitting together in what seems like a private section of the lobby, partitioned from the rest of the room with a couple of bookshelves.

Torrance sits straighter in his chair, his nearly black eyes boring into me. Beside him, Aspen leans his elbows on his knees, finding something fascinating on the empty table in front of him. Berkeley's eyes devour me inch-by-inch. I can't tell if it's because he's trying to find some hidden injury or what, but his sudden attention blooms warmth across my chest and neck.

"Head down, Fiona," Hudson says as a reminder, using my first name instead of my last. "You don't want to attract those assholes' attention. They would love nothing more than to find out if you taste as good as you smell."

I whip my head to look at Hudson, knowing he's not actually warning me but teasing the three of them. Ignoring his suggestion to drop my gaze, I instead straighten my back and toss my long dark hair over my shoulder. In the dim lighting, it looks black rather than the deep purple Rylie dyed my hair. It took convincing a soldier to sneak into the city, but she managed to give me the gift for my birthday.

"That's what I've been told, so they can just assume," I say, smirking. They all make various sounds, including Hudson, and I flick my gaze to look at him. "What about you, Mr. King? Does that work the same for vampires?" I purposely use the name that the guard in the city used on him, knowing it's customary unless told otherwise.

"Would you like to find out?" He licks his lips, stretching his mouth into a smile I can't resist returning.

"If you're offering."

"Only Mr. King would enjoy acting as the donor he most certainly should have remained." A blond vampire with shoulder-length hair stops in our way, blocking a direct line toward the exit. "Desperation for the female's attention looks pitiful on you. No wonder your brother refused to let you stake a claim."

Hudson stands straighter. "Fuck off, Mr. Knightly. Your weak attempt to belittle me reveals your own desperation to try to even breathe in the same air as a woman considering I'm certain you've never done so."

Mr. Knightly raises his arm to strike Hudson. A soft growl sounds from where the guys sit and watch us, causing the asshole to reconsider his actions. He disappears like the coward I knew he would be. I turn my attention to the guys, trying to figure out who did it, but I can't tell.

"That was disappointing, love. I thought you'd stand up on my behalf," Hudson says. "Not even a measly threat to tear Dawson's throat out."

I raise an eyebrow at him. "And risk making you jealous? No way. I fully plan to take you up on your offer to sink my teeth into you."

Hudson smiles wider and nudges me to pick up my pace. If I'm in this weird-ass, hellish situation, I might as well have some fun, despite knowing the danger of teasing vampires. It helps that only Culver was truly like the monsters the elders warned me about hundreds of times growing up. Luckily, I still know better than to let my guard down.

"Careful what you say," Hudson says.

"Never."

His fangs peek out with his smile. "Some take those types of jokes seriously."

"Who says I'm joking?"

He groans under his breath and chooses not to respond. We finally reach another door, one made of glass with a clear view of a hallway with a red floor runner, gold-framed paintings, and what appears to be another lobby at the end. Hudson drops his hand from my back, relaxing a bit as we stroll down the hallway to the other lobby.

A couple of humans, all dressed similarly to me but with the ties, turn their attention from each other. Without Hudson having to say anything, I realize this must be the lobby for humans. It's far plainer than the vampire lounge with its simple white tiles, cream walls, and a small TV. Uncomfortable looking chairs litter the room haphazardly like people just leave them wherever.

"Fiona? Oh, thank God." Rylie's familiar voice draws my attention to her as she sits alone in the corner of the room.

I abandon Hudson and rush toward her. We throw our arms around each other. Rylie tenses, her body stiffening as she huffs in pain. Pulling back, I meet her hazel eyes, nearly the same color as Berkeley's, and frown.

"I'm sorry. I forgot you were hurt," I say, easing my hold.

She blinks the sheen in her eyes away. "I don't care. Don't stop hugging me. I was so scared for you. When the health keeper left me here, I assumed you put up too much of a fight. No one would tell me anything."

I sigh and rest my head on her shoulder. "I'm fine, really. Nothing more than a bruised as hell ass."

She grimaces at me. "You okay?"

"I'm here, aren't I? Only a bit mortified about dropping my pants for the hot as hell practitioner." I cringe at the way my sentence comes out. "He was professional...ish."

She blinks a few times and glances behind me to Hudson. I can sense his closeness without having to check for myself that he's standing in my personal space. "You think that guy is hot?" The look she gives me screams that she finds my admission about finding a vampire attractive to be inconceivable. But she doesn't understand. I barely do. Something about my dhampir nature can't help it.

"Uh, he wasn't the one who checked out my ass," I say, blushing once again at my failure to say something that doesn't sound like an innuendo.

Hudson clears his throat. "That you know of."

Without thinking, I elbow him in the stomach to get him to step back. A couple of people gasp, and Rylie drags me away to shield me from what everyone looks like they expect to be my impending final donation.

Hudson doesn't react to the fact that I hit him. Instead, he smiles at me like we share some sort of secret. And maybe we do. There is no way in hell that I'm telling Rylie about the whole towel incident or the fact that I almost kissed the guy. Or how I also think he's as good looking as Berkeley.

"Come on, Ms. Flamme. It's time to meet the headmistress. I'm sure you will see your friend later." Hudson's voice remains even, and he motions for me to return to his side.

Rylie squeezes my hand, not letting me go right away like she fears she may never see me again, and I have to tug away myself.

I meet her gaze. "I'll come back. I promise. We'll talk later." And by talk, she knows I insinuate devising an escape plan. I'm sure dawn will approach soon. Sunlight is the only advantage we have against vampires, and even then, it's not foolproof.

"Be safe, Fiona. Remember, don't fight." Her words go against everything we've both been taught in regards to vampires. Because Blood Rebels are never to bow down or comply with a vampire. We're supposed to fight regardless of whether or not we can win.

But now? Things are different. Fighting here would end in our senseless deaths. From the look on Rylie's face, like me, she's not ready to die. So complying it is.

"I won't," I say, confirming that I feel the same way she does.

Hudson leads me to a door without allowing me to say more. A small placard declares this to be the way to the headmistress's office. I don't get more than ten feet into the hallway with Hudson before Culver materializes in front of us and flashes his fangs at me, purposefully surprising me and making me jump.

It takes everything in me not to yell at him and slap him across the face. I know he's the type to retaliate. Giving me a once-over, Culver inspects me like someone would inspect a piece of fruit at the dining hall to pick out the best one. His heavy gaze makes me more than uncomfortable. He elicits all sorts of fear and unease unlike his coven brother.

"Thank you for handling my donor, brother," Culver says, turning his attention to Hudson. "It seems she got to

Berkeley, and he couldn't finish his duty as her health keep-er."

"Maybe if you hadn't interrupted during a private ex-am," Hudson says, surprising me. "Cut him some slack. You know he carries a lot of compassion for donors."

"I will, but only because he excels at his job," Culver mutters. "But as the head of our security division, I must ask you to remind all of our brothers about donor protocol. This one is mine."

Hudson retracts his hand from my back. "Yes, brother. I'll remind them."

I don't get the chance to beg Hudson not to leave me with this asshole before he vanishes, leaving only a closing door in his wake. Training my gaze on the floor-runner, I ignore Culver's gaze as he assesses me.

"I'm rather annoyed my brothers brought you here in-stead of abandoning you in the streets for me to return to," Culver says, keeping his voice low. "But perhaps it was a good thing. I'll get to enjoy you far longer this way."

I try not to react, though my thudding heartbeat gives me away.

"Come along now, Ms. Flamme. Headmistress Ras-mussen requested your presence before she agrees formally to release you to me."

Wait, what? Formally releases me? That almost sounds like there's a chance that I won't fall into Culver's hands and under his vicious fangs. He steps forward without touching me, and I force myself to follow behind him, thinking about a dozen things I can do to convince whoever is in charge not to fate me to such a life.

As far as I know from the brief fight Culver had with his brothers over me in the city, the one thing I have going for me in this territory is that I'm female. I can use that, especially if the person in charge of this place is female too.

"Pick up your pace," Culver says, snapping at me. "We don't have all night. The headmistress will be leaving soon, and I don't want to have to wait until tomorrow night to teach you your new place."

I clench my jaw but don't respond. I can't. If I do, I'll lose my shit. If that happens, it's over. I know it. I promised Rylie that I'd return to her, and I refuse to let this asshole force me into breaking my promise.

I keep my head bowed until we reach a set of double doors in the middle of the long hallway. Culver motions for me to get the door for him, and I ease it open, almost afraid of what I'll find on the other side. Cool, rose-fragranced air trickles to me, and Culver pushes the door open completely from above my head, scowling in annoyance by how long I take.

"Welcome, Mr. King," a friendly, masculine voice says, drawing my attention to a young human guy behind a reception counter. "Headmistress Rasmussen has been expecting your arrival."

Culver ignores the guy and crosses the room to a tall

wooden door with ornate designs etched into the wood. A gold placard on the door reads Headmistress Ravenna Rasmussen of the Academy of Vampire Heirs. The light on a small electronic pad on the wall turns green, and the door swings inward without us having to touch it.

"Mr. King, I was starting to believe you had changed your mind about your request to acquire a personal donor." A gorgeous young woman with an ageless face sits cross-legged on a couch with a glass of red liquid in her hand. Across from her rests a massive dark wooden desk with built-in shelving and cabinetry. A projector screen glows on the wall, the video of the moon sinking into the horizon reminding us that dawn approaches.

Culver clears his throat. "My apologies for the delay, Headmistress. I'm sorry to have kept you waiting. It seems Ms. Flamme needed some medical attention, and my brother would not release her to me until he was through."

The headmistress nods. "I find Berkeley's attention to detail and thoroughness quite admirable in regards to the Donor Division. He will serve you well. A region must hold high esteem to its population, and donor health is a top priority." She speaks to him like he needs the reminder, though I feel she might also be mentioning it to me at the same time.

"Yes, ma'am," Culver says. "I fully agree, which is why we were late."

Headmistress Rasmussen offers a warm smile at Culver's lie. "You'll be an excellent addition to our board, Mr. King. Now please, join me. I'd like to meet the one you would like formally to claim."

I find it odd that she speaks of me like I'm not standing next to Culver. I don't know much about vampire customs, but I'm sure I'm about to find out. Now that her gaze turns to me, the headmistress looks like she has a lot to say.

"Please, come sit next to me, Ms. Flamme. I'd like to ask you a few questions." The woman doesn't smile at me, though she sounds friendly enough.

Culver nudges me to get me started until I cross the room on my own. Thankfully, he chooses to stand near a tinted window with a view of the outside too dark for me to see from my position.

I take a seat on the couch next to the woman and cross my legs at my ankles, purposefully mirroring her position. She studies my face while I gaze at my hands. I don't know whether I should look at her or not, but there is no way I'm going to risk and assume I can. She's much more regal than Culver and his brothers and in control of this place, so I know she must be powerful. The best I can do is proceed with caution. Plus, I want her to reject Culver's request to claim me.

"I spoke to your companion earlier this evening, and we had quite the interesting conversation." Headmistress Rasmussen's words work to get me to look up. "She explained that the two of you did not come here with the normal intent someone part of the resistance usually has in venturing into one of Blood Life Corp's regions."

"That is correct," I say, acknowledging her statement.

"The health keeper who treated you confirmed that you admitted the same thing." She pauses to take a sip of what I know is blood from her glass. "Now, either the two of you have corroborated your stories to give us a false pretense of your arrival or—"

"She was not lying." I regret speaking the second the words escape. It's too late to take them back, so I straighten my shoulders and continue. "I want no part of the future laid out for me."

She hums under her breath. "Fortunately for you, Mr. King has agreed to graciously accept you as his personal donor. If you choose to establish the bond I'm sure he hopes for, I can promise your future will not be anything like what you imagined."

Did she just insinuate that Culver desires more than turning me into a blood source? From her peaked brows, I know she definitely did.

I can't stop myself from looking at Culver, who stares at me with something feral in his eyes. "And what if I don't agree...with any of this?"

Culver releases a threatening growl. "It doesn't matter. I caught you in the city. You broke several laws that carry an automatic death sentence."

Headmistress Rasmussen sets down her glass. "If she

were male."

"And because I'm not you expect me to suffer a fate far worse?" My sharp voice snaps both of their attention to me. "This asshole had planned to kill me. If the authorities hadn't arrived, he would've. It wasn't even he who brought me here. He obviously didn't want me badly enough to stick around, so how can you think he will obey the law now? Even one of his brothers said he had a blatant disregard for it."

One second I'm sitting across from the headmistress, and in the next, my back hits the wall and Culver snarls in my face. I cringe and tuck my neck, fear over his fangs begging me to curl in on myself. If he wasn't gripping me by my wrists, I would cover my throat.

"You bitch. No one gave you permission to speak freely," he says.

"Mr. King." Headmistress Rasmussen's sharp voice cuts through his continuous low growls at me. I've never heard something so animalistic before. "If you do not settle down, I will not grant you what you've asked. A region head would demonstrate far more restraint and know how to handle the situation without the use of unnecessary force. She is a donor and not a competitor."

I land on my ass and smack my hand over my mouth to cover my screech of pain. The numbing cream is clearly not as long-lasting as I had hoped. I fall over and curl in on myself to suppress my need to swear to the universe. Culver abandons me to return to his previous spot by his window. The headmistress doesn't move either.

A gentle hand touches my shoulder, and I open my eyes to see Berkeley squatting next to me. He silently helps me to my feet while the others watch. Shifting his body slightly so the others can't see him, he offers me a frown.

"Do you need to return to the health center?" he asks, keeping his voice so low that I practically have to read his lips.

I bob my head, only because I have a feeling if I say yes, he'll get me out of here.

Clearing his throat, he turns to the headmistress. "As Ms. Flamme's health keeper, I must insist she return to the health center for further observation."

"In a few minutes," Headmistress Rasmussen says. "I need to announce my formal decision in regards to Mr. King's request for the record."

I can't stop myself from reacting. "Please, don't let him claim me. I'm better off dead."

Silver flashes in the headmistress's eyes as she glances from me to meet Culver's gaze. "I hereby grant the King Coven Rylie Reynolds as a daylight staff member and Fiona Flamme as a personal blood donor."

"No," I whisper, shock washing over me at not only the announcement of my name but also of Rylie's.

Culver grins and comes to my side. "She will not be needing medical attention."

Headmistress Rasmussen materializes in front of me, stopping Culver from stealing me away. "I was not finished, Mr. King. I have a few conditions you must agree to first."

Culver glares at the woman without a word.

"Both donors must enter the vampire household work program here at the Academy of Vampire Heirs. It will be our staff to teach them what they need to know so that upon your completion of the region head training, they will be properly educated to be a part of your daylight household." She glances at me. "Also, there is a no-bite policy on this campus. While you claimed Ms. Flamme as your personal donor, you will abide by the rules until you return to your home city. She is also allowed a place in the donor dorms if she so chooses. Do you understand?"

"Yes," Culver says with a growl.

"Might I suggest that you use this time wisely to get acquainted with Ms. Flamme. Show her around and do try to make her feel comfortable. Let this be a lesson on building a loyal staff."

"Yes, Headmistress." Culver looks annoyed as hell. Even if she put these conditions in place, it only buys me a little extra time. Why she even did it? I have no idea.

"Good. Now, if you will please head to administration, you can sign your contract there. Also see to it that Ms. Flamme finds her way to the dining hall after her health exam. I'm sure she's probably hungry."

The headmistress waves Culver away, and Berkeley,

who has remained utterly silent, guides me out without touching me. Culver doesn't stick around, and I'm glad for it. His presence alone drives my fear instincts crazy.

Berkeley turns to me in the waiting room. "Would you mind if I carry you? It's much faster."

I shrug. "I guess."

I don't get a chance to react before Berkeley lifts me off my feet and cradles me against him.

He peers at me. "Congratulations on your acceptance here. Only a few handfuls of donors are granted such an opportunity."

Tightening my mouth, I glare at him. "This isn't an opportunity to me. It's punishment."

SIX

PERSONAL BLOOD DONOR

IT WASN'T UNTIL WELL PAST dawn that Berkeley showed me to the donor dorms that can be accessed through a tunnel for vampires while also having an above ground entrance that allows humans to walk through a garden. Because of the sun, I didn't get to experience it. Hopefully tomorrow.

Rylie was passed out on the top of a bunk bed in the room that had been assigned to us. I decided against waking her because she looked exhausted, so I've been tossing and turning, my adrenaline still pumping through me, not letting me relax.

According to Berkeley, we'll now follow a vampire schedule while we're here, which means training classes at night and attempting to sleep in the day. And it sucks.

A strange alarm rings through the air, and I bolt upright and jump to my feet. I rush from the bed and snatch a lamp, holding it like a baseball bat. My heart races, my whole body trembling. Moving to the space next to the door, I wait for someone to throw it open to attack us. The alarm shuts off, leaving my ears ringing.

"Fiona? Oh, Fiona! You're here." Rylie rolls over to the edge of the bunk and swings her legs over to drop to her feet. She rushes me and hugs me against her.

"We've been assigned the same dorm room because we're now property of the Kings." I pout my lip, meeting her gaze.

"What? No one told me." She purses her lips. "I thought they were deciding how to punish us."

"This is punishment. We've been enrolled in the academy to be trained as vampire staff members. Well, you have. I'm supposedly going to be a personal donor." I try not to react. Knowing Rylie, if I breakdown, she will too.

"To which one?" she asks, flicking her gaze to the door.

"Culver."

"F-u-u-u-u-ck. This is so twisted. The elders never mentioned this place. I mean, come on. I haven't been to school in five years. I should be agreeing to a union, starting a family, helping to ensure a good future for our community." She wrings her hands together. "I'm too old for this shit."

"You think you're too old?" The smooth, masculine voice draws our attention to the door. A soft knock occurs, but thankfully the door doesn't thrust open.

Rylie and I gawk at it without moving.

"It's against school policy for me to open your door without your permission, so please, if you would kindly do it for me, I'd appreciate it." Another tap sounds through the air. "It's Torrance, by the way. I'm one of the King brothers." The guy who was adamant about not breaking Blood Life Corp law. I'm not sure if I should be pissed at him for bringing me here or thankful he saved my life. Both. I can be both.

Rylie looks at me with wide eyes, her wild light brown mane partially covering her face. "Don't open it. You don't know what he plans to do. He might sound nice but that's the point. Charm his way in to murder us."

"I don't think he will. He knows I bite, and after he asked me nicely not to, I think he's a little afraid. Plus, if we don't open the door, then what? I doubt he'll just go away," I say.

"She's partially right, Ms. Reynolds. Not about being afraid of a bite but about leaving. I'm here to escort the two of you for a blood draw before breakfast." I try not to smile at his bite comment in front of Rylie. She doesn't appreciate stuff like that like I do.

Turning the knob, I open the door and meet the chocolatey gaze of Torrance. He rests both of his hands on the doorframe, his hulking form blocking the way. I give him a once-over, starting from his full lips, offering me an amused, close-mouthed smile to his dress shirt, slacks, and tie. His blue jacket fits snugly in a good way, showing off the definition of his bulging muscles, and I stare at the crest with a crown on his breast pocket.

"You mean you're escorting just me for a blood draw," I say, crossing my arms over my chest.

Torrance raises an eyebrow at me, glancing at my cotton tank top and shorts I slept in. Unlike his brothers, he has yet to see me showing this much skin, and I can't help enjoying his attention. "No. I said exactly what I meant. Both of you are required to donate blood. Ms. Reynolds, as part of the general donor population supply for students and staff." Leaning closer, he looks down at me. "And you, Ms. King, will donate personally to Mr. King."

My heart drops into my stomach. "Don't call me that. My name is either Ms. Flamme or Fiona."

"Careful, Fiona. It is considered an honor to carry the King name, especially around here. Some people might take offense if you deny the opportunity," Torrance says.

"Then let them."

I attempt to close the door in his face, but he blocks it with his arm. I sigh and turn my back on him instead, meeting Rylie's flustered gaze. She shuffles to the corner of the room and twists her hair between her fingers. Torrance has the gall to step inside with us, though he leaves the door open.

Annoyance rushes over me, and I step into his space and jab my finger into his chest. "Back the hell up and get out. I did not invite you in."

He narrows his eyes, puffing his chest until it feels like I poke a brick wall. My hand takes on a mind of its own, and I spread my fingers and rest my palm over his heart, feeling the beats thud on my fingers. He steps closer, forcing my hand to press harder into him to keep the space between us.

He locks his gaze on mine. Everything in me screams to look away from him. It's been too long since I consumed vampire blood. He could easily manipulate my mind, and there would be nothing I could do about it.

Now that I think about consuming blood, I can't stop myself from inhaling a breath of his fruity scent. Hunger burns in my stomach, and not the kind of hunger for solid food. I try to suppress my worry, because I don't know how I'm going to survive this place without getting the nutrients I need. I can probably last up to a week without getting sick from the lack of blood, maybe two, but I've only had to go so long one time before. Back in the colony, I was allowed to visit the blood sources every three days, and I snuck in a couple of extra times.

I tighten my jaw. "I'm going to ask you one more time to wait outside. If you don't, you will leave me no choice but to show you again what I'm capable of." Flicking my gaze down to his crotch, I silently remind him of the fact that I kicked him in the balls for dropping me on my ass.

"I might like that," he says, smirking at me. "Your bravery is quite admirable."

I groan and shove him back. "Just get out."

"You have five minutes to get ready. If you miss the phlebotomist, Culver will accuse you of attempting to starve him, which might lead the headmistress to allowing an exception to the no-bite clause." His smirk disappears with his words. He sounds sincere enough that I don't think he's joking. I can only imagine the pain Culver will put me through if he gets his fangs in me. I doubt he'll treat me like my favorite blood source in Mount Light Haven would, assuring I always had one helluva good time during a blood exchange.

I shudder at the thought. "Fine. Five minutes."

Torrance lets me close the door on him, and I turn to Rylie. She throws her arms around me, tears pooling in her eyes. I stroke my hand in circles on her back for a few seconds before pulling away and forcing my mouth to smile.

I open the small closet and toss a white dress shirt to her. "Hey, Ry. It's going to be okay. Let's just get through tonight. We'll figure things out come dawn."

She huffs a breath. "Until dawn. I can do this."

"Yes, you can." I touch her shoulder. "And who knows. Maybe we'll learn something we can use."

When I step out of the dorm room, Torrance leans against the wall in the hallway, offering me a smile. Rylie trains her gaze on the ground, already adjusting to the donor rules of this place. Most humans can quickly adapt, and I usually can, but Torrance strolls so closely that his arm brushes mine, and I can't resist looking at him.

"So, will we be escorted everywhere we go?" I ask, filling the silence as he motions us onto an elevator. He hits the button to the basement leading to the tunnel to take us to the main section of the massive estate that makes up the academy.

"Not her," he says, motioning his chin to Rylie. "Just you. You've currently been flagged as a flight risk, and Culver isn't willing to risk losing his investment if you somehow—doubtfully—manage to get past security and escape."

Well, this complicates things. Not only will I be followed all the time, but there also might not be a way for me to try to charm some blood out of a random vampire here. I had intended to entice a security guard or maybe a guy who shows interest in me into a blood exchange, but it looks like I'm going to have to up my game and focus on one of Culver's brothers.

It isn't ideal, but if I don't figure it out, I'll starve. If I starve, my blood hunger will consume me, and my secret will get out. They'll cage or kill me. I can't imagine they'll humor the idea of keeping someone who is their personal predator around.

"And you've been chosen to be my annoying shadow?" I turn my attention to him. Torrance definitely doesn't seem like the type to break any rules, so I hope him escorting me turns out to be temporary. Maybe if I can somehow get to Hudson, he'll do it. He seems like the type—a rule breaker and a huge flirt, the perfect combination in a blood source for me.

"The headmistress suggested that Culver assign the job to one of us considering donor-sitting isn't exactly on his agenda. Not to mention she's well aware of your...dislike of him." He breaks his hard expression to smirk at me.

"Dislike? I hate the bastard," I mutter. "He's lucky I don't kill him."

Rylie hisses at me, snatching my hand to tug me away from Torrance. I don't know if it was her sudden movement, considering he probably forgot she was standing silently next to me, or if my words set him off, but he growls under his breath.

Flashing his fangs, he says, "Remove your hands from Ms. King immediately. You are not to touch her."

Damn. It *was* Rylie.

She lets go of my hand and locks her fingers together, shooting her gaze to the floor. The gesture pokes at my nature, seeing her so frightened that I can't stop from swinging my hand out to slap Torrance.

Big mistake.

He catches my hand before I hit him and draws it to his chest, pulling me into him, so my body is flush against his. I freeze, my heartbeat rapping out of control at his sudden closeness. Breaking his stare, I tilt my head and rest it on his chest. I inhale a breath of his fruity scent.

A strange noise escapes his throat. "Are you sniffing me?"

I groan and try to pull away, but he keeps me pinned to him. "It's called breathing," I lie, heat warming my face.

Fuck. Me. He knows I'm full of shit. I'll never admit that I did sniff him or that I continue to sniff him. It should be a crime for him to smell so edible. I cannot be held responsible for my actions if he's the one daring to risk sharing personal space.

He finally eases his hold on me but doesn't let go of my hand. The doors to the elevator slide open. The empty tunnel greets us, and Rylie gets off first. I tug my hand, pulling Torrance with me instead of freeing my fingers. Rylie gapes at us, no longer staring at the floor. I grimace, baring my bottom teeth at her. She obviously wants me to detach this vampire from me, but I don't know exactly how to.

Torrance swings my hand and chuckles. "What? Is this the first time you've ever held someone's hand? It's nice, right?"

"Oh, so it's okay for you to touch me?" I snap.

"If Ms. Reynolds hadn't rudely interrupted our conversation or handled you so roughly, she would've been fine."

I glare. "You didn't answer my question."

"I'm merely protecting myself from your violent tendencies," he muses. "If it happens to be something we both enjoy, then I don't see the problem."

I shove him, and he grabs my other hand, shifting in front of me to walk backward. I gawk at our hands and then to him, his smirk turning into a full-blown smile. Narrowing my eyes, I drop my gaze to his crotch. I'm not checking out his package, but I fully consider giving him a swift kick to the balls. He's taking his little game too far—at least in front of Rylie. She looks ready to have a coronary while I'm on the brink of teasing him.

"Don't even consider it, Fiona," Torrance says, squeezing my fingers. "If you do, you'll leave me no choice but to carry you like an infant."

I playfully lift my foot. "Not an infant. A back-world blushing bride. You know you want to. You're enjoying every second of holding my hands. I can already imagine how you'll react with your arms around me. Are they as hard as they look?"

His smile fades at my words, his eyes flashing silver. I purse my lips in my own cocky grin, because I got under his skin—pretty sure in a good way.

Dropping my hands, he puts space between us. Whatever crosses his mind stops him from even looking at me now. I should be relieved. I shouldn't care about his rejection. But damn it. His playfulness had me convinced that I could turn him into my next blood source without having to seek out one of his other brothers. Now? I'm not so sure.

Rylie falls into step beside me, staring at the side of my face. I can't bring myself to look at her just yet and keep my focus on the dim tunnel in front of us until it ends at another elevator.

"This is your stop, Ms. Reynolds. Take the elevator to the ground floor and head right. You'll see the lab on the left. They'll be expecting you." Torrance hits the call button on the elevator for her.

"Wait, what about me? I thought I had to give blood too," I say, shifting on my feet.

"Culver has a personal phlebotomist at his disposal. He will not risk any mix-ups," he says, keeping his voice even.

"Oh." I don't know what else to say.

Rylie frowns at the opening elevator door. "He can't draw my blood too? I don't understand why I'm not a personal donor as well."

Torrance sighs. "You've already aged out. To become a personal donor, you must be between eighteen and twenty-two. It allows a vampire to get the maximum adult lifespan as possible. But don't worry, Ms. Reynolds. Your donation to the rest of us lowly vampires is appreciated. You'll provide to our coven once we complete training." He motions to the elevator. "You should get going. You also have time restrictions and shouldn't miss your donation on your first official day. After, check-in in the donor education wing. They'll give you your schedule."

I throw my arms around Rylie, hugging her quickly since I know she won't risk hugging me. She frowns at me until the elevator door slides closed, leaving me alone with Torrance. He peers around the dim tunnel, letting silence fall between us.

"Was that all a lie?" I ask, nudging his bulging bicep with my knuckles.

He meets my gaze. "Huh?"

"You just wanted to get me alone, didn't you?" My. Damn. Mouth. Why can't I control it? It's like it wants me to test my luck to see how dangerous this guy truly is.

Torrance's eyes widen, and he shakes his head. "No, I—"

"Admit it. You want to run away with me. Keep me all to yourself." I offer him a teasing smile, loving his reaction.

Torrance reacts by covering my mouth and pushing me into the wall next to the elevator door. "You can't say shit like that, Fiona. The last thing we both need is for Culver to think I'm trying to steal you from him. I have a position to maintain in my coven, and I'm not willing to risk breaking the rules or disrespecting my brother's authority."

I blink in surprise, something strange, almost fearful lining his voice. He drops his formal tone, sounding more like me. From my blood sources, I know it's something vampires unintentionally do. It's part of their charm to get humans to trust them more. I wonder if he realizes he's doing it with me.

I raise my eyebrows. "Lighten up. I was just teasing. You don't seem like the rule-breaker type anyway. If I was going to ask someone to run away with me, it wouldn't be you." It wasn't him. It was Berkeley, and that was before I realized he was one of the King brothers. It explains why my attempt didn't work.

He tightens his jaw like I offended him. Sheesh. I can't win. He's far too hot and cold that I know I'll never get a drop of blood from him.

The elevator door slides open, and Torrance steps away from me, putting more space than he has since he picked me up. I straighten my dress shirt and comb my fingers through my hair. He silently motions me on, and I enter first.

He doesn't follow me but slaps his hand on a palm pad, turning it green. "One of my brothers will meet you on our floor."

I furrow my brows. "Wait, what? You're not coming?"

He tightens his jaw. "Something's come up. I have to go."

Like that, he disappears, leaving me alone to ride the elevator to a place deeper underground. From the fear coursing through me, I'm nearly certain it might be taking me to my own personal hell.

SEVEN

DONOR DIVISION

"ALL DONE, MS. KING." THE phlebotomist paints a weird gel over the small hole, stopping my blood from dripping. "Make sure you drink a big glass of orange juice at breakfast. I would hate for you to faint."

Rolling down my sleeve, I stand up and glance around the lavish living area of the King Coven's suite. It's larger than any of the houses back home, and from what I can tell, even the coat closet is bigger than the dorm room I share with Rylie.

Aspen puts his com device away and materializes next

to me. He hasn't said more than two words since waiting for me outside the elevator after his brother abandoned me. The only other person in this grand suite was the phlebotomist. At least he was nice.

I thank the phlebotomist for his time and stride to the door that leads to the elevator. I glare at the thing because I have to wait for Aspen to call for it, my handprint turning the damn palm pad red.

From his lack of attention and nicety, I've already crossed Aspen off my mental list of who I'll convince to be my blood source behind Culver's back.

The elevator jerks as it ascends to the ground level. I grasp onto the metal bar to steady myself and catch Aspen staring at me in the mirrored wall. He immediately averts his gaze, turning it toward the ceiling instead of the floor.

"I'm sorry if I inconvenienced the start of your day," I say, finally breaking the silence. "I hope you know it was not my decision."

His hard expression softens, and he finally gives me his attention. "I'm well aware of that, and it's not an inconvenience."

"Okay..." I shift on my feet, uncomfortable by how brisk he is. I guess I shouldn't expect more. I'm only a donor to him—claimed by his brother at that.

"And I apologize if I come off as being short, Ms. King. It is in our best interest if we engage in as little conversation as possible," he says, peering at me in the reflective wall again like he won't risk looking at me directly.

"Why?" I can't help my curiosity. I want to know what makes him different than his other brothers.

He tightens his jaw with the words. "Because I find you perplexingly stunning."

His response throws me off guard, and my jaw drops. That was not what I was expecting him to say. I mean, wow. No one's ever complimented me in such a way.

"And your current reaction is exactly what I was afraid of. My apologies, Ms. King. I didn't mean to make you uncomfortable."

The elevator door slides open, and he bolts away, disappearing and reappearing a dozen feet from me. I run to catch up to him, but every time I attempt to close the space, he uses his vampire speed to keep his distance.

"Hey, come on. I can't keep up with you," I say, stopping to clutch the wall to catch my breath. I plant my ass on a bench just inside the wide lobby.

He rushes back to me. "You can't sit there. This is not a donor commons area."

I sigh and get to my feet. "Then take me to one. I'm not feeling so good."

Aspen combs his fingers through his blond hair, never taking his eyes off mine. I consider planting my ass on the ground to catch my breath, but the last thing I need is for someone else to come and yell at me. My knees shake, my legs not giving me a choice in the matter. My head spins with a dizzy spell.

"Oh, shit," Aspen says, catching me in his arms before I collapse. "Shit."

The world blurs with his speed, and I think I black out for a couple of seconds. A cool hand touches my cheek before a burst of citrusy goodness coats my tongue. I blink the haze from my eyes and catch sight of Berkeley kneeling in front of me. Aspen hugs his arms around me, his body more comfortable than I imagined. His muscles might be hard as bone, but his embrace is nothing short of snuggly.

"Drink some more, Fiona," Berkeley says, holding a glass of orange liquid to my lips. "Your blood sugar is low. It seems the phlebotomist took more blood than he should have."

"Culver demanded he draw more than the daily max," Aspen says, his voice low and husky in my ear. "He signed the waiver to take on responsibility in case of donor death."

Berkeley's fangs peek out from beneath his top lip. "I'll talk to him."

"You know he doesn't actually want her to be his personal blood source, right?" Aspen talks about me like I'm not sitting on his lap, letting Berkeley continue to offer me sips of orange juice.

"He's just in a mood. I'm sure he'll get over his juvenile behavior in a few days. He's never been bested before. She hurt his ego." Berkeley's eyes smile at me, though his mouth doesn't.

"You should've seen her," Aspen whispers, shifting me on his lap a bit. "It was wild."

This time Berkeley does smile at me. "I don't doubt it. Neither do the rest of these pricks. They're too scared to even turn their backs on her."

I flick my gaze up and tense as he purposely and passively addresses the room. A dozen circular tables with red, floor-length table cloths decorate the dining hall. Two crystal chandeliers sparkle light over everything. Brown and burgundy swirl-design wallpaper warms the room, keeping the lighting dim, the atmosphere intimate.

At each table sits a group of vampires drinking blood from crystal goblets like the one the headmistress had in her office. The only thing that would scream more elite than this would be if there was a donor on each table. A few soft voices trickle to me, and I unintentionally lock eyes with the guy who approached me earlier—from the Knightly Coven, I think. He sits with who I assume are his coven brothers, and while they remain expressionless, from the King brothers' various expressions, they are cocky looking enough for me to assume the room isn't scared but jealous.

"You shouldn't give the Knightlys a second of your attention, Fiona," Aspen says into my ear. "Especially Dawson or Monterey. They're douches."

I avert my eyes to another table.

"Don't look at the Godwins either," he adds.

Pursing my lips, I press harder into Aspen and turn my

neck a little. "You try not looking at someone blatantly gawking at you."

The utterly silent room bunches nerves in my stomach. It's creepy. Back home, gathering to eat was always loud as hell. No one ever stared this long either.

A figure blurs toward us, and Hudson appears next to Berkeley. He doesn't greet me with the same smile he had before, so I train my gaze on the glass of orange juice instead. Torrance materializes next and plops into a chair two spaces over. He sets a couple glasses of blood down, acting like I'm not even here.

"Who wouldn't want to look at her?" Hudson says, reaching out to touch my cheek to comb my hair from my face. "She's hot."

I whack his hand away.

He only laughs. "Switch places with me, Aspen. She's more comfortable with me."

Aspen growls. Fear prickles over the back of my neck. I squirm on his lap, trying to get him to loosen his sudden death grip on me. He obviously enjoys my wiggly ass, because I accidentally give him a boner with my movements.

I stiffen and grip my hands into the sides of his legs. "I'm feeling better. Can one of you please show me to the donor dining hall? I would like to eat breakfast without dozens of eyes on me. It's like none of you have ever seen a human woman."

"Don't lump us with them, love," Hudson says.

I sigh. "Whatever. Just take me to the donor dining hall."

"I don't think so. I want you to stay." Culver's gruff voice sends a blip of anger through me. I guess it was wishful thinking to assume he wouldn't join his brothers for breakfast but instead drink my blood in his room or whatever. "If I can't bite you, I want you to watch me drink your blood."

Is he serious?

Aspen slides me into the vacant chair next to him so that I face the table. Culver strolls around to the other side. We face each other, and he glides his tongue over his bottom lip. He's completely serious. Pouring blood from a metal thermos and into a glass, he makes a dramatic show of sipping what I assume is my blood for not only me to witness but also for all four of his brothers. Maybe even the whole room.

He licks his blood-stained lips and grins. "Mmm. I suppose this will suffice."

What an obnoxious bastard. I don't understand how the hell he's supposedly been chosen to run a region. He must be as powerful as hell if everyone tolerates this kind of behavior. Even the horny-ass young soldiers acted more mature than this. And he probably has decades on them.

He takes another drink. "Would be better coming straight from your vein."

I remain expressionless. If he thinks me watching him

drink my blood will get to me, he's wrong. All it does is make me hungry. But not for him. The collection of his brothers' scents wafting around me tantalizes my nature as a dhampir.

I turn my gaze away from Culver's cocky stare to watch Hudson sip his glass of blood. He meets my gaze, his eyes flashing silver. I imagine that he drinks my blood instead of his brother, and hell does the strange fantasy kind of turn me on.

Shit.

Shaking my head, I break his stare, trying my best to suppress my blood lust. I usually wouldn't obsess over it, but because I have no idea when I'll get to satiate my dhampir side, it drives me crazy.

Berkeley plops a bowl of oatmeal in front of me along with a banana. He offers me a warm smile and slides into the chair next to Culver. I hadn't even noticed he left the table to grab me something to eat.

He trains his eyes on me but speaks to Culver. "If you plan on drinking her blood daily, you need to assure she gets proper nutrition. She is a personal donor and not the gen. pop. blood bank. Claiming a personal donor comes with responsibility."

"Do not speak to me as if I'm ignorant, brother. I'm well aware of how to properly take care of my blood source." Culver's face might remain expressionless, but his words burn with anger hot enough to make me sink lower in my chair.

Berkeley clenches his fingers around his glass of blood. "Then you need to stop being purposefully callous. Your attitude will jeopardize our standing with the board. A donor isn't worth the risk of losing the status of region head. I've worked my ass off to get to where I am in the Donor Division. I will not stand by and watch you ruin it."

Culver chugs the rest of my blood in a single gulp. "Do not chastise me, brother. The board will not reject our application based on one female donor."

Berkeley clenches his fingers into fists. "Must I remind you that you need a coven to hold a board member position?"

The tenseness between the two of them leaves me on edge. Everyone in the room hangs onto their discussion. I lean closer, whipping my gaze back and forth between them. While Culver has obvious power, I think Berkeley can handle himself.

While I know it's not all about me, it still revolves around me, and I silently cheer Berkeley on. I like him even more now. I wish he'd punch Culver to get him to shut the hell up.

"Are you threatening to sever our coven union? Because like your thoughts on a donor not being worth jeopardizing our future position with Blood Life Corp, I believe a donor is also not worth the risk of losing your coven." Culver twists his lips up in the corner, glowering at me.

Torrance pounds his fist on the table, startling me. I drop my spoon, and it clatters to the floor. All five of them, along with seemingly everyone else in the room, turn their attention to me. I wipe my mouth with my napkin and drop it on the table. Pushing my chair back, I get to my feet despite Culver demanding I sit here.

"Where do you think you're going?" Culver asks me.

"You're finished drinking my blood." I motion to the glass. "And unlike you, I have somewhere to be."

Culver growls when I turn my back on him, but Berkeley tells him that it is in his best interest if he lets me go.

Peeking over my shoulder, I smile at Berkeley. He remains expressionless. Maybe I did misinterpret his chivalry. It isn't about me but about their standing.

Swiveling back around, I manage to stroll across the dining hall without incident. I head into the hallway alone but only manage to get a few feet away. A shadow sneaks up on me. I recognize Aspen's mouthwatering scent, so I don't have to look up to know it's him. He falls into step by my side, his body close enough that our arms brush together.

I clear my throat. "Next time, maybe take me to the actual donor health center. That was awkward as hell being under everyone's scrutiny like that. I'm sure your brothers would have also appreciated my absence since they seem to hate me for merely existing."

"Does that mean you plan to pass out every day?" he asks, staring at the side of my face as I refuse to look at him.

He avoids commenting on my observation about his brothers' feelings about me, basically confirming that I'm right.

I shrug. "I'm nearly certain I won't have a choice in the matter. Culver is set on killing me one glass filled with the maximum amount of blood at a time."

"Which is why I want to offer you this." Aspen chugs his glass of blood before rolling up his sleeve. He bites his arm, surprising me. It takes everything in me not to snatch his hand to latch onto his arm. He doesn't give me the chance, though. Instead, he dribbles his blood into the glass and offers it to me.

I scrunch my nose. "You can't expect me to drink that."

He frowns, glancing at the glass like my words offend him. "Oh, I'm sorry. I just assumed you'd be okay with drinking my blood with your background. I didn't realize you had a preference as to whom you'd accept an offering from."

I raise my eyebrows. That's why he looks offended. He thinks I don't want his blood because of him. "As long as this isn't an attempt to slow down my death so Culver can enjoy me longer..."

"I'd prefer if he didn't enjoy you at all." Aspen holds my gaze, trying to read my reaction to his thoughts. I like how honest he seems to be, like with the whole compliment thing earlier.

"Then I most definitely want your blood," I'm quick to

say. A little much? Maybe. But something about how he acts like he might like me a bit prods at my nature. Not to mention I'm afraid to pass up the chance to get what I need from him with little effort on my part. "Just...not from that glass. It's contaminated."

He gapes at the cup. "Oh, the human blood."

I nod. "Yeah, it's gross to me." Reaching out, I lace my fingers around his wrist and pull his arm up to my mouth. "This way is fine."

The second my lips caress his skin, he releases a soft gasp of a moan like my mouth on him is the last thing he expected. Sliding his free hand around my waist, he tugs me into him close enough to feel his hardening desire. And hell do I enjoy his reaction. It means I wasn't off in my thoughts about him.

I meet Aspen's gaze as tingles burst over my tongue and down my throat. A need so intense consumes me that I can't find the will to pull away. The blood donation got to me. So has Aspen. He was the last one I expected to drink blood from, especially because he didn't ask for anything in exchange. He's purely giving me his blood for my benefit. Such an act, giving up an ounce of control to me, gives me a serious lady boner. Blood drinking has never been only about getting what I need to survive.

I never wanted my blood sources back home to feel like a meal like vampires make humans feel. And obviously, that idea is the last thing on Aspen's mind as his hand slides down to my ass, watching my eyes to see if it's okay. I give him silent permission by lifting my leg up so that he can pick me up and let me straddle his waist.

"Fiona," he whispers, my name a breathless plea on his lips. "You're so beautiful."

His words set me off in a good way, and I ease from his arm only to plant my lips to his. The world spins as he relocates us out of the hallway. My back hits a wall, and Aspen deepens his kiss, testing the seam of my lips with his tongue until I open my mouth to feel the soft sensation of his tongue caressing mine.

He eases away to smile at me. "I haven't been able to get you off my mind since the moment I laid my eyes on you."

I close the space again and explore his mouth with mine. He whispers my name again, and I slide my fingers into his blond hair and down his neck, memorizing his body through his clothes with my fingers.

Lowering me a bit, he presses his now raging boner between my legs, testing the barrier our clothing creates between us. I moan softly into his mouth, squeezing my thighs tighter around him. I can't believe I'm kissing him, that I'm the reason he's incredibly turned on, or that he hasn't even asked for a taste of my blood. Just the thought sends a rush of desire through me.

Aspen slows down, easing away from me to look into my eyes again. "I wish I were the one to claim you. Culver doesn't deserve a donor like you."

His words snap me from my blood lust-induced haze, and I slap him across the face. He growls in shock and drops me. I manage to land in a crouch before hitting my knees. He's so lucky that I consumed his blood, and the ache of my tender skin doesn't bother me.

"What the hell?" he asks, twisting his features in confusion. Despite my scowl, he risks closing the space and holds out his hand to me. "I'm sorry. I didn't mean to drop you. What did I do wrong for you to hit me?"

"I should've known you weren't being nice for no reason." I turn away from him, wishing that I never let him so close to me. I knew better. Just because he offered me his blood doesn't mean anything. In his eyes, I'm a donor. Beneath him. "I'm such an idiot."

I stride across what looks like a storage room of blood draw equipment to the door and fling it open to head into the hallway.

Aspen blocks my way out, holding up his hands. "Fiona, wait. I don't understand what you're insinuating about me being nice. It's not an act or anything. I find you so...enthralling. I thought we were having a good time."

"We were, but now it's over." I shove past him, not letting his size intimidate me. "Donors like me have places to be. Now, if you'll excuse me, I need to go and figure it out since I'm pretty sure I wasn't supposed to have my breakfast in a donor-restricted area. The last thing I need is to get into more trouble."

He groans and follows me, keeping at my pace. "You wouldn't have gotten into trouble. You're Culver's personal donor. It's expected that you'd share a meal together even if he can't bite you."

Like that makes it any better.

Instead of saying so, I bow my head and walk like I've seen the other humans of the academy do. I treat Aspen like how I've seen vampires treat the humans, acting as if he's not walking by my side. I'm afraid to give him any more of my attention.

Give a little and they take it all, according to Elder Newberry and his reasoning in trying to keep me from the blood sources. They don't think the same as humans. While I was enjoying Aspen's closeness, he was clearly dreaming about laying me on a table to drink my blood instead of all the other fun stuff he should've been thinking.

Why does it annoy me so much?

"Fiona..." He obviously wants to say something but realizes his charm over me wore off the second I slapped him.

I swing my gaze to him. "Don't say my name like I'm the one who hurt your feelings. You don't even know what those are. You're clueless."

The soft murmur of voices draws my attention in front of me, shutting down anything else Aspen can say. I spot a few humans striding in different directions through a lounge area with dozens of doors all facing a central reception counter. A sign declares I've found the Donor Division wing, and I slow down to peer at the man sitting at the desk in the center of the lobby. He glances up to me for a second before shifting his gaze to acknowledge Aspen beside me.

"Nice to see you, Mr. King. I hope you're having a lovely evening," the man says, leaning back in his chair. "I had expected your coven leader to check in Ms. King and Ms. Reynolds."

At the sound of Rylie's name, I jerk my attention to the row of chairs lined against the wall. Rylie sits with her head bowed without looking in my direction. At her feet rests two black bags. She's far better put together than I am. Someone must have helped her tie the dumb tie around her neck so that she fits in with everyone else.

"My brother couldn't spare a moment today, and I still need to get in my Donor Division hours, so I'll be taking his place."

"Donor Division hours?" I wish my curiosity would control itself. I don't want to open a line of communication with the guy who wishes he was the one to claim me as his possession just because I kissed him.

"All region and city heads are required to accrue a certain amount of hours among the donor population. It helps give a better understanding of..." He lets his voice trail off.

"How to control us? Assure you know how to keep us placated so we don't resist? Learn how to manipulate us to do whatever the hell you want?"

"Ms. King!" The man behind the counter stands up and smacks my hand with a wooden rod. "You cannot speak to Mr. King, or any other vampire for that matter, that way. Now show me your wrists so I can offer you another reminder."

What the hell? The guy's commanding voice pushes my body to comply, and I stretch out my arms in front of me. I guess I shouldn't be so surprised by a violent punishment. I'm sure other humans fare much worse in actual vampire households.

The man swings the rod, and I close my eyes, preparing for the pain to ensue. I hear the stick smack against something. A soft groan gets me to snap my eyes open when pain doesn't swell through me. I gawk at the man standing with his arm cradled against his chest.

Aspen points the rod at the man. "Mr. Croft, do not ever attempt to punish Ms. King in that manner again. She has permission to speak freely within my coven, and she knows not to extend that same informality to anyone else."

The man, Mr. Croft, blinks a few times and nods. "Yes, Mr. King. My apologies. I'll inform Ms. King's instructors of your request."

Aspen sets the rod on the counter. "Good. I expect you have the schedules in order?"

"Yes, Mr. King. Here are Ms. King and Ms. Reynolds' work tablets. If you'd allow me, I can show them how they work."

Aspen swipes them off the counter. "No, thank you. As the head of my coven's innovation and technology division, I have it handled."

Motioning to me, Aspen gets me to leave the counter. I stop a few feet away and turn to glare at him.

"You did not have to do that," I snap. "A word of warning would have worked on that guy."

Aspen glowers right back at me. "Would you like me to allow him to hit you next time?"

"Actually, yeah. I better get used to it seeing as Culver will probably tear out my throat the second you guys complete your training here." I dodge past him and catch sight of Rylie gaping at us.

Fingers link to my shoulder and spin me around. "What the hell is wrong with you? What did I do to piss you off? I still don't understand why you're so...annoyed, especially after..."

I close my eyes for a second before I drown myself in the light blue color of his gaze. "Are you that oblivious?"

"Did I get the wrong impression? I thought you enjoyed my company, or do you kiss everyone like that?"

I release a shocked laugh. "For your information, I've only ever kissed two other people and definitely not like that."

He leans closer to lower his voice. "Then what the hell is wrong?"

I wave my finger between us. "This. This is. I'm not

something you can possess and play with. You cannot act like you have some sort of right to claim me."

He tilts his head, studying my face without a word. "I *don't* have a right. You belong to my brother."

I sigh. "You know what? You're right. None of this is important anyway. I don't know what I was thinking. I'm no different than every human here."

Spinning on my boots, I don't give him a chance to respond. Instead, I rush to Rylie and throw my arms around her.

"You okay?" she asks, whispering in my ear.

I shake my head, blinking my eyes. "We need to figure a way out of this. And soon."

EIGHT

PERSONAL DONORS SUPPORT GROUP

"WAIT, SO LET ME GET this straight. Personal donors aren't allowed to pursue a romantic relationship with another human?" I shift in my seat, staring at the small tablet with a list of rules and etiquette I must learn to fulfill my position as Culver's personal donor.

The eight other guys in the small class look at me, amusement crossing their faces.

"Am I the only one who doesn't think this is fair? I have needs." I blush as the words escape my mouth. I didn't mean for them to sound like my needs fall into the whole sex category, but I'm pretty sure if I can't have a companion outside of Culver...fuck. My rebel gaze darts over to Aspen as he leans against the wall. No one follows my line of sight, pretending like he isn't even in the room.

A chuckle erupts from the cute guy sitting across from me in our circle of desks. "Don't we all. I'm sure your mister would be happy to fulfill any of your requests."

That makes another guy tip his head back and laugh. "Some of us are doomed to have relationships with our hands."

My mouth drops open, and I crinkle my nose. "You say that like you wouldn't be doomed already."

Another guy whacks him with a howl of a laugh. "Damn. I'm jealous as hell of whoever claimed you."

I throw my hands up. "This is ludicrous." I flick my attention to Aspen again. I can't help myself, even if I'm still a little angry. My wandering thoughts just can't stop replaying the feeling of his mouth against mine.

"But it's necessary." An older man, probably the oldest looking one I've seen this whole time on campus, straightens his back and looks at me. "Can anyone explain to Fiona why that is?"

"Vampires would rather kill a donor than share," the cute guy across from me says, smiling rather than giving me the news of what will surely be my fate if I can't stop glancing at Aspen.

"That's right, Elliott. Possessiveness," the man says. "And unfortunately for you, Fiona, you'll have a much harder time if you don't recognize things that might trigger your mister's deep-seated nature. Can anyone name what types of situations a personal blood donor should avoid?"

"Eye contact," Elliot says, responding before anyone. "A personal donor should not look at anyone directly besides their mister or mistress."

I flick my gaze to Aspen again. He finally meets my stare, gazing at me from across the room. I shift in my seat and look away.

"Purposely touching someone without permission," the guy next to me says.

"Not completely, Bryan," the guy on the other side of me says. "Right, Mr. Craig?"

"Right, Pete. While you should avoid physical contact, it's more of when someone else touches you without first getting permission from your mister," Mr. Craig says. He shifts his attention to me. "Why don't you try to think of a scenario, Fiona? An important part of guaranteeing your safety is to recognize and be aware of certain circumstances."

I purse my lips, hating that the instructor put me on the spot. The weight of Aspen's stare draws my attention to him, and I can't stop my mouth from blurting. "Making out with one of your mister's coven brothers."

Silence greets me as all the guys stare at me like I said the most ridiculous thing in the entire universe. I shift uncomfortably and glance at my work device again, though nothing has changed.

"Fortunately for you, the likelihood of that occurring is nearly unfathomable. Vampires take possessive claims, especially over personal donors, rather seriously. And from what I know about the King Coven, their tight-knit bond would never allow such an occurrence."

Aspen has the nerve to smirk without comment.

I lick my lips. "Then I would say accepting blood from another vampire."

Once again, I'm greeted with silence.

"You know, in case you get seriously injured or something," I add.

Mr. Craig scratches the back of his head, trying to gather his thoughts for a moment. I guess these types of situations have never been brought up before. It's not exactly something I imagined to happen either.

"Wow," Elliot says, speaking up. "It's not often someone makes Mr. Craig speechless."

Mr. Craig snatches a wooden rod from a holder on his seat and whacks Elliot on the knee with it. "Show some respect."

Elliot rubs his knee. "Sorry, sir. It's just that her questions are strange. She should know that a vampire would never willingly share blood—not for something like that."

I frown. "Tell that to my blood sources..." I cringe as the words fall from my mouth. I thought everyone looked at me like I was crazy before. But now? I'm pretty sure I've suddenly grown two heads.

Mr. Craig claps his hands together. "All right. We're getting a bit off topic. Fiona, I want you to read the section about the intimacy of a blood exchange in your guidebook before tomorrow's class. As for the rest of you, I want you to make a list of everything you know about the resistance and Blood Rebels. We'll continue class tomorrow with an open mind. I'm sure Fiona would love to enlighten us on her experience growing up unregistered. This way, we can better help her adjust to her new life as a personal blood source."

Ah hell. I don't like the sound of any of that. I raise my hand, getting Mr. Craig's attention. "I'd rather not. I'm sure no one wants to hear about my boring-ass life, anyway."

Elliot grins. "What are you talking about? You're the most exciting person to have enrolled in the academy."

I automatically look at Aspen. Surprisingly, he smirks again like he agrees with the guy.

Mr. Craig offers me a smile. "We are here to support you, Fiona. That is the goal of this class and why it's only open to those selected as personal donors. No one will understand you like we do, but we can't unless you help us out. Everything that you share will remain confidential. No judgments either."

Yeah, right. I can already see the list of people these dudes plan to tell about my "needs" as soon as we leave here. They'll probably hold on to their thoughts for themselves later, too. Ugh.

I don't have it in me to argue with Mr. Craig, so all I do is nod and swipe my bag off the floor. Tossing my work device into it, I go to sling it over my shoulder when Aspen locks his hand around the strap and takes it from me.

"I'm capable of carrying my own bag," I snap, trying to steal it back from him.

"You're still pissed off." It's not a question.

I don't respond to him, feeling the weight of everyone's gazes on us. Striding to the door, I exit the small room and back into the lobby where the same guy as before remains seated behind the enclosed reception area. We're the first ones out of class, and I head toward the row of seats along the wall and plop my ass down.

According to my schedule, the Personal Donors Support Group was my last class of the day, but I annoyingly have an assignment to do in each of them from basic Reading Comprehension to Household Management, and embarrassingly Human Hygiene, like I don't know how to bathe properly or some shit. This school is the worst. I wish I could take things more beneficial—like combat, vampire law, anything that'll give me a better understanding. But like the rest of the human population, I'll always be deprived. I'll have to teach myself like always.

"Fiona, will you let me apologize?" Aspen asks, breaking the silence. "My behavior...it was inappropriate. I got carried away after, you know." He motions to his arm without rolling up the sleeve. His bite would already be healed anyway.

"You should've told me that accepting your offer put my life at risk." I wring my hands together. "I might be just a donor to you, but—"

He rests his elbows on his knees. "I'd never put you in danger." His voice comes out so softly that I strain to hear his whisper.

"Did you not hear the instructor? I'm a dead woman. The second Culver finds out—"

Aspen cuts my words off with a kiss that steals my breath away. I hum with desire, caught off guard yet surprised in a good way at his sudden closeness. I clutch his face and swivel in my seat to kiss him deeper.

"Fiona." Rylie's sharp voice erupts panic through my heart, and I scramble away, falling off my chair in the process.

Someone catches me from behind and rights me on my feet. I stiffen, gawking at Rylie standing ten feet away and Aspen still sitting in his chair. He tightens his jaw and growls, the deep, throaty noise setting off my fear instincts.

"I'd say I got you, love," Hudson says, his breath tickling my ear, "but it seems my brother had you first. Way to make a guy jealous. And to think I had already planned our future together."

I close my eyes, trying to suppress my panic. "It was an accident. Please don't kill me."

"Your mouth on his was an accident? Kill you?" Hudson eases his hands off my hips. "Both of those things are absurd. Killing you isn't even on the list of things I want to do to you. Kiss you like my brother did is currently number one, though. Because, damn."

I shiver at his soft voice caressing my cheek as he whispers in my ear.

"He won't tell if you want to," he adds.

Aspen tightens his jaw, obviously hearing his suggestion and noticing my unintentional reaction. I had almost kissed Hudson already, and it was Aspen's interruption that had stopped that.

"Fiona, want to go to the library?" Rylie asks, braving to speak up and break both Aspen and Hudson's attention on me. "We could stop at the dining hall first. The rest of the night is ours to do as we please."

Swallowing my nerves, I nod and step away from Hudson. Rylie keeps her eyes trained to the floor even though Hudson stares at her. Aspen joins him, and a strange sensation crawls across my skin. I can't explain it, but I fight to resist the need to deny Rylie to ask the two of them to hang out.

Instead, I offer my arm to Rylie. "I'll see you two later."

"You bet you will, love," Hudson says, grinning at me.

"Love?" Rylie mutters under her breath. "What the hell?"

Before Hudson can respond, I drag Rylie away. It only

takes me twenty feet to realize that the two of them follow us. I peek over my shoulder and glare. Hudson mouths the words "flight risk" with a smile, answering my silent question of why they're creeping behind us. Twirling his finger, he motions for me to turn around.

I pick up my pace, tugging Rylie with me. "I'm sorry you saw that," I whisper, trying to keep my voice inaudible to Aspen's vampire hearing. While I am sorry I got caught, I'm not apologetic the kiss happened...twice. I didn't expect the shy, aloof vampire to be such an amazing kisser. I can already imagine doing it again.

Rylie puffs out her bottom lip, stopping my imagination from turning into a fantasy. "And I'm sorry you felt you had to do that."

"What do you mean?" I stare at the side of Rylie's face. I expected a far worse reaction. The fact that we grew up together, and I know her feelings about vampires hasn't escaped me yet. And right now, she's handling her feelings pretty well.

"I know you're doing what you have to do for the sake of surviving." She says the words in such a way that if Aspen and Hudson do hear her, I doubt they'll speculate that she refers to my need of vampire blood. "Do you think you'll get what you need?"

I rub my lips together and offer her a smirk, silently telling her that I already have.

She reads my expression, her eyes widening. "No wonder they're stalking us."

"Hey. We are not stalking," Hudson says from behind us.

"You're also wrong about Fiona. She does not have to do anything she doesn't want to for the sake of surviving." Aspen obviously takes offense to the notion that I kissed him for any other reason than I wanted to.

Rylie flares her nostrils and spins to face him. "My best friend would never even look at a vampire otherwise."

Scrambling to get between them, I hold my hands up. "Please, don't hurt her. Rylie's like my family. The only person I'd consider so. She's protective of me."

Aspen automatically steps away. "I wouldn't. It's against the academy's rules to harm a donor."

Rylie glares. "So you'll just wait until we're out of here."

"Rylie!" I snap, pushing her away. "What the hell? Do you have a death wish?"

"Do you?" she accuses. "You were kissing that asshole where anyone could see you. What if he's setting you up? I know that you will do what you need to do, but try not to be stupid about it, okay?"

"Just trust that I know what I'm doing, Ry. Please." I lean in close to her. "We need someone on our side. That's what I'm doing."

"Are you sure about that?"

I resist responding how I want to—with a yell that everyone on campus would be able to hear. The last thing I need is to remind her that I'm different. What she sees as danger, I see as a good time.

"Yes, I'm sure. Now, come on. I'm starving and have a lot of assignments to complete for tomorrow." Ignoring the gazes of Aspen and Hudson, I get Rylie to pick up speed, though it's her who has to lead the way. I don't know where anything is in this place. I just keep walking and eventually end up where I'm supposed to be like everything is inter-connected. It helps that with one of my ever-present vampire stalkers, I'm not restricted to donor-only areas.

Rylie leads me into a noisy dining hall with a long counter that lines one of the walls. A variety of different foods in different trays waft delicious scents through the air. It's almost as good as the vampire dining hall in that way.

I gawk at the massive selection far superior to the oat-meal I had for breakfast. My mouth already waters at the sight of a dozen different kinds of food I've never tried before. Mount Light Haven relies heavily on the land, the community mostly eating stuff we grow unless traveling soldiers brought stuff in. This stuff is definitely far from the vegetarian basics.

"Whoa, is that beef?" I ask, pointing at what I'm pretty sure are hamburger patties. The cattle in our community were used for dairy products and not the meat.

A hand touches my shoulder. "If you're not used to eating particular items on the menu, I'd suggest you start small."

Spinning around, I face Berkeley as he stands a foot away from me, staring at my overly full plate of food. "Are you seriously monitoring my diet?"

"Yes, it's part of my job as your health keeper. I figured I'd stop by since Aspen said you missed lunch, and I suspected you might gorge yourself." He glances at my plate.

Heat flushes my face, and it takes everything in me not to chuck all my food onto his pristine white shirt. "I'm not gorging. Just because I have a little bit of everything on my plate doesn't mean anything."

He smirks. "Whatever you say."

I turn back toward the line, catching the gazes of a few familiar guys from my classes. Ignoring Berkeley's presence, I continue to fill my plate despite his warning. Rylie waits for me at the end of the line, her plate not even half as full as mine. She raises an eyebrow, and Berkeley chuckles from behind me.

"Don't judge me," I mutter to her. "That asshole already does. "You've already had two meals here. All I've had was overly sticky, unsweetened oatmeal, which I didn't even get to fully eat."

Rylie grabs a plate with a piece of cake on it and sets it on my tray. She grabs a cup of some sort of chocolate cream stuff next and squeezes it on next to it. "Then you definitely want these too."

Berkeley closes the space to me and swipes my plate to

carry it for me. "Fi, I'm not judging you. I'm looking out for you. There is a difference. And you should've told me you didn't like what I brought you for breakfast."

"Whatever." I don't bother trying to snatch my plate back and instead follow Rylie. I want to limit as much conversation with him as possible after this morning. Though he was nice to me from the moment we met, he makes me nervous on all sorts of levels. One, he butts heads with Culver, and I'm more likely to get caught in their angry crossfire. Two, he's ridiculously attractive. Rugged, muscular, dreamy as hell. And three, I kissed one of his other brothers.

A few guys, including Elliot from my last class, wave in our direction. Rylie picks up her pace to head to their table. Nerves bunch my stomach. The weight of the stares from the all-male table penetrates the two of us before flicking to where I know Berkeley remains like a shadow.

"Hey, guys," Rylie says, her cheerful voice drawing a smile from at least half the table. "Have you met Fiona yet?"

"Hello again, Ms. King," Elliot says, keeping his eyes glued to the table instead of looking at me when he speaks. He obviously knows how to separate what was supposedly a private discussion in class, even with Aspen present, from the rules of how to treat personal donors in the donor commons. I, on the other hand, take a moment to look at each of the guys.

"Is it okay if we join you?" Rylie asks, already setting her tray on the circular table. She takes a seat next to a guy from my hygiene class, who I think is named Patrick, and she bumps her shoulder to his. She turns her attention to me. "Come on. There's room for you to squeeze in."

I turn to grab my tray from Berkeley and see that he already arranges my dinner at the empty table behind the group. He smirks and motions for me to join him without even looking at the table of my new classmates gawking at me.

"Fiona?" Rylie asks, drawing my attention to her. "Come on. Sit."

The guy next to her, Patrick, leans in and says, "Maybe she shouldn't."

"Yeah, there's a space rule when it comes to personal donors, and it looks like it already applies to her," Elliot says.

Rylie huffs. "But that's not even—"

I touch Rylie's shoulder. "It's fine. I'll just sit behind you."

She frowns but relents, obviously not wanting to make a scene in front of her new friends. I pat her shoulder and join Berkeley, who sits right next to the place he set up for me. I slump onto the bench seat and rest my elbow on the table, trying not to let the whole situation get to me. I'm not exactly used to being treated like this. In Mount Light Haven, no one would have ever suggested it would be better if I didn't include myself.

"You should start with the spinach salad," Berkeley

says, forking the lightly dressed leaves for me. He holds it up, and I just stare at the fork.

"Uh, I can feed myself," I say, swiping a piece of melon with my fingers from my pile of fruit instead of accepting his offering.

He blinks, his brows furrowing, and then he sets the fork down. "I guess you can."

"I've been doing it since I was a toddler." I grab a piece of tangerine next and nibble a bite, the juice splashing my chin.

He smirks and offers me a napkin. "That explains a lot."

Narrowing my eyes, I pick up a strawberry next and chuck it at him. I gasp and cover my mouth with my hand as it splats against the middle of his forehead. He didn't even move, allowing me to throw my food at him.

I rush to wipe the glob off his forehead with my napkin, shifting in my seat to check to see if anyone noticed. People did. Silence falls over the room, the other donors probably anticipating my punishment.

Berkeley ignores everyone and graces me with the best smile, even with his fangs. Offering me the forkful of spinach salad again, he waits until I relent and let him feed it to me.

"Throwing food is also a tendency of young donors, besides the lack of using utensils," he teases, his smile widening even more with my glare.

I grab the fork from him to feed myself, the stares of the other donors making me nervous. I know Berkeley probably doesn't intend for his gesture to seem like he's feeding a pet, but from the look of the one of three other females besides Rylie and me in the dining hall, it's misconstrued as such.

"I didn't expect you to let me hit you." I lower my voice, hoping if people can't hear us, they might stop paying attention.

"Now what would be the fun in teasing you if I didn't let you tease me back? You're cute when you get your way." He bumps his shoulder to mine. "Plus, I realize my presence caused you some inconvenience with the others."

I lick my lips, making sure I don't have dressing on my mouth. "I've never felt so rejected in my life. How stupid, right? Not like anything can ever come of it."

Something indecipherable flickers in his eyes, and he scoots a bit closer until I can barely manage to eat without elbowing him. His sugary scent fragrances my breathing space, and I can't stop myself from shifting toward him until I can meet his hazel eyes. Our knees brush together, the subtlety of our bodies touching eliciting tingles through me.

"You're far from rejected, Fi," Berkeley murmurs.

I tighten my lips. "They're afraid of me."

He shakes his head. "No, they're afraid of *me*. They're fearful that I'll notice how the male population can't take their eyes off you. How they shift closer to hear the melody of your voice. How they wish you'll grace them with your enchanting smile."

I raise my eyebrows and laugh. "Yeah, sure." I motion my hand to the table across from us. "Look at that guy's hand. He's shaking."

"Because he realized I heard him whisper something inappropriate about you to his friend." Berkeley's eyes flash silver with his words.

The guy hops up from the table and trips over his own feet, clearly hearing our conversation. Berkeley vanishes from beside me, and I tense at the sight of him now standing over the guy. I clench my fork in my hand, fully prepared to throw it if I have to, but Berkeley only helps the guy to his feet.

"So you know, Mr. Sampson, I agree with you," Berkeley says, flicking his gaze to me.

Everyone watches the guy go without looking back at us. Murmurs whisper through the room, and I hear my name a couple of times. I don't even have to hear to know that Berkeley's presence is unwanted here, and they're silently blaming me.

Setting down my fork, I slide off the bench and grab my bag from the floor. I step the couple of feet it takes to reach Rylie and rest my hands on her shoulders. She startles, dropping her fork onto her plate. It's enough for me to realize that coming here was a mistake. Eating with the King Coven in the vampire dining hall might have been awkward and agitating with Culver's presence, but at least people didn't look like they were going to make a run for it.

"I don't think I'm up to go to the library. I'm not feeling well," I say, meeting her gaze. "I didn't get much sleep."

She tightens her lips. "Want me to come with you? I'm nearly finished." Her gaze darts to the guy, Patrick, and I can tell she doesn't actually want to come with me.

So despite wanting to talk to my best friend in the privacy of our dorm, I wag my head, sending my dark purple hair sweeping back and forth. "It's okay. We'll talk later."

This way, I'll have time to think things through. I wanted nothing more than to escape the fate the elders wanted for me, but this wasn't the life I imagined, feeling like an outcast among people who would've treated me like a gift to humanity if they weren't subjected to serve vampires.

"Okay, I won't be too late," Rylie says, giving me a half hug.

Turning away from her, I meet Berkeley's frown. I don't say anything as I stroll past him and to the arched doorway that exits into the hallway I think will take me to the path back to the dorms.

"You okay, Fi?" Berkeley asks, falling into step beside me.

I don't respond to him. I don't even look at him. Instead, I keep my eyes trained on the floor and let him follow me outside and into the night.

NINE

BLOOD SOURCE

I PACE AROUND MY ROOM, staring at the sun shining through the tinted window. The special tint is meant to protect vampires, but it really gets on my nerves. I'm not used to things being so dim all the time, even if I should sleep. But I can't. Not alone like this.

Rylie came in a few hours ago only to peek her head in to check on me. I could hear Patrick's murmur of an invitation to his dorm room, so I pretended to be asleep. She should at least enjoy herself in this prison of a school, and Patrick seems just like her type.

A soft knock on the door draws my attention from the window. I frown and cross the room, flinging it open, expecting to see Rylie finally returning. Berkeley stands in the hallway with his hands hidden in the pockets of a hoodie. His dark brown hair hangs in a damp wave to the side. I can't help drinking in how sexy he looks in casual clothes, his face flushed from what I can only assume is the heat of his recent shower.

"I hope I didn't wake you," he whispers, rocking on his heels. "I know it's late...or early. I couldn't sleep."

I open the door wider and step back. Berkeley straightens his shoulders, glancing over my head and into my dorm room as he checks for Rylie.

"She decided to spend the night with someone else," I say, answering his silent question. "I hope that's okay. I didn't see anything against it in the code of conduct for donors."

He smirks at me. "We're all adults here. There is nothing against spending the day with someone...except for you. You are only permitted to join Culver in our coven's suite."

I grimace at the thought. "Maybe if he were you I'd consider it." I cringe as I accidentally say my thought out loud. "I mean, you don't seem like you want to murder me in my sleep."

His eyes flash silver. "If I could claim your contract and you chose to room with me, the one thing I can promise is that. But in all honesty, I doubt either of us would be sleeping."

Fuck. Me.

Blush crawls up my chest and to my neck, and I shift my weight from one foot to the other. Berkeley reaches up and traces my jaw without touching me like he can somehow absorb the warmth of my skin.

"I'm sorry, Fi. I shouldn't have said that," he murmurs.

I rub my lips together. "Probably not." Because now my damn mind wants nothing more than to turn this unexpected encounter into a full-blown fantasy. "But I don't mind. I prefer you to speak freely, because I can't read you."

He chuckles, his voice nearly breathless. "That's probably for the best. I do hope you know that I don't agree with the situation my brother forced on you at all. While you technically broke a couple of laws in Nocturnal Crown, you do not deserve to be the victim of his unwarranted cruelty."

"Thanks for saying that." Waving my hand, I motion to my room. "Would it be inappropriate to invite you in? I kind of don't want anyone seeing you in the hall. I still haven't recovered from dinner."

His face hardens into a frown. "I am sorry about that. Next time I'll mind your space. I just..." He doesn't finish his thought and accepts my invite into the room, looking once behind him before closing the door.

The room suddenly shrinks with his presence, Berkeley's muscular form dominating the space in front of me. He silently looks around, taking notice of the two made beds, my pile of laundry on the floor, and my unfinished assignments on the single desk.

"This is quite inadequate," he says, mostly to himself.

I swipe my bra from the chair and stuff it under my comforter. "It's fine." I roll it out for him and take the spot on my bed. "So what brings you here? They don't make you guys babysit me all day too, do they?"

"That's the daytime security's responsibility since you're not exactly wandering." Straightening his shoulders, he reaches into the front pocket of his hoodie and brings out what looks identical to the thermos I watched Culver pour my blood from.

"Please don't tell me I have to fill that up. I know the limitations of the human body, and with how much the phlebotomist took the last time, any more will put my health in jeopardy." I scoot down on my bed to put space between us. "As a health keeper, you should know that."

Untwisting the thermos, he shows me its contents. I nearly snatch the cup away to chug it, smelling the scent that I'm certain is his blood. I inhale a shuddering breath, meeting his gaze. His features harden but not in a bad way. He swallows and licks his lips, his anticipation nearly as palpable as mine. And after the Personal Donor Support Group, I realize that him offering me his blood without me asking him is a huge deal.

"I do know that, Fi," he says, keeping his voice low. I love how he shortens my name, calling me something different than everyone else. "And while the information you might have learned probably contains back-world medical science that doesn't apply much now with our blood production enhancers, I do fear for your health under Culver's desire to push you to your limit."

"So you want me to drink your blood?" It's obvious from the thermos, but I have to ask. My desire to hear him say it prods at my very nature as a dhampir.

He clears his throat. "Vampire blood carries regenerative qualities that will assure you can handle the blood loss without having to go through a blood transfusion. After speaking with Aspen—"

I frown, twisting my lips. "He told you?"

Berkeley rolls the thermos between his hands. "Yes, as a precaution in case you experienced any side effects from his blood apart from the mild lust he said you experienced."

I groan and comb my fingers through my hair. "That wasn't all because of the blood." I regret saying the words immediately. I just can't seem to control sharing my thoughts. Berkeley makes it far too easy to talk to.

"You don't have to explain anything. I'm not here to talk about your encounter with my brother. I just want to assure your safety against Culver's undeserved wrath." He extends his arm to hand me the cup. "So will you please drink this?"

I frown without taking the thermos. I had no idea I'd be so disappointed by the fact that he's solely here because he's my health keeper. And it's utterly crazy for me to be upset. I mean, what the hell? I kissed his brother. I nearly kissed his other one. Now, I'm sitting here, thinking about what it would be like to kiss him too. I shouldn't want to kiss him or any vampire. I've never desired something so much, at least, not when it came to the suitors the elders have sent my way. All of this makes me wonder if there is a reason for my lack of...interest in the humans. This makes me think so, but I can't be sure.

"Fiona..." His soft voice draws my attention to him. "It's okay if you don't want to. I'm sure Aspen would be willing to give you some of his if you want. I can call him."

"No, don't," I'm quick to say. "I'll drink yours, if that's what you want."

He makes a whispery, sexy noise and licks his lips. "I do."

Berkeley shifts from the chair to sit in the space on the bed that I put between us. I don't grab for the thermos right away and instead meet his gaze again. The way he devours me with his eyes, trailing them from my lips and to my breasts showing cleavage from my tank top, continuing down to my bare legs on display because I chose a pair of cotton shorts to sleep in—he makes me feel so sexy even though I'm not trying to be.

"You know, I wouldn't mind if you wanted me to drink from your arm." I bite my lip with a smile, loving how he reacts with a moan at even the idea.

He shifts, pressing his leg into mine. "I might regret this, but I don't trust myself enough with you to do that. I..." He chuckles and shakes his head.

"You what? I told you I like when you speak your mind," I say.

He combs his fingers through his hair. "I shouldn't. Things are complicated enough." Caressing his finger to my shoulder, he pushes my long hair to my back and looks at my throat. "I shouldn't even be this close to you."

"But you are," I say, my voice coming out as a whisper.

"I am."

Before I realize what I'm doing, I find myself closing the space to Berkeley to kiss him. He reacts with such passion that I don't get the chance to straddle him before he's pushing me back onto the bed to deepen our kiss. His elbows cage my head as he keeps the weight of his body off me while resting his legs between mine.

I slip my tongue into his mouth, tasting the sugariness of his kiss that sends tingles through me, turning me on. Breaking his mouth from mine, he trails his lips to my jaw and works his mouth over my neck. I moan as his weight shifts, and he slides his hand down my stomach, testing me to see if I let him continue, his hunger to explore my body too prominent that I want to take this wherever it happens to lead.

I give him silent permission by guiding his hand to the waistband of my shorts and arching my hips up a bit. He glides his fingers down my pelvis and between my legs, releasing a moan just feeling exactly what he does to me.

Gasping as he rubs my slick, sensitive skin, I reach down to graze my fingers over the zipper of his pants, pretty intent on feeling for myself what I do to him as well. His breathing quickens as I manage to unhook his button with one hand and trail my fingers lower to lace my fingers around his erection.

"I want you to be mine," he whispers into my ear, his finger putting more pressure on my clit, creating a far better sensation than I've ever done myself.

I hum under my breath, pulling his cock free from his pants to stroke my hand over it. I might not have a lot of sexual experience when it comes to going all the way, but I've at least been this far a couple of times, just never to completion. If I were caught with one of my blood sources, they'd have been put in the daylight cages. They were nice enough that I hated the idea. But now? I don't have any elders to worry about.

I squirm under Berkeley's touch, the blood hunger he elicits inside me with his offering quickly turning into an uncontrollable lust I want to explore. He does too, his mouth returning to mine as he draws his finger over my body in such a way that I can't stop the short bursts of gasps escaping my lips that he continues to steal away with his kisses.

"Fiona," he murmurs, going further to slip his finger

inside me. "I want to taste you."

The subtle click of his fangs extending turns me on even more that I almost agree to a bite. I tilt my head to expose my throat and shoulder to him. But he doesn't ask and just slowly eases his body next to me so he can link our free hands together to bring my finger to his lips. He kisses the pad of my index finger, watching my reaction.

"Just a prick," he whispers, his breath tickling my palm.

I nod my consent, and he sucks my finger into his mouth and pierces his fang deep enough to draw blood. He hums under his breath, the vibration of his desire building my own until I feel like I'm going to explode.

His lips meet mine once again, sweeter than ever, and I gasp at the taste of his blood from him biting his lip for me to taste him. I suck his bottom lip into my mouth, the sugary flavor setting off my dhampir side. I nearly lose control and bite him, but my body has other plans as my muscles tighten, and I arch my back and grab my pillow to muffle the moan of pleasure escaping me way too loudly.

My chest rises and falls as I catch my breath. Berkeley shifts the pillow from my face and smiles at me before kissing me again. He pulls me closer to wrap his arms around me, just hugging me by the waist as we lie on our sides on the tiny bed, facing each other.

"You're more incredible than I thought. I don't know what it is about you, but I've never been so attracted to anyone in my life." He leans in and kisses me like he can't get enough. Like if he stops, he might never get to do it again.

"You sure you don't want to run away with me yet?" I ask, keeping my voice low.

His jaw tightens, his muscles flexing with his thoughts. "Fiona, I can't. I'm training to be the lead of the Donor Division of my coven's region. I can't do that to my brothers. We've all worked hard to get to this stage."

I swallow my disappointment. "And I'm not worth it. I guess I shouldn't have thought otherwise, huh? Stupid me."

He turns his gaze from me. "Fi, please. It's not that. You're—"

"I get it." I sit up and slide my legs over the edge of the bed. "You don't have to say anything more." Because I don't want to hear it. I don't want to hear how great he thinks I am. In the end, it doesn't change the fact that I'm a donor to him. "You should probably go. Getting caught with you isn't worth costing me my life, even if I'm already on death row in your brother's eyes."

He looks like he wants to say something, but I don't give him the chance and open the door for him. A shadow in the hallway catches my attention but disappears too quickly toward the tunnel. Berkeley releases a soft growl and comes up behind me, tugging me away from the door.

Picking up the untouched thermos of blood from its spot on the floor, he holds it out to me. "You should drink this."

I take it from him but don't bring it to my lips. "Who

was there? Should I be worried?"

Shaking his head, he says, "Only if you're afraid of Hudson."

"Hudson was spying on us?" I can't stop the annoyance from rushing through me. "Will I ever get privacy again? Do you guys sneak around while I shower too? I know I've been deemed a flight risk, but it's not like I even have anywhere to go."

A soft tap draws my attention away from Berkeley to a hulking figure in the doorway. Hudson meets my gaze with a frown while also holding a metal thermos in his hands. I gawk at it in surprise. Because...seriously? I thought it was going to be a lot harder to get my mouth on vampire blood, and here they are giving me more than I need.

"Since Berkeley told you I was here, I want you to know I was not spying on you, nor would I want to. Especially if—never mind." He clenches his fingers into a fist for a moment. "I'm not a creep."

"It seems my brother had the same idea as me," Berkeley says, standing awfully close. Too close.

I struggle to breathe with the fragrance of him tantalizing me and reminding my body about how good it felt to be with him even if my mind knows this whole situation is utter bullshit.

"I just wish he didn't beat me here," Hudson mutters under his breath.

Annoyance rushes over me, and I step forward and

snatch the thermos from his hand. I cradle the two containers to my chest. Narrowing my eyes, I say, "Thank you for your concern and the blood, but you both need to leave. I think you've gotten the wrong impression. I'm not some plaything you can toy with until Culver decides to rip my throat out. I shouldn't let any of you get so close."

"Fiona, no. It's not like that," Hudson says. "Sure, you're fun to tease, but—"

"But I'm a donor. Your brother's personal donor." I clench my jaw, trying to suppress my suddenly wild emotions that make me feel like utter shit. "Just get out. I'm starting to think my life is just a competition to you. So leave. I'm exhausted and need space. I can't think with you guys around."

Hudson looks ready to argue, but Berkeley nudges him toward the door. They exit the dorm room and stare at me from the hallway. I'm about to shut it in their faces when I notice Rylie and Patrick gawking at us from what must be Patrick's room a few doors down across the hall.

Berkeley twists to follow my line of sight, and Patrick slams the door. I huff out a breath and shake my head.

"Fucking great," I mutter. "Just what I need."

"Fiona—"

"I meant what I said. I'm done tonight. I just want to go to bed." Shutting the door, I stroll toward the storage cabinet with a tiny built-in fridge and stick the thermos Hudson gave me inside.

I chug Berkeley's blood, hoping it'll settle my wild heart and stop me from calling them back.

Another tap on the door pulls my attention to it. "Are you kidding me? That better be you, Rylie. I've had enough of the King brothers for one day."

Swinging the door open, I prepare to tell one of them off, knowing that Rylie would just come in since our lock works with the both of us with a single touch of our hands. Fear explodes through me at the sight of Culver standing on the other side of the door.

I try to shut him out, but he rushes in, locking the door behind him.

Linking his fingers into my hair, he holds me in place and snarls. "How dare you sneak around with my brothers. You are mine."

"I wasn't sneaking," I say, trying to grab his wrists.

"You are mine," he repeats, his deep voice cutting through me. "Mine!"

Culver jerks my head, exposing my neck to him. He extends his fangs and tries to lock me in his gaze. I know what he's trying to do, and instead of resisting, I slacken in his arms, faking the fact that he can't manipulate my mind because I just drank Berkeley's blood.

"Don't move. Don't scream. You will let me bite you," he says, his breath sending strands of hair from my face.

I try not to react, afraid he'll give me my final donation if he discovers otherwise.

He leans in closer. "Tell me you want me."

The words stay locked in my throat. I can't do it. I won't do it.

Instead, I scream.

TEN

FINAL DONATION

THE SHRILLNESS OF MY VOICE shocks Culver, stopping him from sinking his fangs into my neck. Jerking my leg, I knee him in the groin, getting him to drop me. He doesn't leave me on the floor for long. Grabbing me by my long hair, he hoists me back up, recovering wicked fast from my attempt to harm him.

"You little bitch," he says, extending his fangs even longer.

This is it. This is the moment I knew would come all my life. I'll die by a vampire's fangs like the elders predicted.

"Which one of my brothers gave you their blood?" His chest heaves, his eyes flashing silver as he keeps them locked on mine.

I don't respond, flailing in his grip. Strands of my hair rip free from my scalp, but I don't stop. I don't care if I end up bald. I'm not going down without a fight.

"Tell me!" he yells, releasing me only to shove me.

I crash into the desk. The pain of the edge ramming into my back sends me to my knees. I feel around the floor, my eyes watering from pain, but I refuse to stop looking for something, anything, to use as a weapon.

"Who gave you their blood?" he asks again, stepping on my hand hard enough to make me scream.

I jab my free fist into his knee. His leg buckles, and he roars and stumbles, catching himself on the bunk bed. Rolling over, I squeeze into the small space under the bed. I knock my hand into a bag Rylie must've hidden. Culver latches his hand onto my ankle and drags me out. I swing the bag, whacking him upside the head. A handful of utensils clatter across the floor, and I swipe up a fork and stab it into his calf.

He falls on top of me, pinning me to the floor. Panic rushes over me as he restrains my hands between us and smooshes my face into the floor. I cry out and try to bite his fingers digging into my cheek. Light bursts into the room from the door, and I scream for help, praying that maybe Berkeley or Hudson chose to remain nearby.

"Get off of her!" Rylie yells, charging into the room. She throws a decorative vase from the hallway, sending glass cascading around me. It's enough to get Culver off me, but he launches at Rylie instead. She doesn't even get to swing her fist before he locks her in a hold.

Culver captures her in his gaze. "Don't fight."

Rylie slackens in his arms, sending panic through me. Her wide eyes don't move along with the rest of her. Culver's mind manipulation paralyzes her. She's utterly defenseless to his attack. Combing his fingers into her hair, he bends her neck too fast for me to do anything. He sinks his teeth into her throat harder than I've ever seen a vampire bite. He doesn't plan just to drink her blood but to kill her.

Fury sweeps over me, pushing me to my feet. I grab a steak knife from the scattered utensils on the floor and race toward him. Culver doesn't release Rylie upon my approach. Underestimating my capabilities gives me the chance I need. I know I'll only get one, so I focus on putting all my strength into the force of my jab.

Culver hollers and snarls, jerking around to launch at me. Rylie falls to the floor, her blood staining our rug. She doesn't move, her open eyes not even blinking. My focus on her distracts me from Culver, and he manages to latch his hands to my waist.

"Tell me which of my brothers gave you their damn blood, Fiona," Culver demands. "If you tell me, I'll let your friend live."

I blink a few times, my heart ricocheting around my chest. "You're lying."

Culver drops me to the ground and kicks me in the stomach, sending me rolling. I hit my back on the wall and heave a breath as his force steals the air from my lungs. Scooping up Rylie, Culver holds her against his chest, drawing his tongue across the bite mark he left on her neck.

"If you tell me, I'll give her my blood, and she can live. If you don't, I'll break her neck," he says, brushing his fingers through her hair to show me her face. He shifts her slightly to look into her eyes. "Beg Fiona for your life."

Rylie suddenly releases a cry, her eyes darting to me. "Fiona, please. Please don't let him kill me. Please."

The desperation in her voice breaks me apart piece by piece even if I know she was manipulated into pleading with me.

"I don't want to die," Rylie says, tears burning pink lines down her cheeks. "You have to do something. It's your fault I'm here. You put me in this position. You should've just accepted your duty."

"Three seconds, Fiona," Culver says. He bends Rylie's neck more, making her scream.

"Fiona!"

"It was Berkeley!" I scramble to my feet, trying to get to Rylie. "Berkeley gave me his blood."

Culver flashes his fangs and drops Rylie to the floor to close the space to me. "I wanted to drain you, but I thought of a far worse punishment," he says, his deep voice stabbing fear into my heart. "Punishment for you and my treacherous brother."

I spit in his face. "Fuck you."

He snaps his teeth at me, making me wince. "Berkeley will never want you again once you transition. He couldn't resist you because you're a helpless little donor bitch."

I only glare.

"You can spend the rest of time an outcast like the worthless piece of shit you are."

He extends his fangs to bite me, and I grab the front of his shirt to keep a few inches of space between us. He snaps his teeth again and again, and I manage to swing my fist up, clocking him in the jaw. The force of my punch surprises him as his head snaps back, his neck now exposed to me.

I don't hesitate and sink my teeth into the skin of his throat, biting him so hard that his blood floods my mouth. I'm dead set on performing his final donation first. Locking my arms around him, I squeeze him as tightly as possible, refusing to let him go. I swallow his blood by the mouthful, my blood hunger controlling me. His hold on me loosens just enough to where I can break free.

He growls, clutching his neck. "What the hell?"

I lick my lips and rush him again, his vampire speed and strength weakened by his blood loss. His eyes widen, setting me off like nothing ever has. I've never seen a vampire afraid in my life, and I want nothing more than to savor every second of it.

Culver tries to dodge out of my way, but Rylie somehow manages to get to her knees, and she trips him. He falls to the ground for a few seconds, still managing to get to his feet. Instead of running like I expect, he spins and rushes me, slamming me into the wall. I don't have time to react to his burst of speed. Pinning me in place, he extends his fangs and sinks them so deeply into my neck that hot, fiery pain shoots through me like his teeth pierce me to my soul.

My vision hazes, my head dizzy with pain flooding through me. Culver pulls back and grins at me, enjoying the uncontrollable whimper that escapes my mouth. His smile pisses me off, his sick-fuck attitude making me want to cut his heart out to devour it. A flash of silver crosses his gaze, his cocky expression vanishing. I realize it wasn't his eyes flashing silver at me, but mine flashing at him.

He releases me, bolting toward the door. I beat him to it, my sudden speed overwhelming him. I punch him in the chest, my hand sinking slightly into his body. He yells as the power of my punch shatters his sternum. Shadows crowd the edges of my vision, and I lose control, feeling like a monster rises from inside me to take over.

I knock Culver off his feet, thrusting him hard enough into the wall that his body sinks into the plaster. He stumbles to stand and glances at the tinted window. Swinging his fist, he punches the glass, but it doesn't shatter. All it does is crack under the pressure. His desperation, one intense enough that he's willing to risk the sun to escape, only fuels me more.

Grabbing another steak knife from the floor, I stalk him, hissing under my breath like the true predator I am. He thrusts his fists into the window again, a fissure of light exploding across his face. He cowers like the weak asshole he is, and I launch on top of him, straddling him.

Fear and anger—something so dark and wild that I can barely see—takes control of my body completely. It's like I watch a savage predator attack Culver from the outside, stabbing him over and over with the knife until my hand sinks into him, his heart a pulverized pile of goo that seeps with the rest of his guts out of his back and onto the floor. I've never been so strong in my life.

I pull my arm free of his chest cavity and pop a finger into my mouth, tasting the strangely satisfying spicy sweetness of his blood. A small cry draws my attention away from my kill, and I see Rylie trying to drag herself toward the door, the color gone from her skin.

I collapse to my knees, my adrenaline vanishing as my actions sink in. I killed Culver. I manage to obliterate his heart. I am so screwed. If I can even get up, I doubt they'll let me live long. I'll have to think of something. Blame someone else. I'm dead otherwise.

"Ry-Rylie," I whisper, fear and pain suffocating me, sending me curling in on myself. "Get th-the b-blood. Fridge." It's the only thing I can think to do to help her.

A strange noise cuts through the pounding in my head, and I manage to pull Culver's com device from his jacket. My vision disappears completely, leaving me blind. Pain radiates through me like a fire licks across my veins. The bite makes it hard to concentrate on anything else. I've never had a bite hurt like this. It scares me.

"Help," I whisper, feeling the com device's smooth screen with my finger. "Help."

"Fiona?" It's Torrance.

"Help," I repeat.

Torrance growls, but I can't see him.

Someone swears.

I lose consciousness completely.

⚜

Soft arguing tugs me from the dark recesses of my mind. Pain burns on my neck like the time I accidentally and unthinkingly lifted a hot pot from the stove and scalded my fingers. My chest tightens with fear, and I try my best not to move.

Something icy touches my throat, causing me to startle. "She's regaining consciousness." Berkeley's scent wafts over me, his closeness sending a dozen different emotions through me—lust, fear, anger, and even a tiny bit of comfort.

"I've managed to link into his security feed. I'll have their video in just a minute." It's Hudson, his voice an angry tone I can't recall hearing.

"Hey, Fi. Fiona? Can you open your eyes for me?" Berkeley asks.

I don't answer him and continue to inhale slow breaths.

"Give her a couple of minutes," Aspen says. Cool fingers interlock with mine. "She's probably terrified. Whoever attacked her bit her hard."

"Much harder than Rylie." Torrance's mention of Rylie gets me to snap my eyes open.

"Ry! Rylie!" I screech, my voice sharp enough to make Berkeley wince.

Aspen squeezes my hand, pulling it toward him to get my attention. "She's going to be fine, Fiona. It's you we're worried abo—shit."

I blink a few times, my bottom lip quivering uncontrollably.

"What?" Hudson drops to his knees in front of me, closing off the circle his brothers create around me.

Berkeley grasps my chin to get me to look at him. "Oh, fuck," he says, his hazel eyes widening. "She's transitioning."

"What do you mean she's transitioning?" Torrance asks.

Aspen combs his fingers through my hair to pull it from my neck. "Her attacker bit her with venom." Venom? I should've guessed that's what Culver meant about throwing me to the shadows. Such a punishment, turning a Blood

Rebel into something they hate, is far worse than death. But not to me.

"Someone must've really had it out for us if they went through the trouble to not only murder Culver but also turn Fiona." Hudson scoots closer and touches my knee. "Hey, Fiona. Can you tell us what happened?"

His question sends cold dread down my back, and I don't answer him right away. He thinks someone attacked us—including Culver. It's better than I could've hoped for.

Pressing my lips together, I think for a second before I nod. "Culver came to my room to...sneak a bite. But he was followed. A...huge guy—" I glance at Torrance. "Taller than you, Torrance." I touch Hudson's shoulder. "More muscular than you. Bigger arms, dark hair. Scary."

Aspen growls so softly in his throat I'm not sure if I'm hearing things. "Could be Monterey."

My eyes widen. I know I heard him speak, but Aspen's mouth didn't move. "What the hell? Did you just project your voice into my head?" The second the thought escapes my mouth, panic engulfs me. "Can you listen to my thoughts?" Ah, hell. If that's the case—

"Shit," Aspen murmurs. "Not only are her eyes flashing like crazy, but she's also gained her super hearing."

"What?" My voice rises in pitch. I reach up and prod my teeth with my finger. No fangs. I'm not transitioning. I can't be. I feel the same as I did before. Just sore and achy.

The four of them inch even closer, caging me in between their muscular bodies. Berkeley tightens his jaw, turning his face expressionless. His brothers look to him like they want him to do all the talking.

"Fiona," Berkeley says, touching my hand until I let him hold mine. "The vampire who bit you released his venom. You're transitioning into one of us."

Hudson's com device chimes, and he breaks our circle and swipes it off the coffee table from next to another device, one covered in blood. It's Culver's. I know it. I can smell his blood on it from here. For the first time, my attention draws to the rest of the room. I'm in the Kings suite on a couch. I'm alone with them, and from the video feed displaying the sunset outside, I've been out for hours.

"I got it," Hudson says, returning to sit on the floor in front of me. He taps the screen a few times, and a projection lights up from his phone.

A part of me dies.

Anger bursts through me, and I manage to scramble to my feet in an attempt to block the projection on the wall, one that leaves me cold and empty—completely grossed out and mortified. The video feed is from my dorm room. They had a camera in there. They were watching us.

"You sick bastards!" It takes everything in me not to attack all of them. "I can't believe this. I thought you guys were different."

"Fi, no. Wait. It's not what you think." Berkeley closes the space to me.

"How? That's *my* room. You were recording my room. You're sick." I rake my fingers through my hair. Two soft voices—mine and Berkeley's suddenly whisper through the air. I spin to look at the projection, tears burning my eyes. "OhmyGod. Turn it off!"

Berkeley swears under his breath and races to Hudson to grab the com device, but it's too late. Everyone watches our passionate kiss turn into more. Tapping the screen, he flicks the projection off and continues watching the screen as if he can't pull his gaze away.

His eyes flick to mine and back to the screen. My heart thrums in my chest, my emotions hot and wild. If I stay, I might attack. I want to attack all of them for invading my privacy. I don't know why I thought any differently, that this place wasn't full of twisted monsters. And it's not only the Kings I'm pissed at. I got too close. Too trusting. I let them charm me, thinking that maybe I was different to them.

Blinking the tears from my eyes, I head toward the door. I refuse to stay in the same room with them. I need out and fast. I need air. A weapon.

"Don't let her leave," Berkeley says without moving from his spot.

Hudson materializes in front of me. "Sorry, love. You heard our first in line. You gotta stay, especially if someone's out for us."

For them. Yeah. Of course he'd think only about himself and his brothers.

I surprise him by grabbing the front of his shirt and swinging him around, my muscles crazy-strong. He stumbles, and I jerk the door open and rush into the hallway.

"Don't let her go!" Berkeley calls. "I mean it."

Aspen appears in front of me next, and I spin to dodge him. Torrance catches me from behind, lifting me off my feet. I jerk my leg up and kick Aspen in the groin, sending him to his knees, dropping a whole slew of F-bombs.

I thrust my head back, refusing to get dragged into the room, head-butting Torrance. The scent of his blood snaps something dark inside me, and I thrash hard enough to kick off the wall, sending us back. I land on top of him and flip too fast for him to catch.

He releases a warning growl at me, and I full-blown yell in his face, unleashing my rage at him. I open my mouth to bite him, nearly getting his throat, but strong hands rip me away. The world blurs, and I land hard on my ass in a grand bedroom with a king-sized bed, mahogany furniture, and plush rugs over shiny dark wood floors. An ornate-framed mirror reflects my image to me from its place over a dresser, and I scream and pick up some sort of metal statue and chuck it, shattering the mirror into a thousand glittering pieces of glass.

"Someone's going to hear her," Hudson says from the other side of the door. "Why are we doing this?"

"I have to show you something," Berkeley says.

"If you even try to share that video feed of you and Fiona, I'll cut your throat out." It's Aspen.

"I should hold you down and let her kick you," Hudson adds.

Berkeley growls, the guttural sound piercing my heart with panic. "Shut up and listen. We caught who killed Culver."

"Was I right? Fiona described someone who sounded like Monterey," Aspen says.

Berkeley doesn't respond, but I hear Culver's familiar voice cut through the air as he plays the video of me killing Culver.

"Shit. I don't believe this," Hudson says. "That can't be right. She's a donor. A little feisty, but what she did...impossible."

"Do you need to watch it again?" Berkeley asks.

"No, what I need is to talk to her," Hudson says.

"Look what she did." Something crashes as Torrance's voice booms through the air. "Fuck that. She killed Culver. She could kill you."

"You're damn right I will!" I yell, pounding my fists on the door. "You betrayed my trust. You used me. You're cowards. All cowards."

The door to the bedroom flies open, and Berkeley rushes me. I fly off my feet and hit my back on the bed. I snatch a pillow and chuck it at him, sending feathers dancing through the air. He grips a dagger in one hand and a thermos in the other.

"You need to calm down, Fiona." His commanding voice stops me from arguing. "I want to give you the benefit of the doubt but you're making it difficult."

"Are you kidding me?" I ask, clenching my fingers into my palms.

He holds out the thermos. "Drink this. It'll help settle you down so we can talk like rational people."

"I think we should report her to the headmistress," Torrance says.

Berkeley chucks his dagger at him with perfect accuracy, sinking it into his shoulder. Aspen and Hudson restrain Torrance before he can retaliate, and Berkeley rushes and slams the door on them.

He returns to me and hands me the thermos. "Drink."

Fear forces me to accept his offering. I untwist the lid and bring it to my mouth. My stomach rolls at the gross scent. I sip it anyway.

Cringing, I cover my mouth, but I can't swallow. It's not vampire blood. It's human.

I spit the blood in Berkeley's face.

ELEVEN

UNEXPECTED INHERITANCE

"SHE'S NOT A VAMPIRE." BERKELEY'S voice remains even as he speaks with his brothers on the other side of the door. "The venom didn't take. I don't know why yet, but her eyes stopped flashing and she doesn't have fangs."

I clear my throat. "Of course I haven't changed. I've been vaccinated against turning into your kind." It's a flat out lie since I grew up in a rebel community and only those in the city get any sort of vaccines, but they don't know that.

"There is no vaccine against vampirism. The Vampire

Uprising was started by a bunch of vampire vigilantes that decided to cull the human population to stop the trashing of the world we're stuck living on for a long-ass time," Aspen says. "The donor population believes what Blood Life Corp wants you to believe. The Blood Hunger Plague was caused by the most powerful of our kind biting humans with venom and then abandoning them to cause chaos that they could swoop in and act as heroes by getting everything in control."

I frown at his words. That's not exactly what I was taught about how things went down, but it's pretty close. The asshole vampires responsible—they should pay.

"So like Aspen said, you were not vaccinated," Berkeley says.

"Like you would even know. You've never been to my colony. We're not human-only. Vampires are part of the resistance too. They have their ways." I don't care if they believe me or not, but I'd rather claim a vaccine stopped me from turning completely than letting on to the fact that maybe since I carry the dhampir mutation, I might not change. I never thought about it before and never needed to.

"Maybe she's immune," Hudson says. "You know how kids and the elderly don't transition and die. Maybe her immunity resisted and instead of killing her, she worked through it."

Berkeley sighs. "That's an interesting theory."

"Who cares why," Torrance says, his deep voice full of throaty annoyance. "All that matters is that we get our story straight. I don't know about you, but there is no way I want the headmistress and board to find out about Fiona. I want her contract. Culver didn't lose his life so that she can be taken. And then what? It would be a waste."

I can't believe what I'm hearing.

Berkeley releases a strange noise. "As first in line, I'm going to have to deny your request. She is mine now. We've already proven our compatibility and attraction."

"The hell? That's not how this works," Aspen says. "She'll be my blood source. I was with her first."

Something crashes. "Screw the lot of you. I'm requesting to transfer her contract to me." The door flies open, and Hudson stands in the doorway. "Come on, Fiona. We're going to Headmistress Rasmussen immediately."

I stand in shock, overwhelmed by their desire to claim me for themselves. "What? No. I'm not going anywhere."

He tightens his jaw. "You killed the head of our coven. The board drains for far less. Is that what you want? Do you have a death wish?"

"No, but—"

"Then come on," Torrance says from behind him. "We're wasting too much time. We will stick to your story about an intrusion, but don't think we're through here. You destroyed everything we worked for."

Fury rushes over me. "You guys are fucking assholes.

Just like Culver. I can't believe I even fell for your charm."

Hudson presses his lips into a thin line. "We could say the same."

I don't get the chance to run or fight. Hudson sweeps me off my feet and tosses me over his shoulder like the property he thinks I am. I stretch my arms and drag up the back of his T-shirt to scratch my nails into his skin. All he does is shift me, dropping me a foot to scare me into thinking I'll crash to the floor. Swinging my fist, I punch him right on the ass cheek.

Torrance catches me before I smash into the ground. All four of them growl at each other. The rumbly noise sets off my fear instincts, and I thrust myself away from Torrance only to find myself in Berkeley's arms. Swiping a dagger from who the hell knows where—his jacket or something—he aims it at his brothers, stopping them from trying to steal me away.

"We're not settling this like a bunch of outcasts," Berkeley snaps. "She can't be a personal donor if you all rip her apart."

I squirm in Berkeley's arms. "Put me down! I'd rather go with any of them over you. You fucking creep. Do you always record acts of intimacy or was it just to show your brothers that you managed to seduce me in a moment of weakness?"

Berkeley releases me, but no one takes his place. "Fi, no. I swear. It wasn't like that. We had no idea security did that until Hudson used Culver's access code to check the security feeds in the hall. The headmistress didn't inform us. I don't think Culver even knew. The only time security reviews anything is by request or if there is an incident, and it usually goes through the proper channels. We were fortunate that Hudson and Aspen excel in security and technology. No one will see those feeds. I swear."

I clench my fingers into my palms. He sounds honest enough, but I don't know if I believe him. "Yeah, right."

Berkeley releases a groan and grabs my hand, tugging me away. He spins me so that his brothers can't see me. I yank my hand back and hold my palms up, pressing them into his taut chest. Stupid muscles. Why do they have to feel so good touching them through his shirt?

Leaning down, he risks closing the space. "Please, you have to believe me. I wouldn't have gone so far if I had known. I'd—"

"You'd have just ensured I wouldn't find out. Now you're saying all this because you don't want me to put up a fight against the insufferable claim you want to put on me. Fuck off, Berkeley. It's never going to happen." I try to step away from him, but he moves with me.

"Fi, I know you're freaked out. I'm sure you didn't intend to kill Culver. But the fact is that you did. If you fight against me, you'll ruin your chance at a happy life. I understand donors far better than my brothers. I know we could move past this. We can build a relationship we both enjoy.

I'll be good to you. Unselfish." His hazel eyes capture mine but not in the horrible mind manipulation way. "I can forgive you for what you did. I wasn't as close to Culver as they were."

"Forgive *me*? *You* forgive *me*?" My chest rises and falls with my deep breathing, his words jabbing at my control. "Fuck you, Berkeley. Do you know why Culver was in my room to begin with?"

He rubs his hand over his neat beard, pinching his chin in the process. "He expressed his desire to bite you, so I assume it was because of that."

I close my eyes. He knew. They probably all knew what he was planning to do. "Do you know why I killed him?"

"Isn't it obvious?" he asks, lowering his voice. "He pushed you too far. He threatened the one person you consider family."

Standing up on my tiptoes, I hover my lips close to his ear. "All of that might be true, but I killed him for trying to punish me because of you. He bit me with venom because of you. He wanted to transform me and cast me to the shadows so that you wouldn't want me."

He shivers under my soft breath. "He was wrong."

"Then prove it. Don't let your brothers stake a claim. Bite me with your venom." I don't know where the thought comes from, but I can't stop the overwhelming need to do anything I can to get out of this academy. Out of this position as a blood source. I'll give up my humanity and turn to the shadows to guarantee it.

"Fi," he murmurs. "You don't really want that."

I scowl at him and ram my hands into his chest, sending him stumbling back. "The hell I don't. Anything, and I mean anything, will be better than ever getting claimed by any of you."

A strange bell rings through the air, drawing everyone's attention toward a small screen inlaid into the wall by the door. The King brothers look at each other and then to me. It sounds similar but softer than the alarm that went off in my dorm room at the start of the night yesterday.

"We have to go before anyone realizes Fiona and Rylie aren't in their dorm," Hudson says.

"Where is she?" I feel like the shittiest person in the world at the mention of Rylie's name. I was so concerned about me that I had forgotten about her. I should've insisted on seeing her the second I woke.

"In her new room. She's under sedation," Berkeley says.

"New room?" I ask.

Torrance laces his fingers behind his head. "Enough with the questions. We have to go. Now."

Torrance doesn't give me a chance to argue. Snatching my hand, he pulls me against him and lifts me off my feet. The world blurs.

⸺ ♛ ⸺

Headmistress Rasmussen sits behind her grand desk, just

staring at the King brothers. Her tight mouth gives nothing away. I don't know exactly what I was expecting from the announcement of Culver's death, but it wasn't this.

It's like the death of a vampire doesn't garner any sort of emotion apart from annoyance and inconvenience. For calling Culver their brother, the Kings show no grief or sadness. It's weird as hell. If I had just lost a sibling, I'd be devastated. All these guys seem to want is to figure out how to divide their unexpected inheritance.

"We'd like to personally allocate resources to the academy's security force to assure something like this doesn't happen again." Hudson's gruff voice draws my attention away from the headmistress.

"We'd also like to file the proper paperwork to ensure my new position as head of the upcoming King Region." Berkeley straightens his shoulders.

Again, Headmistress Rasmussen doesn't react.

"We are all willing to take on the necessary classes to fulfill the requirements needed to continue the region head training program without Culver." Aspen shifts, curling and uncurling his fingers.

"And if you'd allow us a few extra minutes of your time, we'd like to discuss Culver's donor contracts." Torrance flicks his attention to me. He remains expressionless despite the tension stiffening his tall frame.

Headmistress Rasmussen stands up from her chair and ignores the four of them to saunter across the room where I planted my ass on the couch while the brothers ignored me to tell the headmistress a half-assed story about Culver getting attacked and killed in my dorm room.

She tilts her head slightly, searching my face. "Ms. King, you are excused. Please make your way to your third class. Do not speak of the day's events to anyone. Do you understand?"

I bob my head. "Yes, Headmistress."

"Torrance, please escort Ms. King and return here promptly." She doesn't look at him as she says the words, keeping her gaze on me. "Someone will retrieve you at the bell to take you to the rest of your classes. I'd like you to return to my office after dismissal."

I scrunch my nose. "So this is it? I just continue as if nothing happened?"

"If we put a halt to the training program every time someone was attacked or killed, we'd never get anything done. So yes. Carry on with your day and appreciate that you didn't succumb to the same—or a much worse fate— than Mr. King."

This. Fucking. Academy. The last thing I want to do is to return to the list of bogus classes that teach everything I've spent my life standing against.

It takes Torrance touching his hand to the small of my back to get me to move my feet. The rest of his brothers watch us go, a variety of expressions marring their handsome faces. I turn away from them when we enter the hallway, and Torrance surprises me by picking me up and running at vampire speed until I find myself in the familiar lobby of the donor education wing.

The place is empty, all the classes already in session.

"Would you like me to run to the cafeteria for you to pick up a late breakfast before I go? I'm sure you're hungry," Torrance asks, peering at the man behind the counter.

"No." The last thing I want to do is eat. I'll probably barf my brains out if I even try. My stomach twists and turns, still upset by everything. It doesn't help that the only thing it wants is some vampire blood. The pain worsens the more I think about it, so I step away from Torrance to put some space between us. If I don't stop catching a whiff of his delectable scent, he might very well be my next victim.

"You have to eat something," Torrance says, keeping his voice low. "It's been too long. Proper nutrition will keep you healthy."

"And good health assures you get all the blood you want from me." I glower at him. "Which isn't happening."

He leans in with a scowl that matches mine. "Let's get one thing straight, Fiona. You might think you're some kind of victim, but you're far from it. You've killed two vampires in only a few days, which is two more than the death count you think we carry."

"Would you like me to make it three vampires?" I ask.

Torrance growls and knocks his hand into my shoulder. "You're something else. You think we're the monsters, but you haven't shown any remorse for your actions. I was wrong to think that you deserved better. You weren't much different than him. I don't care if you think he deserved to die or not. Culver was still my brother. He brought our coven together. Now I don't know what's going to happen."

Damn him and his dark eyes. He has no idea, and I shouldn't feel even a tiny bit bad about doing what I had to do to save myself. But just seeing the sudden spark of sadness reflect in him does make me feel bad. Just not for Culver.

I rub my lips together. "Your mind games won't work on me, Torrance."

He sighs. "Whatever, Fiona. Just go to class."

"Gladly."

Torrance disappears from in front of me, and I thrust open the door to my third class of the day—which also happens to be the weirdest and dumbest one—Human Hygiene. Everyone's gazes dart away from the instructor, an older man with graying hair, a round belly, and a long, unkempt beard that doesn't exactly make him look like the role model of human hygiene, and to me.

Mr. Adkins taps his cane on the floor. "Ms. King, you're late."

"I'm sorry."

I slide into the only empty desk next to a guy who I think is in at least two other classes of mine. Patrick sits a few seats away, refusing to look in my direction. Mr. Adkins stares at me from my face to my feet, raising an eyebrow in the process. He couldn't be more obvious that he's judging my wrinkled clothes, ones that one of the Kings grabbed for me from the pile on my floor instead of the closet. It's also now that I realize a few drops of blood spatter decorate my sleeve.

"And what is your excuse? Did you oversleep?" Mr. Adkins asks.

I sigh. "Yeah, sure."

"And what's the number one rule in assuring good donor hygiene?" His dull brown eyes bore into the top of my head because I refuse to look at him directly.

"I honestly don't give a shit." I thunk my head on the desk, letting my hair spill forward.

Mr. Adkins hits his cane to my desk. "Ensure you have enough time to properly bathe, brush your teeth and hair, and dress in clean clothes."

"So basically be good enough to eat," I snap. "No thanks."

"This is about keeping your mister or mistress happy. A happy mister means a more pleasant life for you. If you find yourself in a position that you do not have the proper amount of time to follow the rules of human hygiene, then it is better to be late than to be gross for your mister. And right now, you're disgust—"

The door to the classroom flings open and hits the wall with a clatter. Mr. Adkins startles and throws his cane in my direction. Torrance appears between us, catching the heavy wooden stick. He extends it back to Mr. Adkins without saying a word. No one moves or speaks, watching as Torrance closes the space to me. He sets a small paper bag on the desk in front of me without even reacting to everyone's stares.

I swallow, my nerves shot from being humiliated in a room full of guys. The fact that there are very few females at the academy does not help.

Torrance turns toward the instructor. "Mr. Adkins, do you know what the number one rule is for a vampire who possesses a personal donor?"

Mr. Adkins gawks at us, a blank stare stuck on his face like he's incapable of uttering anything incoherently. The rest of the class doesn't fare much better. If I didn't know any better, I'd think everyone transformed into a vampire by how silent they are.

"Anyone else?" Torrance asks, directing his attention to the guy hunkering down in the desk next to me.

"You a-are supposed to take care of their personal needs," the guy murmurs, practically lying in his seat to get under his desk.

Torrance flashes his fangs at him and stands straight. He moves to hover behind me, resting his hands on my shoulders. "Correct. Unfortunately, Ms. King's mister was unable to provide her proper care this early evening. Because of this, the duty fell to me, and I accidentally grabbed

Ms. King improper clothing nor did I assure she ate her breakfast. I also escorted her here, late, so the fault of her unkempt appearance and tardiness falls on me."

It's my turn to sink lower into my seat. I thought I was embarrassed before, but I'm mortified now. This asshole just confirmed that I'm a hot mess. Even if it was no fault of my own, I can't stop my cheeks from blushing.

"Get out, Torrance," I mutter, training my gaze on the wall. "You're making it worse."

He leans down to look at me. "How so? This reprehensible supposed instructor clearly has no idea what he's talking about in regards to you. You are far from uncleanly, and I highly doubt you could ever smell bad, or in Mr. Adkins' crass words, disgusting. I find you quite appealing."

I turn in my seat to look at him, his dark eyes flashing silver at me with undeniable desire. He looks at my mouth, his face close enough that all he'd have to do is close the two inches of space to kiss me.

And fuck me, do I want him to. How can I be so attracted and so pissed off at someone at the same time? He basically slapped a "property of the Kings" across my throat earlier. He accused me of screwing up his life. He blames me for Culver's death when he should blame that dickwad for trying to mess with me.

"I look forward to claiming you, Fiona," he murmurs, bringing his hand up to push my hair behind my ear.

His words snap me from my sudden blood lust that has

me all sorts of crazy thinking about what it would be like to let him put his mouth all over me—and have him let me return the favor. But fuck it. I'm not one to be claimed. I'm more than that bullshit.

I whack his hand away from me and glare. "You've interrupted my class long enough. I don't care if you think I'm still good enough to eat. I don't need you standing up or defending me. This class is for donors, and you are sure as hell not one. So please leave."

"Fiona, I—"

"Leave!" I screech, pointing at the door.

Torrance disappears from next to me and reappears in front of Mr. Adkins. Resting his palms on the instructor's desk, Torrance bends down and glares at him. A blip of fear squeezes my heart. I'm afraid he's going to do something terrible to the old man, who even though he embarrassed me was only doing what this school of vampires made him.

"Mr. Adkins, if I ever catch you speaking so obtusely to Ms. King, I will not hesitate assuring it never happens again. You do not call out and humiliate a woman in such a way. Do you understand? If you have concerns about Ms. King you will bring it up directly to her in private."

"Yes, Mr. King," Mr. Adkins says, lowering his gaze.

"Actually, I take that back. Do not speak to her at all. She is only in this class because it's a requirement. You will pass her regardless."

Mr. Adkins nods his head and glances toward me. I

cover my face with my hands and take a few deep breaths, waiting for the sound of the door closing behind Torrance.

A hand knocks on my desk, drawing my attention from the imaginary hole I want to bury myself in. I look at the guy next to me, the one who answered Torrance's question that Mr. Adkins couldn't.

"I've never seen anyone correct Mr. Adkins before, which he deserved. I wonder what he said." He smirks at me. "Hopefully something that will have him in need of focusing on his own personal hygiene."

I raise my eyebrows and laugh. Hearing him wonder what Torrance said makes me feel tons better. I realize that my hearing must still be out of whack from the venom bite that continues to throb on my neck. "Hopefully."

The guy offers me a wide smile and extends his hand. "I'm Ivo Nowak and hopefully the future head of daylight security of the Daybreak Hills Estate in the future King Region."

Well, if that isn't a mouthful. I don't even know what the hell I'm supposed to be called besides a personal donor. "You're going to live with the Kings?"

Ivo's brows pinch together like I've said the most ridiculous thing. "I'm training to serve the Knightly Coven, not the Kings. Their city is within the future King Region. How do you not know that?"

"I'm not from this territory," I say.

"Maybe we can meet in the library sometime. I doubt

anyone will go out of their way to teach you the real things you need to know." Ivo shifts closer, ignoring Mr. Adkins as he starts his lecture.

I look at Ivo, and I mean really look at him. He's cute enough with his neatly combed dark hair, caramel eyes, and clean-shaven face. Something familiar lies in his gaze. He might be in one or two of my other classes. I can't be sure since I barely paid attention.

"Do you have a death wish?" I whisper, trying to figure out if he's messing with me.

His smile widens. "Actually no. Had it been yesterday, I wouldn't have even considered it. But after..." He licks his lips and gets as close as possible, the scent of his minty breath slightly strange since I'm used to scents much sweeter. "I know what you are, dhampir."

My blood cools. "I don't know what you're talking about."

He touches my knee under my desk. "It's okay, Ms. Flamme. Your secret is safe with me."

TWELVE

ACCEPTABLE COMPROMISE

THE REST OF MY NIGHT flies by without much incident. I haven't seen any of the Kings since Torrance scared the shit out of Mr. Adkins. The guy wouldn't look in my direction, even though I silently begged him to get Ivo to stop looking at me.

I was wrong about his familiarity from class, because I haven't seen him past the Donor Hygiene lecture, so I must've just seen him around. Maybe in the dining hall. No matter what, I'm on edge. Not only because of the Kings but because Ivo left me with a ton of questions. The biggest one being how the hell he knew what I was.

So, after my Personal Donor Support Group, I wait for the lobby to clear to see if one of the Kings will show up. No one comes, and I refuse to go looking for them. Instead, I stroll to the reception counter.

Mr. Croft peers up at me with pinched brows and wrinkles lining his forehead. "How may I help you, Ms. King?" he asks, his voice sharp with annoyance like I interrupted something important, though all I see is a blank computer screen.

"I need directions to the library," I say, resting my elbows on the counter.

He purses his lips. "You can find a map of the school on your work device."

"I don't have my work device." I sigh. "You know what? It's fine. I'll figure it out."

Spinning on my feet, I stomp my way toward the archway that leads to one of the grand hallways on the side I think leads to a donor commons area. I'll probably have better luck asking someone there anyway.

"Wrong way, Fiona." I stop in my tracks and swing my arm in an attempt to clock Torrance for startling me. He catches my fist and pulls my hand down without letting go.

I huff and yank free of him. "It's rude to sneak up on someone."

His jaw twitches. "It's rude to try to punch someone trying to help. Are you this aggressive with my brothers, or is this just the way you like to act with me."

"I'd kick all of you in the balls given the chance, so no. Don't consider yourself special."

I expect him to scowl at me, but his dark eyes light up with the smile that stretches across his handsome face. I get caught off guard by how hot he looks when he's not glowering or humiliating me.

"You know, my brothers are wrong about you," he says, motioning for me to stroll with him back into the lobby and across to the other side where another grand hallway awaits. "They think you're a bit wild and overly confident to hide the fact that you're scared out of your mind by being here. They also think you're far more fragile than you let on to be."

"I'm not afraid," I snap.

He looks at me in his peripheral vision. "I know that. I don't think you're fragile either. I mean, look at that bite." Shifting my hair from my shoulder, Torrance tries to look at the throbbing mark left behind by Culver.

I swing out and punch him in the solar plexus. He bends forward, a growl escaping his throat. I take the chance to dash away from him and deeper into the hallway. Without a sense of direction, I just keep moving and hoping to stumble somewhere familiar.

Torrance speeds in front of me and blocks my way. His fangs flash from beneath his full lips, a stark contrast from the smooth dark hue of his skin. Stepping into my space, he gets close enough for me to breathe in his mouthwatering scent. My stomach burns with hunger, my dhampir side awakening at Torrance's presence.

I try to put more space between us, but my back hits the wall, and I have nowhere else to go. "You need to step back and learn what boundaries are."

Torrance shifts on his feet, actually listening to me. The movement surprises me, the sudden empty air between us far greater than my body wants. Something deep-seated comes over me, and I grip onto the front of his tailored jacket with a crown crest on the breast pocket, spinning him around. He lets me cage him in, my hands digging into the taut muscles of his broad chest.

"I thought you wanted space," he murmurs, his voice coming out in a breathy hum that sends tingles between my legs.

I inch my face closer. "I don't like to be cornered."

"It triggers your fear instincts." It's not a question. All vampires know exactly what to do to scare humans. Stalking them, cornering them, chasing them—anything that feels like they're hunting us is enough.

"It triggers my need to bite you," I say, stretching even closer so that we share the same breath. "It also confuses me."

He licks his lips. "In what way?"

Without responding, I slide my hand to the back of his neck and pull him to me until our lips meet. Torrance stiffens in surprise for a second before reacting to my unexpected affection with a wild passion that sends me jumping into his arms. His tongue slips between my lips as he explores my mouth. His hands rub down the length of my back until he pulls me even closer by my ass.

His mouth tastes as amazing as he smells. My blood hunger shifts into blood lust, and all I can think about is figuring out how to turn a kiss into something more satiating. Torrance moans a breath into my mouth, something more intimidating than I imagined hardening against my thigh. I'm not the only one turned on.

I nip his lip, testing to see how hard he'll let me bite him. He drops me an inch lower, flexing his raging hard-on between my legs, the fabric of our clothing seemingly not much of a barrier between us now.

Torrance bites his own lip, sending a burst of tangy yet sweet, like a citrus dessert, flavor across my tongue. And damn does it set me off.

I suck harder on his lip, not even letting him pull away from me. A hot moan vibrates across my mouth from him. "If we don't stop, I will bite you," I say through a kiss. "Your blood...it tastes amazing. Unlike anything."

"You want more?" he asks, pulling back slightly to meet my gaze.

I suck my bottom lip between my teeth to bite it. "Does that weird you out?"

"That's the last thing your desire does to me." Torrance

raises his arm to his mouth and sinks his fangs into it.

A breathless moan escapes my mouth, my hunger and need kicking my body into action. I pull his arm to my mouth without hesitating and latch my lips over his bite. Blood fills my mouth along with a wave of hot desire, and I reach down and caress my hand over his erection, just feeling exactly what I do to him.

"Just a little," he whispers, his eyes locking onto mine. "We're not in private."

I draw my tongue over his skin. "And why is that?"

"Can I take you back to my room—"

Something clatters in the hallway, and I throw myself away from Torrance and land on my ass. He's quick to help me to my feet, hooking his fingers around my waist as he pulls me protectively into his side. Rylie and Berkeley stand a few feet away. Rylie gawks at me while Berkeley glowers at his brother. My heart pounds in an attempt to escape my chest, and I try to step away from Torrance, but his hold on me, while not painful or tight, still feels unbreakable.

"We had an agreement not to touch her until the final decision about her contract was made," Berkeley says, his voice soft and even, his mouth unmoving.

I realize he's doing that whisper thing that prevents ordinary humans from hearing vampires when they don't want to be heard. I remain expressionless. I bet Berkeley hasn't considered the possibility that the side effects of Culver's bite might not have worn off like he thought. And there is no way I'm going to tell him. Hearing them speak about me gives me an advantage.

"I didn't touch her first. She came on to me," Torrance says just as lowly.

Berkeley's eyes flash silver in anger. "You could've denied her."

Torrance growls. "Bullshit. You wouldn't have, brother. I know how much she gets to you. I'm nearly certain you're not even broken up about the death of our brother."

"Like you are—"

"Rylie, what are you doing with Berkeley?" I can't take the whispering argument between the two of them about me, so I break their supposed silence.

Berkeley automatically steps away from Rylie and crosses his arms over his chest. I raise my eyebrows at his sudden movement. He obviously doesn't want me to assume anything, but I don't know why. Maybe he thinks giving her even an ounce of attention will push me back into Torrance's arms. At this point, I think only another offering of his blood will do that, because the look Rylie gives me makes me feel like a traitor to humanity.

"I was escorting her to our meeting with the headmistress," Berkeley says, answering for her.

"Oh, okay." I grab Torrance's hand and manage to detach it from my side. "I was just on my way to the library."

"The library? No. Torrance was supposed to escort you to the same meeting, considering it involves you, Fi." Berkeley flicks his gaze from his brother to me. "And so you know, the library is down the other hall."

I tighten my jaw and jerk my attention to Torrance, who surprisingly meets my gaze. Any other person would probably look elsewhere considering my annoyance twists my features into a scowl. "You told me I was heading the wrong way."

He doesn't react. "You were...for our meeting."

I backhand him across the shoulder. "You should've told me."

His lips pull up on one side in a half smile. "You looked like you'd put up a fight, so I went with the surprise approach." Reaching up, he caresses his knuckles across my cheek like he can't resist touching me. "Surprise. We're going to find out who gets to claim your contra—"

I swing my arm, whacking Torrance in the shoulder again. He doesn't move out of my way, just letting me, and it pisses me off more than it should. I can't help the reminder that he could've moved and didn't, in a twisted attempt to make me feel like I'm the one in control.

Raising my arm, I prepare for another punch. I'll keep doing it until he stops me if I have to. It's Berkeley who intervenes, stepping up behind me to lock his fingers around my wrist. I try to elbow him, but he shifts and presses his chest into my back. Torrance doesn't move either, the two of them squishing me into an infuriating vampire sandwich. And my rebel body. I like being between them way too much. My stomach growls obnoxiously loud, exclaiming that I better take my chance and try to devour them.

"Did you not feed her?" Berkeley whispers to Torrance from over my shoulder.

I groan and knock my head into his bone-hard peck. I thought the super hearing was cool, but now I'm just annoyed. "Someone better step back and give me some space."

They both ignore me, and Torrance says, "I watched her eat lunch in the donor hall."

"And what did she have?"

I shove myself back into Berkeley because the two of them continue to whisper about me. If I couldn't hear them, standing here in their supposed silence would be creepy as hell. And by the quiet scuff of Rylie's shoes on the floor, I know I'm not the only one who thinks so.

"Are we just going to stand here or are we going to meet with the headmistress?" I ask, raising my voice a little louder so that they can't ignore me. "I have a lot of assignments to complete and really do need to head to the library." Not that I actually want to do the work. I just can't get what Ivo said in class off my mind. He knew what I was, and the only people I know of who know that sort of information are Blood Rebels. It wouldn't be too shocking to discover another one here. Blood Rebels are everywhere. Soldiers sometimes hide in plain sight.

Berkeley and Torrance both extend their hands out to me. "Sorry, yes. We should be going," they say in unison.

I frown. "God, you guys are creepy as hell sometimes."

Torrance chuckles. "When you live with someone so long, sometimes you have the same thought."

"It's obnoxious," Berkeley adds.

They both keep their hands out, waiting for me to choose who I want escorting me to the headmistress's office. Rylie stares at me in silence, the same question crossing her tired features. I consider ignoring both of them, but their eagerness digs into me, and even though I shouldn't—and I mean, really fucking shouldn't—give either of them more of my attention, I relent and take both their hands.

"This is new." The voice comes from behind me, and I twist my neck to glance over my shoulder at Hudson. He stands next to Aspen, and the two of them stare at the three of us. "I didn't think either of you would ever dare try sharing."

I twist my lips in a scowl. "Sharing?"

No one responds to me. Hudson and Aspen close the space, and Aspen motions for Rylie to walk ahead of him. I don't get the chance to repeat my question. Berkeley and Torrance pull me along with them, forcing me to keep a brisk pace that I nearly have to run between them to keep up.

"This shouldn't take long," Berkeley says, glancing at me. "We've already submitted our applications to transfer your contract. Headmistress Rasmussen will take into account the history we share, so the likelihood of becoming my personal donor is quite high. You will be able to start providing your blood immediately."

I flare my nostrils with my deep breath. "Great." Sarcasm drips in my voice. He sounds way too excited, which annoys the hell out of me. This isn't some matching game. I don't want to be anyone's personal donor.

Torrance squeezes my hand. "Don't mind my brother's wishful thinking. The headmistress will assure you are placed with someone you'll be happy with."

"Which is hopefully me." Hudson winks at me from over his shoulder. "I haven't been able to get you out of my head since our little fall together."

Fuck me. How the hell they can go from being pissed and angry earlier to practically jumping over one another for my attention is beyond me.

"I don't even know what you're talking about," I say to Hudson, purposely lying. I don't think I'll ever forget smooshing him with my boobs and how close we came to kissing, but there is no way in hell that I'm going to let him know that.

Hudson fake-glares at me, seeing right through my words. "Careful, love. I'm fully prepared to remind you the second I sign my name to your contract and make you mine. I'd love to finish what we started."

I open my mouth to tell him that his fantasy will remain just that, but we enter the small lobby outside the headmistress's office. The receptionist buzzes us in, and I find Headmistress Rasmussen sitting at her desk with four stacks of papers in front of her. She tilts her head up to glance at us but doesn't give us an ounce of expression to give away what is going through her mind.

"Ms. King, Ms. Reynolds. Please take a seat," she says, motioning to the two chairs in front of her desk. Looking to the Kings, she nods her head toward the sitting area and adds, "The four of you can wait over there. I have a few things I'd like to discuss with your staff before I finalize my decision."

None of them argue, but each of them takes a moment to touch my shoulder. It's the oddest thing. They obviously don't see the imaginary wall I put around myself to assure my personal space from others, and it seems worse right now, like they're silently claiming me.

Headmistress Rasmussen turns her attention to Rylie first. "Ms. Reynolds, not much will change with your staff contract, though as restitution for your injuries, they'd like to offer you the opportunity to decide on the final staff member they'll be adding to your daylight household in the coming year."

"So you basically want me to punish someone else as a way of making it up to me." Rylie directs her attention to the Kings instead of the headmistress.

Headmistress Rasmussen taps her nails on the glass top of her desk. "I don't think you understand the generosity of their offer, Ms. Reynolds. The position of a household staff of the King Coven happens to be coveted by many. All of our current donor students have not been sorted into households yet apart from you. If you happen to enjoy someone's company, now would be the chance to solidify his or her position. Transfers between covens tend to be denied."

Rylie side-glances me. "Let me get this straight. The offer is meant to be personal? I've been here for like two seconds. What if I end up hating the person I pick? Again, not exactly making up for this shit show."

I can't stop the bubbling laughter from escaping my throat. Because she's right. "This is ridiculous. Why not offer her something more valuable?"

"This is the most expensive thing we can offer," Berkeley says, scrunching his nose like I've insulted him.

"Clueless bastards," Rylie whispers under her breath.

Hudson growls. "You don't have to accept the offer, but perhaps you can talk to your classmates and get their opinions. A certain male seems to have a thing for you and would probably love to be asked."

My mouth forms an O as I realize exactly the meaning behind the offer. "Seriously? You want her to pick someone with the intention of a union?"

"That tends to make happy households, which is something we desire," Aspen says, speaking up.

"And what about me? Do I get the same offer? I did not leave home just to end up somewhere else with the same procreation expectations." I lean back in my chair and cross my arms.

"Don't be ridiculous," Headmistress Rasmussen says, drawing my attention to her. "Such scenarios would never be risked. Pregnant donors cannot provide blood."

Rylie and I look to each other. If only something like that wouldn't mean expanding the donor population. That's the difference between the Blood Rebels and Blood Life Corp. Rebels want to assure we survive outside of the cities. Larger numbers mean more people to fight. But for vampires? It means assuring a future food source.

"Fuck. Is she considering what I think she is?" Hudson whispers under his breath to his brothers.

"No male donor in this school would be that stupid," Torrance responds.

I twist in my seat and glare at the four of them. "So I'd actually get contraception if I find someone I like?" I know the answer already—that there is no way I'm allowed ever to be intimate with a donor, but it's way too good of an opportunity to screw with them after everything.

Headmistress Rasmussen presses her lips together. "Ms. King, such radical ideas cannot come to fruition in your case. You have been claimed by the King Coven. If you feel like you need more from your contract outside of the basic needs that must be provided to you, you can discuss such things with your mister."

I rub my lips together. "So intimacy isn't considered a

basic need?"

Rylie grimaces at my remark. "Fiona."

It takes everything in me not to react. "It takes more than food, clothing, and conversation to assure my happiness, which according to the Personal Donors Support Group is what you teach vampires to be the key to their own happiness with a personal blood source." I glance over my shoulder, noticing that the four brothers cling onto my every word.

"That is correct, Ms. King. We find unwilling blood sources to be quite exhausting, and we are not barbaric. We believe the key to civility lies in how well we treat the donor population. Why do you think I put the no-bite clause on your contract? I fully believe you'll grow out of your disdain toward the idea." The headmistress smirks at the Kings. "And from the applications on my desk, it sounds like I was right."

Damn her. Damn them.

"It's only been a few days, so I can't be so certain."

Berkeley softly growls, the noise low and barely audible that I shouldn't be able to hear it. But I'm glad I can. There's something satisfying to my dhampir side about the intense attention they give me in this moment.

I decide to push my luck and add, "While the Kings are pleasant enough, I don't know if they actually understand the concept of a woman's needs. They are quite insistent about their desire for me to fill their...insatiable hunger that

I don't think I could ever be truly happy. And since that's your teachings here for a blood donor...maybe you'll find it in your heart not to force me into a situation I hate."

"Is she fucking kidding? All I can think about are the hundreds of different ways I can make her cu—"

Berkeley whacks Hudson on the shoulder. "Headmistress Rasmussen, I'd like to point out that Fiona has only ever vocalized her dissatisfaction with Culver. She cannot possibly know that she'd hate her life as a King with one of us."

The headmistress turns her attention to me. "I have to agree, Mr. King. My decision stands on her contract remaining with your coven."

"Shit," I mutter.

"But, since Ms. King has gone through the trouble to express her desire of a life where her personal needs encompass more than what must be done for her survival, I will include that in her contract based on what she wants and agrees to." She turns to me. "I hope you find that an acceptable compromise."

I nearly fall out of my chair at her words.

And then I nearly die at the sexy grin each of the King brothers gives me. They are far too happy about the task.

"So, if that's all settled, we'd like to know who will acquire Fiona's contract," Aspen says, flashing his fangs at me in a way that totally makes me unintentionally smile.

Ah, hell.

"Due to these unconventional circumstances, I've decided to let Ms. King choose between you." Headmistress Rasmussen waves her hand. "Now, go on, Ms. King. Tell me who you'd like to establish a personal donor relationship with."

What the hell? I get to choose? That concept goes against everything I know about Blood Life Corp and donors. We're not supposed to have the ability to make these types of life-changing decisions.

My heart thrums wildly under the sudden silence and anticipation. Turning to Rylie, I meet her gaze. She searches my face, trying to figure out who I'll pick before I say the words. I shrug my shoulders without looking at the guys. I don't know who I should pick. I don't want any of them to claim me.

"Pick who you think can provide *everything* you need," Rylie says, reaching over to rest her hand on mine. She's talking about blood. And right now, I'm pretty sure I could get it from any of them. None of them act like the idea repels them. Hell, Torrance wanted to take me back to his room so I could drink as much as I liked.

The memory sends a shiver through me, and I meet his dark gaze. He smiles at me like he knows exactly what I'm thinking about. Blush crawls up my neck, and I avert my eyes to Berkeley. He cocks an eyebrow, daring me to even try forgetting our moment of passion together. Aspen leans forward, his blue eyes begging me for attention. He licks his lips, reminding me of our hot kiss outside of class and how he unintentionally satiated my dhampir need by trying to help my donor side after the blood loss. He seems like the type to care for me on every level I need.

Hudson clears his throat to get me to meet his penetrating gaze. "I know we haven't gotten to know each other like you have my brothers, but I can promise you that our relationship will be nothing short of blissful, love."

His words make me want to find out exactly what he means. Because he stopped by to offer me his blood to protect me from Culver, I can't shrug him off without consideration. Our attraction helps.

"Well, Ms. King?" Headmistress Rasmussen asks, tapping her nails on her desk again. "We don't have all night."

I take a deep breath. "No."

She frowns. "What do you mean *no*? No isn't a choice."

"You asked me to pick, and so I'm picking no one." I cross my arms and lean back in my chair, turning my gaze to the ceiling.

Headmistress Rasmussen flies from her desk and yanks me from my chair. I don't get a chance to fight before I find myself pinned to the wall. Four distinct growls sound through the air, and she twists her neck to snarl at the King brothers closing in around us like they'd risk fighting the headmistress for me.

Turning back to me, Headmistress Rasmussen attempts

to lock me in a mind manipulating gaze. I automatically force my body to relax in an attempt to fake my way through it, considering I just drank Torrance's blood. I'm shocked as hell that none of them mention it. I know Berkeley saw.

"Ms. King, tell me which of the King brothers you want to take your contract," the headmistress says, leaning in so close that her silver flashing eyes are the only things I can see.

"I don't know," I say, keeping my voice even.

"Ms. King—"

Soft murmurs whisper to me as Berkeley, Torrance, Aspen, and Hudson all talk among themselves too quietly for us to hear.

Berkeley clears his throat. "Would it be unrealistic to request that we split her contract and share her as a part-time personal donor?"

Headmistress Rasmussen sets me on my feet to turn to face them. "That's a bit dangerous, considering our possessive nature, don't you think."

"I'm good with sharing," Hudson says, smirking at me. "I trust my brothers to play fair. We wouldn't have gotten to our position as future region heads otherwise."

Oh, shit.

"We all agree that we can manage. Perhaps it'll be easier on Ms. King. She seems to enjoy the idea of being with each of us but not the idea of being a personal donor." Aspen meets my gaze.

I break out in nervous laughter. "Are you serious?"

"Incredibly serious," Torrance says, his sultry voice wrapping around me in a way that makes me squirm.

"We'd still follow the health guidelines for personal donors as well as continue to drink gen. pop. blood," Berkeley says.

Hudson materializes in front of me and brushes my hair from my shoulder, devouring my blushing throat with his gaze. "And this way we can guarantee to fulfill your every need in the way you desire."

Whoa, shit. He's getting to me in a good way, and he knows it. I wet my lips and swallow to try to get my voice to respond but then decide against it. I'm doomed. Completely doomed. There is no possible way this could end in any way except for me dead. The headmistress is right about a vampire's possessiveness. If the blood sources back home even saw me with one of the others, they'd go psycho. They were never kept together in the bunkers and had their own spaces.

Headmistress Rasmussen gathers the stacks of papers on her desk and sorts them into a tall pile. She hand writes something illegible across the top and places the paperwork in a bin. "You have convinced me to allow you to split her contract on a trial basis through the rest of the term as a test. If you can manage to fulfill her basic needs, keep her in good health, and also keep your good standing with no internal conflicts, I'll bring forth the idea in front of the Blood Life Corp board for final approval once your city head training is complete."

"Shit," Rylie and I whisper at the same time.

I can't believe this is happening. I don't even know how I'm supposed to feel.

"Excuse me, Headmistress," Berkeley says, closing the space to me while keeping his gaze on her. "Did you say *city head* training?"

She remains expressionless. "I did."

Torrance growls, tensing. "But that would mean—"

"I'm sorry, Misters King. Without Culver as your leader, your coven no longer qualifies to obtain control of an entire region. You have shown great skill, intelligence, and authority during your training that the board agreed to transfer your status so that you can remain at the academy." Headmistress Rasmussen links her fingers together, not letting the sudden heat pouring through the room at the Kings' anger get to her.

"This isn't right. There has to be something we can do," Berkeley says. "My brothers and I worked hard for this."

The headmistress turns to me and Rylie. "Ms. King, Ms. Reynolds, you two may be excused. The rest of the meeting is none of your concern. Per your misters' request, we have moved your living quarters into their suite, so that's where you'll remain for the rest of your time here."

Rylie hops to her feet and takes my hand, despite the warning growls rumbling from Aspen and Hudson. No one follows us as we reach the door. I glance back once, the tension in the room so palpable that I can feel it sink into my bones.

The King brothers' attention darts to me, and without having to ask them, I know this is bad. Not only was I responsible for killing their brother, now I've ruined their chance at running a region.

With the looks the four of them give me, I'm afraid of what this means for me.

My life is about to go from weird to awful, and there's nothing I can do about it.

Nothing short of dying or running away.

I might end up doing both.

THIRTEEN

THE RESISTANCE

I PACE AROUND THE TABLE Rylie sits at in the library. The room is unlike any of the libraries I've seen in back-world movies. Instead of shelves and shelves of dusty books, giant screens glow from the walls with digitalized books that you tap to send directly to your work device. I've never seen such a collection. Blood Life Corp outlawed the creation of books to control the education of the donor population. There were a few salvaged from the uprising in our community, but nothing like this. I can't believe they even allow us access.

I stop in front of the wall and swipe my finger across a collection of educational textbooks.

"You can look at the covers, but you'll be denied access to all of the Blood Life Corp Politics, Vampire Law, and Donor Division books." The familiar masculine voice draws my attention from the digital library and to where Ivo stands a few feet away. He brushes his hand through his dark hair and peers around like he's checking for one of the Kings. "I see you managed to lose the shadows."

"Don't know for how long," I say, turning to where Rylie sits, staring at us.

She gawks in our direction in surprise and then hops to her feet. Rushing toward us, she thrusts her arms around Ivo. He chuckles and lifts her off her feet in a hug. I just stand awkwardly, staring at the two of them. Rylie clearly knows this guy, which confirms my earlier thought about his connection to Blood Rebels and the resistance.

"Ivo, I can't believe you're here," Rylie says. "I thought—I thought you were dead. The elders said you were."

He looks around the room again. "Because of the sensitive nature of my task to get a position among one of the leading covens." Shifting, he glances to me. "And you being here jeopardized everything I've worked for, Ms. Flamme. When the elders sent word that you abandoned your duties... What were you thinking? You put yourself in danger without producing an heir."

I reach out and slap my hand over his mouth, shutting him up. "Don't you dare try to chide me. You have no idea."

Rylie touches my shoulder. "Relax, Fiona. He's only thinking about the future."

"Not *the* future. *My* future. And my future is none of his damn business." I glare at Ivo. "I don't know what you expect to do, but I don't want any part of it."

"All I have been tasked with is to get you out of here, so someone can take you home." Ivo reaches for my hand and grabs it before I have a chance to pull away. "Now might be the only chance we get. Come on."

I stiffen, fighting against his pull. "You can help me out of here, but there is no way in hell I'm going home."

Rylie takes my other hand. "Fiona, please. We'll talk about this. He's right about it being our only chance. Now that the Kings split your contract—"

"They what?" Ivo asks, his brows scrunching.

Rylie pouts her lip. "It's awful."

"Oh, be quiet. Don't be so dramatic. They can't even bite me. And even if that were the case..." I need to shut up. My rebellious mouth will end up with Ivo murdering me in my sleep because such words would make me look like a traitor. "It's fine. I can handle myself."

Ivo tugs my hand again. "It doesn't matter if you can. It's not a risk the elders want to take. Now, if we hurry, we can get outside easy enough."

"Do you have a weapon I can use?" Rylie asks Ivo.

He tightens his jaw. "You don't need one."

She scowls. "The hell I don't."

"You're not coming. My task was Fiona only. The elders want you to stay."

Color drains from Rylie's face at his words. Without having to ask her, I know this situation is her worst nightmare. She planned to remain in the community, raise children, and enjoy a life outside of vampires. If she is forced to stay here, none of that will be possible.

"No," Rylie whispers.

"She means, *hell no*," I snap. "Plus, I'm not leaving her behind. Unless you plan to take us both, you can screw the hell off."

"Fiona, no. It's fine. If this is what the elders have tasked me with—I'll survive." Tears pool in Rylie's hazel eyes. "I'll be okay. You are the most important. Humanity needs you."

"And I made you a promise."

"Screw it. We're out of time." Ivo hooks his arms around my waist and throws me onto his shoulder. He's surprisingly strong but not vampire strong, and I thrash hard enough to throw him off balance. I screech as we topple over. Ivo tries to overpower me, straddling my waist, but I punch him in the nose. His blood splatters across my face, and I shove him off to climb on top of him. He scowls at me, unable to fight against my sudden strength triggered by his attack.

"Fiona, stop. Stop," Rylie begs.

"No! The asshole tried to—"

A growl reverberates through my bones, cutting my words off. Ivo's eyes dart above my head at whoever created the giant-ass shadow blocking out the overhead light. I don't look up or move, afraid of what will happen when I do. I'm nearly certain violence isn't tolerated, especially violence that causes a donor to bleed.

"Tried to what?" Hudson asks, his voice deepening with a hidden threat.

A dozen responses swirl through my mind. If I say the wrong thing, Ivo is dead. As much as his little stunt pissed me off, he doesn't deserve such a fate.

"Tried to stop me from smashing the screen with the chair," I say, tipping my head back to look up at Hudson. "This library sucks. Everything I want to read is restricted."

Hudson smirks at me a second before he slides his hands under my arms and lifts me from on top of Ivo. "Easy now, love. Seeing you pinning him down with blood all over his face makes me incredibly jealous."

I swipe my finger across my face, smearing the blood. "Don't be. He's not my type." And by type, I mean blood type. Because there is no way I want any of Ivo's blood on me. "But he might be yours." I extend my finger out to him and tap it against his mouth.

Hudson shocks the hell out of me by lacing his hand

around my wrist. Ever so slowly, he tugs my hand back to his mouth and sucks on my finger. I remain utterly still under the weight of his stare as he tries to read my reaction. Instead of giving him one, I draw my finger across his lips until I reach his sharp fang peeking out.

He flares his nostrils, his eyes flashing silver. I tease him just a little, scratching the pad of my finger across the point. I expect him to snap his teeth at any second, but he manages to resist, though his heart thrums in my ears, louder than everything else in the quiet library, the donor section empty of everyone apart from the four of us.

"You're testing my restraint, Fiona," Hudson whispers, his hand sneaking up to rest on my hip.

"I hope it's awful." I take things further by piercing my finger with his fang. A drop of blood splashes his lip, and he draws his tongue from his mouth, closing his eyes as he savors the small taste.

He groans in his throat. "The worst."

"Good."

A chair squeaks from behind him, and he shifts me with him to glance at Ivo shuffling toward the exit. Rylie remains frozen in place, a dozen emotions flickering across her face. She looks like she's torn between wanting to cry and yell at me, but her fear keeps her silent.

I exhale a small breath, pulling myself together. "It's getting late. We should probably head back to our room."

I say the words to Rylie, but it's Hudson who responds

with a nod.

"To comply completely with your contract, I've changed the sleeping arrangements. You'll now be sleeping in my room on my day with you." Hudson smirks at me like a cocky bastard, daring me to argue with him.

"Then where will I go? Do I get to return to the donor dorms?" Rylie asks, speaking up.

Hudson doesn't look at her as he says, "And risk you getting hurt? You might not be a blood source, but you're a highly valued member of our staff. I'm nearly certain my little love here will murder the entire school if something happens to you. So no. You will now just have your own room in our suite."

Rylie throws her hand out. "That's not fair. How am I supposed to have a life?" Or privacy. I know that's her greatest concern.

"You're free to come and go as you please. You're not a prisoner. While I don't think the guests you try to invite over will show, with proper permission, you can bring whomever you want over. How else will you pick another member of the donor population to join our staff? Head-mistress Rasmussen has generously granted you until the completion of the training program."

"Oh." Rylie shifts on her feet.

"But be prepared. If word gets out, you'll probably become the most popular donor at the academy," Hudson adds.

I turn my attention toward the exit, expecting to spot Ivo hiding in the shadows, but he took off the second he could. I don't blame him. I wouldn't risk seeing how this plays out either, considering he failed his mission to get me out of here.

I never believed I'd ever think this, but I'm grateful for it. I'm glad Hudson interrupted. I can't imagine ever leaving Rylie behind. With my sudden contract split between the four King heirs, I can now use it to my advantage. One of them might give in to me. If I charm the hell out of them, I could get them just to let Rylie go—at least after we leave this place. I'd remain a blood source forever as long as it helps her go free.

She'd do it for me. Her being here made it quite obvious.

When neither of us responds to Hudson's comment, he slides his fingers off my hip and touches my hand, testing to see if I'll let him take it. I do, despite the look Rylie gives me. I just hope she'll understand what I'm doing or why I gave up the chance Ivo offered to help me leave.

"Ready, love?" Hudson asks with a gorgeous smile. "I can't wait to show you my room. It should be fun."

I raise my eyebrows. "Whatever you say."

He flashes his fangs. "Just wait and see."

♔

"All done, Fiona," Berkeley says, pressing his cool finger to the spot on my arm where he extracted my blood. He quickly rubs a cotton ball over it and applies an invisible gel that dissolves to mimic my skin. "Was that okay? I didn't hurt you too much, did I?"

His flurry of questions surprises me, and I turn my attention from the tube of blood he hands to Hudson and to him. His tight lips hide beneath the scruff of his facial hair as he waits for my response.

"It was better than the last time with the phlebotomist," I say, rolling down my sleeve.

"Here," Hudson says, holding out a chocolate cupcake to me. "I asked the kitchen to make you something sweet."

I stare at the cupcake like it'll somehow disappear or that he'll stretch his arm up and not allow me to take it. Hudson smirks at me and brings it closer to my face until it hovers an inch from my lips.

"Why won't she take it?" Hudson whispers, his question to Berkeley not intended for my ears.

Berkeley gathers his blood draw equipment. "She doesn't like to be handfed."

Just to spite the two of them and their annoying whispering, I lean forward and lick some of the chocolate frosting from the top. Hudson chuckles, amused by the fact that I proved his brother wrong, even if he doesn't know it was on purpose.

I hum at the burst of sweetness. "I haven't had a cupcake like this before. It's so good."

"Want another bite?" Hudson asks, his smile widening

as Berkeley stops what he's doing to watch the two of us.

I nod. "Can we take it into the room? I'd like you to feed it to me while I finish up my assignment for Human Hygiene."

Berkeley clears his throat. "About your classes..."

I slowly turn my gaze to him. "What about them?"

"We changed your schedule to better suit our situation. Human Hygiene is the last class you need," Hudson says.

I groan and shake my head. "Then what am I taking now? I just got used to them."

"Come on. I have everything in our room. Things will change slightly depending on who has you for the night, but I can at least go over tomorrow."

Our room? A change in classes regularly? I can barely keep up with things as it is.

"Don't worry, Fi. You'll be fine," Berkeley says. "We'll assure it."

Berkeley cuts us off, blocking my way for a second before Hudson can drag me into his room. The two brothers look at each other for a moment, and then Hudson nods slightly as if giving Berkeley permission for whatever he plans.

He steps into my personal space and tilts his head. "Would it be okay if I hugged you?"

I stand in surprise. "Uh, yeah, I guess."

Wrapping his arms around me, he pulls me against him, burying his face into my shoulder. "I know things are weird right now, and there might be some tension between all of us, but I just want you to know that we are all attracted to you and figured with the low female-to-male ratio...we agreed that sharing you would make us all happy. I mean, if you're okay with it. I'm grateful for getting even a piece of your contract. We will show the board that this will work. They'll see that we are still fit to run a region."

It's like he says the words to convince himself. Because I don't care whether or not they run a region. I don't care if he's grateful that he got his way. I don't even know what I care about in this moment. Maybe just being alive and here and not either dead or forced into a life I know would feel far worse to me than providing a little blood to a coven that I know will return the favor.

I pull away. "I'm sure they will, Berkeley."

He smiles at me. "Have a good sleep, Fi. If my brother gets on your nerves, you have every right in your contract to call on me."

I tip my head to look at Hudson. "I'm sure I'll be fine."

Hudson grins. "Damn straight, you will be."

As we pass Rylie's room to head to Hudson's, I stop in front of the door and peek in to see her fast asleep with her back facing the door. She didn't say a word when we got here and went straight to bed. I can't help the worry that clings to me for my best friend. As soon as I get a moment alone with her, I'll make sure she knows that I have a plan.

"She'll be fine in a few days," Hudson says, nudging

me to close the door.

Behind the first set of double doors that faces the large living space is his room. The door palm pad turns green under my touch, and the door opens for me. I hover in the doorway with Hudson behind me and stare at the grand room. This is far from being a bedroom. It looks more like a swanky apartment with an open floor plan with a bed and an entertainment area with a couch and projector screen. A small office space rests against the far wall with giant monitors that flicker with videos from the security feeds around the property.

I flick my attention to the small rolling cot set up next to the king-sized bed with fluffy pillows and a gray and white feather-filled duvet that reminds me of clouds. It looks as soft as them too.

Strolling to the bed, I flop back on it, proving my thoughts correct. The bed cuddles my whole body, nearly as good as Berkeley's goodnight embrace. I stretch my arms over my head and arch my back. This bed is ten times better than the lumpy bunk bed in the donor dorms.

Hudson releases a soft, sexy, almost purring sound in his throat. "Damn, she's on my bed."

I don't respond to his whisper.

Berkeley chuckles from somewhere outside the door. "You can tell her the cot is intended for her."

"No way. You should see her. I don't want her to move. I want to climb in and join her. I didn't think she could get any sexier."

I thought I could use my super hearing to my advantage, but it's impossible to pretend I can't hear Hudson. Sitting up, I say, "You want to join me, huh?"

Hudson darts his gaze from my exposed stomach where my shirt pulled up and to my eyes. "Is that an invitation?"

I twist my lips to the side. "I was only commenting on your conversation with Berkeley."

"Fuck," Hudson whispers. "She still has enhanced hearing."

"What?" This comes from Aspen. I didn't even know he was here.

I clear my throat. "Hudson's right. I can hear you still."

The door to Hudson's room swings open, and Berkeley hovers in the doorway. "When were you going to tell us?"

"Never, but having you talk about me like I'm not here was getting on my nerves." I sit up on the bed. "But I'm not in the mood to talk about this right now."

Torrance appears behind Berkeley. He drinks in the sight of me sprawled out on Hudson's bed. "Damn," he murmurs under his breath. I don't think his swear was about my super hearing, not with the way his eyes practically burn my clothes off.

Aspen shoves him, taking his place. "This can't be good."

"Maybe for you," I say, propping up on my elbows. "So mind your mouths."

They all just gawk at me.

"And tomorrow, I'm setting some rules," I add. I wave my finger and point at the tiny bed. "Like sleeping arrangements. You can have the donor bed. I like to sprawl out."

The looks they all give me speak volumes. I might have to fight them to get what I want.

I narrow my eyes, focusing on Hudson first. "You will follow them if you don't want me to drive you crazy."

"Too late for that," Hudson says, sitting on the edge of his bed.

I smirk and play-kick him. "You have no idea."

He pretends like he's going to grab my foot but purposefully misses. "It looks like I'm first up to find out."

I laugh. "Damn straight. You guys were sorely mistaken to think you could just claim me. So you know, I can't be claimed."

I won't be claimed.

And now that I'm here, knowing I'm not going anywhere, I'm fully prepared to prove it.

FOURTEEN

JUST A POSSESSION

I ROLL OVER ON MY side and gawk at Hudson sleeping in his bed. The bastard moved me once I fell asleep. And hell. I must've been really out. Something like that should've woken me up.

Getting up, I pad across the soft rug to his bed. I might not be strong enough to relocate him, but I'm not letting him get off easy for the sneaky-ass move he pulled. I hover over him like a creep to figure out where exactly I need to tug on the blanket to get him off the bed. With how he twisted the blankets around himself, he tossed and turned all day. I wonder if he's always so restless or if it's because of me. Not that I'll ask.

Finding the end of his sheet that he lays on, I gather it between my fingers. This could end badly, startling a vampire like this, but I'm willing to risk such a move. Putting him in his place like he attempted to do with me is totally worth it.

I clench my jaw and silently count to myself. It takes me up to ten before I gather my nerves completely. Yanking the sheet as hard as I can, I manage to roll him to the side of the bed where I finish pulling him off. I scramble to jump over him as he falls to climb onto the bed.

Hudson releases a growl, shooting to his feet. I pull the blankets up to my chin, my fear instincts going off like crazy. He aims a dagger at me, his chest heaving, his eyes crazy silver. He must have weapons everywhere. I didn't take that into account. I was willing to risk getting bit but not stabbed.

"Don't hurt me," I say, grabbing a pillow like it could possibly protect me.

Hudson's face softens at my words. "What the hell were you thinking, love? You can't sneak up on a sleeping vampire. If you wanted to sleep in bed with me, all you had to do was ask. I'd have heard you."

My wild heartbeat settles down now that I know I'm not about to die. Hudson plops on the bed next to me without a word and pulls the blankets around us. I lie in surprise as he turns on his side, taking up the tiny sliver of bed between my spot and the edge.

"Do you always watch people while they sleep?" he murmurs with his back to me.

I blush crazy-hard and attempt to push him off the bed. He doesn't budge this time. My fingers dig into his shirtless back, his skin warm from the blankets compared to the usual coolness of a vampire's skin that I'm used to.

"Are we really going to play this game now?" he asks, rolling over.

My hands move with him, and we stare at my palms pressing against the taut planes of his chest. The blanket drapes low over his chiseled body, revealing the band of his underwear—what I think are boxer-briefs. I was too caught up on my fear when he was standing to get a good look at him.

"Fiona?" My name sounds out softly on Hudson's lips, his eyes meeting mine. "Are you okay?"

I realize I haven't said anything to him since asking him not to hurt me, and he doesn't know that my lack of words is because his closeness—how hot he looks lying beside me, how he acts like this is the most normal thing to do—gets me in a good way. My mind wanders to places it shouldn't go.

Licking my lips, I manage to nod my head and say, "I'm fine. It's just...you moved me, you bastard." I finally break his stare, his charm losing its effect on me. I now remember why I did what I did in the first place.

He chuckles. "Damn straight, I did. I tried—and I really mean it—to give you what you wanted, but that bed sucks. I fell off it twice. I tried to wake you up, but you're grumpy as hell in your sleep, so I moved you. I'd apologize, but I'm not sorry."

I glare at him. "I am not grumpy."

"You snapped your teeth like a wild beast."

I try to shove my hands into his chest, but he's quick to move, and I fall into him. I freeze, resting my cheek against his shoulder blade with my arm dangled around him. I inhale a soft breath, the sudden heavy silence between us speaking volumes. I love this way too much. So does he.

"Fiona..." Hudson shifts to his back so that I nestle in the crook of his arm, the front of my body resting against the side of his. "You were right about driving me crazy. I need to get up before I try to kiss—"

I cut off his warning with my lips, totally turned on by his admission. Because I want nothing more than to kiss him too. Hudson pulls me on top of him so that I can kiss him deeper, not even caring that we both just woke up. I moan softly, his mouth tasting as sweet as he smells.

His hands slide down the lengths of my sides to dig into my hips, pushing me slightly lower until I feel how hard he is for me. "Your kiss tastes as amazing as your blood," he murmurs, drawing his tongue along the seam of my lips to brush his tongue to mine.

I ease back a little to put an inch of space between our mouths. "I wouldn't know about yours. I never did get a chance to taste you like I have with your brothers."

His eyes flash silver with my comment. "You love testing me."

"What? Are you afraid?" I smirk at him. "Can't lose your power over me now, can you?"

A frown hardens his features, my words striking a nerve with him. "I'd never manipulate your mind without your permission, Fiona."

I think I actually believe him. "Why not?"

He sits up with me still on top of him so that we face each other on an even level. My legs remain slung over his, though the space between our bodies allows me to think more clearly. Being this close to Hudson, kissing him, prods at my deep-seated nature as a dhampir. I enjoy letting my blood lust control me more than I should...if it's even that. My attraction to Hudson is far more than wanting to taste his blood.

"Because I want you to like me by your own free will. The only time I'd ever use that ability on a human is if they were trying to hurt someone, saw something that could jeopardize not only their life but others, and maybe to link minds to create a fantasy...upon request, that is." Hudson grins at my reaction to his last comment. "But reality is far more fun."

His admission leaves my mind whirling. Hudson is far

from being anywhere near the asshole that Culver was. And maybe I've known it all along. The same goes for his brothers. Apart from this weird-ass agreement and their desire to claim me, they're not as bad as the shadow dwellers I spent all my life training to fight against.

It's something I should've known. Hudson—and the rest of his brothers for that matter—act pretty similar to the blood sources the elders kept in our community. The only difference is that the blood sources gave up their status and power, allowing humans to control them in return for a constant blood supply. I don't see that happening any time soon with the Kings. But what I can see is more compromise than I ever imagined.

"You do make it so," I say a little late, pulling myself from my thoughts. "This morning has been...entertaining."

He raises his eyebrows. "Entertaining?"

I bob my head and lean forward a bit. "Enlightening."

Closing the space, he kisses me again. "What else?"

"Not like what I imagined."

"Better?" he murmurs, tightening his hands around my back to pull me onto his lap.

"A little."

Resting his forehead to mine, he kisses me again like he can't get enough. I hope he never does. I never thought I could wake up in a place like this, with someone like this, and actually enjoy myself. "What would make it fucking amazing?"

"If we didn't have to get up. I don't exactly enjoy spending the night with a bunch of people who are afraid to be near me." I purse my lips. "Thanks for that, by the way."

"I'd apologize but I like it this way. You're mine, Fiona—well, I guess now ours—and I see how the other donors look at you. The other covens too."

"Well, you don't have to worry about other covens. I kind of like yours."

"And the donors? Seeing you on top of that guy, with his blood on you, fuck."

"Well, I do have a plan to get out of the whole personal blood source thing," I tease. "I can't exactly fulfill that task with you."

He play-growls at me and pushes me onto my back. "We can try."

He rests his body between my legs, his desire as hard as the rest of him, and I dig my fingers into his shoulders in anticipation. I don't know exactly what I'm doing but I like how Hudson makes me feel. It's far different from the few hookups I've had with the blood sources in Mount Light Haven. This isn't about blood. It's more.

A soft alarm rings through the air, declaring breakfast will start soon. It's the only thing that stops me from teasing him back. I meet his gaze, his desire for me making it hard to think about anything else. If the alarm didn't go off, I don't think we'd ever leave this bed. That I'd even want to.

"Or not," I whisper, my heartbeat matching the sudden

quickness of my breath as I pull myself from the lust Hudson arose in me.

He slides his arms around me and kisses me for a bit longer. With a groan, he rolls off. "I think I might hate my classes now too."

"Which I assume are far better than mine."

Hudson offers me his hand to help me to my feet, and he lets me get ready in his private bathroom. A fresh uniform rests on the bed, awaiting me when I stroll out of the bathroom in only a towel. I head to the partition in the corner to change. Hudson did go all out to make sure cohabiting wasn't going to be awkward for me, which I appreciate.

Berkeley waits for me at the table with his blood draw equipment ready to go. I can't stop the frown crossing my face at the reminder. I don't know why, but I find that I feel more like a blood source getting my blood drawn this way. The times I let the vampires back home drink my blood, it was far more fun. They made it so it felt like we were reciprocating fulfilling our needs and not actually treating each other like food.

Berkeley looks up. "Headmistress Rasmussen thought keeping the splitting of your contract would be better left in private. We will only ever drink gen. pop. blood in the dining hall."

Strong arms wrap around me from behind, and Hudson rests his chin on my shoulder. "I hope this is okay."

I let him nudge me toward the table. "It's fine. I just need a little time to get used to this idea of being someone's breakfast."

Hudson holds my free hand while Berkeley extracts my blood. "I don't consider you my breakfast. You're not a meal to me. More like...the beautiful, irresistible, hot as fuck woman I'm lucky enough to survive on."

Warmth blooms across my chest at his words. "Laying on the charm rather thick, aren't you?"

He kisses my shoulder. "Never, love."

If it weren't for Rylie's door opening, I might have turned to kiss him on the lips like he obviously wants. Instead, I sit straighter in my chair and force my mouth to smile at her. She flicks her gaze to mine for a second and strides across the room to the bathroom.

Turning to glance at us, she says, "You need to adjust the sound of the alarm in my room. I didn't hear it go off. Now, I'll barely have time for breakfast. Unlike some people, I have to follow the rules. I will not get humiliated by getting whacked like an animal by my instructor for being late."

"I'm sorry, Rylie. I would've woken you up had I known," I say, glancing at Hudson.

"Whatever." She slams the door to the bathroom, cutting off anything else I could try to say to make her morning better.

Berkeley gets to his feet. "I'll grab her something to eat

from the kitchen."

"Maybe see about stopping the whole punishment thing with her too? You guys did it for me," I say, pushing my chair back.

He nods. "I'll see what I can do. Personal donors are treated a bit differently."

Berkeley disappears, leaving me alone with Hudson. I peer at the closed doors of Aspen and Torrance's rooms, but I don't hear any movement. They might have already left for the day. Without vampire speed, I know I've slowed Hudson down. Berkeley too.

"We can stop by the dining hall to say hi to them before class if you want," Hudson says, tugging me toward the door.

I flick my gaze to his. "Is that okay?"

He nods. "They'll be happy you thought about them."

"What about you? Does it bother you that I do?" I can't stop myself from asking, especially knowing Headmistress Rasmussen's concern over dealing with the possessive and jealous nature of vampires. The fact that they need contracts and other bullshit even to maintain peace shows exactly how hard it is for them to share.

He chuckles. "Far less than I expected."

Before we reach the door, Hudson stops and rolls up the sleeve of his dress shirt. I freeze in anticipation, excitement and confusion washing over me. He sinks his fangs into his arm, sending dark ruby blood dripping in rivulets to his elbow as he extends it to me.

"Will you drink my blood, Fiona? Your concern about mind manipulation might have been unfounded with me, but with others…I don't want to risk it. It was something my brothers and I discussed last night. It'll also make sure you recover more quickly from the frequent blood draws. Blood Life Corp technically doesn't allow the exchange, because of the lack of control it allows, so please don't mention this."

"So why didn't you just give me some in bed?" It takes everything in me not to snatch his arm. My hunger burns worse than ever since it's been what feels like forever since I had blood. And that fact worries me. Before, I could go longer than this. I think the venom bite might have enhanced my dhampir mutation more than I realized.

"It would've been far too dangerous," he murmurs. "I can tell you're not ready for that kind of intimacy with me, and you already test my restraint as it is."

"It's too bad you just assume what you think I'm ready for." I grab his arm and pull it to my mouth to drink his offering of blood. I can't help the soft moan that escapes me, his blood satiating more than just my hunger. It quenches my curiosity about how he tastes—incredibly delicious like his brothers—far better than the other vampires I've encountered. No one tastes exactly the same, and I'm lucky I like him this much.

Sliding his free hand around to the small of my back,

Hudson pulls me even closer, trailing his hand down to squeeze my ass.

"This is unlike anything I've ever experienced," he whispers, leaning into me to brush his lips to my neck. "My brothers were right."

I frown and pull away from his arm. "Wait, what? You guys talk about what you do with me?"

He takes a step back, his brows lowering on his head. "We tell each other everything."

Fury explodes through me, and I push him away from me. I can't believe this. "Just when I thought I could possibly like you all. I should've known better." I storm around him and fling the door leading to the hallway open.

He tries to grab my wrist, but I swing out my fist and don't give him a chance to grab me unless he wants to get punched. "Fiona, wait. What's wrong? What did I do?"

I throw my hands into the air. "You somehow think it's okay to discuss my personal business with your brothers. That's not cool. It's—it's—I have to go."

Spinning away from him, I dash down the hallway and toward where I know I'll find the elevator to take me up. I get on alone and lean my back on the wall, feeling stupider than ever. I'm never going to be more than just a donor. More than just a possession they share.

Why is it so hard for me to accept that this is my life now?

Because I know I need more.

I deserve more.

I hit my back on the mat and gasp a breath. Hudson lands on top of me and pins me down. The sound of his fangs clicking in my ear unintentionally turns me on instead of scares me, which I know was his intent. For the last hour, he's been purposely setting off my fear instincts—per our instructor's command.

"Shit," he says, breathing into my ear. "You're supposed to try to push me off you and not surrender. Definitely not expose your neck like that. Or hold me in place with your legs. Now isn't the time to express your needs. You know I can't properly fulfill them. You got pissed off just by me talking about them with my brothers."

His words knock some sense into my head, and I take advantage of the fact that he relaxes on top of me, totally turned on himself too, to break my arms free. I swing out and punch him in the throat. He gasps and falls onto his back. Rolling, I get on top of him and aim my imaginary dagger at him. I won't get a real one until Mr. Jimenez can trust me enough not to try to cut out the heart of every vampire in the room.

"You know, Mr. King, letting Ms. King win won't help her if someone starts a blood feud with your coven." Mr. Jimenez crosses his arms and stares at us. So does the rest of the class, the first one I've been in that contains both donors and vampires.

"I wouldn't expect her to fight," Hudson says, pushing up despite my being on top of him. He lifts me in his arms as he stands and sets me on my feet.

The class continues to gawk at the two of us.

From this class so far, I've learned that the vampires who work on the security forces, like Hudson, must learn to work with donors. It took me by surprise, and annoyed the hell out of me when I had to partner with Hudson after storming out on him, but he's let me burn off my anger by letting me get some punches in.

"Even so, she needs to know how. Why your coven didn't immediately enroll her in this class baffles me. As a personal donor of someone from a prestigious coven such as yours, she has a target on her. The fact that she's female...just don't take it so easy on her. She'll never learn if you coddle her." The instructor notices the silence and turns toward the rest of the class. "This isn't rest time. Come on, donors. Show your potential employers what you've got."

I watch a burly human launch at a vampire only to be knocked on his ass. The humans in the class are all training for daylight security positions. It gives each coven a chance to see if they're worth being part of their staff.

And for the first time, I actually doubt my skills. The students here are far better trained than I am even if I've been practicing combat with the Blood Rebels for most of my life. It doesn't help that I never had access to equipment that could build my muscles and strength. The only thing I seem to excel at is endurance. I still feel as I did the moment I stepped into the room while the rest of the donors are sweaty and struggling to catch their breaths.

"All right, Ms. King. Let's try something different." Mr. Jimenez turns toward an open door that leads to his office. "Mr. Nowak!" he yells. "Come join us for a moment, will you?"

I groan under my breath as Ivo strides from the office. His gaze darts to me like he might've known that I was part of this class now. Mr. Jimenez turns to look at me as well, his fangs peeking out from beneath his lips. Unlike the other vampires, he doesn't retract them, probably as his way of intimidating the donors in the room.

"Mr. Nowak, I'd like you to work with Ms. King for the rest of class," Mr. Jimenez says.

Hudson releases a growl. "No. I don't fucking think so."

"If you have a problem with my teaching methods, you can take it up with the headmistress, Mr. King," the instructor snaps. "If you feel you can't control yourself, then you can leave. It's not like I ask that you allow Ms. King to work with someone from the Powers or Saint Covens."

Mr. Jimenez's comment tugs another growl from Hudson, but he doesn't argue and instead heads out of the room. I gape at the door closing behind him in surprise. I try not to react at suddenly being abandoned, because I shouldn't care, but now I'm nervous as hell.

"Hello again, Ms.—" Ivo leans closer, lowering his voice. "Ms. Flamme."

Without waiting, I launch at Ivo and knock him on his back before he can even put up a fight. I swing my arm to punch him in the nose, but a cool hand locks around my fist, stopping me from clobbering Ivo.

"How about we try that again when Mr. Nowak is ready, shall we?" Mr. Jimenez says, smirking at me.

I glower at Ivo and shove my hands into his chest to push off of him. Mr. Jimenez calls the class to watch us. Annoyance rushes over me at being forced into the center of attention, the last place I want to be.

"All right, Mr. Nowak. You know the rules. No combat. Ms. King must learn how to free herself first to be able to fight."

I position my body, dreading that Ivo will lock his arms around me at any second. It was a bit harder for Hudson to set off my fear instincts because my mind kept wandering into fantasy mode because of our kiss in bed this evening. Even if I'm still angry about the whole kiss and tell closeness of his brothers, I'm still attracted to him.

Ivo's presence sets off my fear real quick, probably since he's human. I'm not used to feeling threatened by them. It helps that I don't trust the guy. He was instructed by the elders to take me. What if he realizes it's more than about Rylie behind my reason for not wanting to go?

Ivo comes at me. I scream, scrambling away from him, my body not wanting him to touch me at all. The door clatters open, and Hudson fills the frame, his eyes flashing silver as he enters attack mode. Mr. Jimenez intercepts Hudson, stopping him from reaching me. It's enough to make Ivo hesitate.

"You okay, Fiona?" Hudson asks, pushing slightly against the instructor. I have a feeling that Hudson could easily outmatch the vampire and only the fact that everyone in the room watches him might be the only reason he doesn't.

I take a few deep breaths. "I'm fine. I was just startled is all." And creeped out.

Mr. Jimenez shifts out of Hudson's way. "Go on and reassure Ms. King that she is safe here. It seems that your absence did the trick to prod at her natural fear instincts, though I'm surprised she reacted so heavily to a donor." His low words are intended only for vampire ears. "Take note and respect the bonds your donors create, class. In Ms. King's case, she already relies on Mr. King to protect her."

Come the hell on. I do not rely on Hudson to protect me. It takes everything in me not to react to the instructor's words. Hudson raises his eyebrows at me, a cocky smile crossing his face. He knows I heard the instructor and loves every second of the fact that my supposed nature doesn't want me to be without him. That's far from the case. I just don't want Ivo getting within a foot of me.

Engulfing me in a hug, Hudson turns me away from the class and snuggles his face into the crook of my neck before I can fend off his affection. Not because I don't want it. I want way too much of it. And he knows it.

"I'm sorry I abandoned you, love. I was standing right outside the door. The only time I'd actually leave you was if you were spending time with one of my brothers." His soft voice tickles my skin. "But I had to leave. I don't like seeing others put their hands on you. It makes me want to kill everyone in the room, and that would guarantee expulsion from the program."

Ah, hell. How can he piss me off and make me swoon at the same time?

I groan. "It's fine. I'm not some damsel. I just—go sit in the corner and face the wall."

He chuckles. "You better kick that prick's ass. I don't like the way he looks at you. Since I can't do it, you have to."

I tilt my head up and grin at him. "Gladly."

He surprises me with a quick kiss, leaving my body buzzing as he disappears to do what I asked him. He stands rigid, his broad back and muscular arms rippling as he flexes. I drink him in for a moment, totally checking him out. He must feel my gaze on him, because he shifts and smiles at me over his shoulder.

"All right. Let's try this again," Mr. Jimenez calls. "Mr. Nowak, Ms. King, please take your positions."

I tighten my jaw and shift to face Ivo. His smug expression morphs to something darker, probably because of the small exchange Hudson and I shared. I can read the Blood Rebel's face clearly. He's disgusted that I even let Hudson touch me, let alone kiss me.

"I need to get you out of here," Ivo mouths. "You deserve better."

I guess I read him wrong. He knows I'm a dhampir after all. He'd think the same as Rylie, and that I do what I do because I have to. He'd probably attempt to kill me right now if he knew I do what I do because I want to. I've never been so attracted to anyone like I am to all four of the King brothers. It's strange and exciting, especially because I know they want me back.

I don't respond to Ivo and instead tense in preparation for his attack. He steps forward to lock his arms around me again. My fear instincts scream like crazy, causing me to yell. Someone grabs me from behind, locking their fingers into my hair while covering my mouth with a hand.

"Mr. Knightly. Release Ms. King immediately," Mr. Jimenez says.

A guttural growl, along with the click of extending fangs, cools my blood.

Hudson flies at me from across the room, dodging a few guys that try to get in his way.

But he's not fast enough.

I close my eyes and prepare to get bitten.

FIFTEEN

BLOOD FEUD

IVO RIPS ME AWAY FROM a scary-ass vampire who is part of the Knightly Coven. Hudson collides into the asshole, sending both of them sprawling. Growls sound through the air, and the vampires blur in a fight. The donors rush to get out of the way.

"Settle down!" Mr. Jimenez hollers, attempting to break up the fight closest to him.

Ivo yanks me off the ground and drags me toward the door. Reaching for his belt, he unsheathes a dagger to protect us. Hudson yells my name, distracted by Ivo rushing me from the room, and the vampire punches him in the nose, sending his blood spraying.

"Hudson!"

My scream rips through the air, drawing the attention of another vampire, sending him my way. The asshole blond guy from the Knightly coven rushes at me, fangs extended and ready to snap his teeth into me. Ivo shoves me out the door and jabs his dagger, catching the vampire in the side. The move surprises the vampire enough to stop him in his tracks. I bet he never expected a human to injure him.

"Come on, you have to run," Ivo says, locking his fingers around my wrist. "They'll kill us otherwise."

Ivo doesn't give me a chance to hesitate, dragging me away with him. Other donors scramble out of the way as a team of vampire security personnel flood the hallway to enter the fight behind us.

"This way." Ivo points to a door on the right. "It leads to the tunnels."

"The tunnels to where?"

A figure materializes in front of the door, blocking our way. Ivo pulls me to a halt and stands protectively in front of me like any good soldier of the resistance would do. I tense for only a second until my brain catches up with me to register that Aspen stands in front of me, and he's most definitely not a threat.

"I've got it from here, Mr. Nowak," Aspen says, his

light blue eyes flashing.

I push past Ivo and throw myself at Aspen, whose arms feel so utterly safe the second they wrap around me and lift me off my feet. He releases a small chuckle into my hair, stroking his hand over the length of my back in an attempt to stop my body from trembling.

"Get me out of here," I whisper to Aspen, brushing my lips to his ear. "I want to go to our room."

"Soon. First, cover your ears," Aspen says, setting me back on my feet.

The second my hands cup over my ears, Aspen's hands join them, muffling the world around me. A blaring alarm rings through the air, the sound intense and jarring despite the fact that I protect my eardrums. Aspen cringes slightly, but he doesn't pull his hands away to cover his own. Ivo drops to his knees, the sound loud enough to even hurt his human ears. The method to break up a vampire fight isn't so different than when Rylie used the horn to slow down the vampire who attacked us outside the city.

After what feels like an eternity to my sensitive ears, the alarm shuts off, though my ears still ring. Aspen pulls me back to him, engulfing me in another hug like he can't resist himself. I stay glued to his side, ignoring Ivo's gaze as it burns into me as he manages to get his shit together to get off the floor. He quickly softens his face under Aspen's scrutiny and bows his head.

"My apologies, Mr. King. I was only trying to protect

Ms. King. She was nearly attacked by two members of the Knightly Coven." Ivo flicks his attention toward the classroom where guards lead beaten and bloodied students, including Hudson, into the hallway.

Hudson breaks away from the group to rush to me. I reach up and touch his chin, inspecting his split lip. A bruise starts to shadow over his right eye, and I can't stop from gawking at the bite mark that tore through his white dress shirt, staining the fabric with blood.

I touch the spot and automatically bring my bloody finger to my mouth. "Ouch. That looks painful."

Hudson's eyes flash silver at my gesture, but he doesn't react otherwise. "Fuck, Fiona. I'm so sorry," he finally says, ignoring my comment while giving me a long once-over. "Are you hurt?"

I shake my head. "I think I'm okay. Just shook up."

Hudson turns to Aspen. "Take her to Berkeley anyway. I want to be sure."

"Mr. King. Mr. Nowak. Please join us. Ms. King can meet us in the headmistress's office once she gets the medical exam you feel she requires." Mr. Jimenez waves to Hudson and Ivo, but only Ivo shuffles forward with his head bowed.

Hudson cups my cheeks and leans in to kiss me on the lips right in front of Aspen. I stand on my tiptoes and unashamedly caress my mouth to his before sucking his split lip between my teeth.

"You're going to get me in trouble if you keep kissing me like this," Hudson murmurs.

"Then maybe you shouldn't taste so good."

"I never expected to love a little role playing with you. Maybe you can bite me later." He detaches from my sudden death grip on him, my body buzzing as his words totally turn me on.

I stare after him as he returns to the group of vampires that vanish a split second later, taking a few donors with them. I shudder a small breath and shiver. Aspen slides his fingers through mine, drawing my attention to him. I shake off the desire Hudson abandoned me with to deal with on my own, and I bare my teeth in an awkward smile.

"You better not pull that shit with me," I say, swinging his arm with mine.

He grins at me, sliding his free hand around to the small of my back to pull me flush against him. "I'd never."

He lifts me up by my ass, and I automatically curl my body around his. The world blurs with his vampire speed. I find myself straddling him while he plops down on the couch in our living room.

I don't get the chance to catch my breath before he kisses me. I smile into his mouth, enjoying his sudden affection. His hands play with the strands of my hair cascading down my back, and I shift on his lap to press harder into him, letting my desire carry me away.

"I can't wait for our time together," he murmurs, tightening his hands around my waist to slow me down as I grind against him.

"When is that?" I ask, pulling back. "Do you have a schedule or something, or will it be a surprise every day for me?"

He shrugs. "Not sure yet. We haven't had time to discuss anything. Hudson got the first day with you because...of reasons."

I roll my eyes and shift off him. "Okay, whatever."

He sighs. "I'm sorry, Fiona. I'll be honest with you. My brothers and I talk, and from what Hudson told us about your fight this morning, we agreed to wait until we can all sit down together before we decide anything."

"And what about me? Do I get to decide anything?"

"I did say *we*, didn't I?" He reaches for me and pulls me closer like he can't stand letting space get between us. "And for this to work, you need to be included. I don't know if you realize this, but I enjoy everything about you. I don't want you to be just a blood source."

I lift my gaze from our intertwined fingers and to his sky eyes. "You want me to be your bed companion. We've discussed those in the Personal Donor Support Group."

The face he gives me, wide eyes and crinkled nose, a tint of blush crossing his cheeks, makes me bubble with laughter. I reach up and feel a spot of warmth on his face. How I made this hard-ass, intimidating vampire flush makes me all sorts of excited.

"Or am I assuming wrong?" I add.

"You're teasing me," he says, mostly to himself.

I smile. "Gotta entertain myself somehow."

"I look forward to helping to entertain you too." Berkeley stands in the doorway, a soft smile on his face, though his eyes don't light up. He shares a look with Aspen, who tightens his jaw. "As soon as I give you a quick exam and escort you to a shit show of a gathering happening right now."

I groan and cover my face. "What's going to happen to me? I didn't even instigate or tease any of the bastards. That one asshole just tried to bite me for no reason."

I shiver as Berkeley growls deep in his throat, an uncontrollable reaction to my words. Aspen reaches out and flicks his shoulder to get him to stop.

"And what about Hudson? He was trying to protect me." I rest my head on Aspen's shoulder. "This is Mr. Jimenez's fault. He insisted I practice my defense moves with Ivo."

Berkeley narrows his eyes. "With who?"

"Mr. Nowak, the prospective head of daylight security for the Knightly Coven," Aspen says.

I cover my mouth. "Oh, shit. He stabbed one of them."

Berkeley and Aspen look at each other.

"He protected me," I add. "They're going to give him his final donation, aren't they?" As much as Ivo pissed me off, and how nervous he makes me, I can't feel good about being responsible for his death, even if it was partly his decision and partly due to his upbringing as a Blood Rebel.

"That'll be unlikely. He didn't actively seek to harm anyone. If anything, his bravery will be seen as a commodity when it comes time to apply for positions." Berkeley glances at me. "I'd even consider him if my brothers agreed. It's not often that a donor protects someone other than themselves if there is no bond or blood relation."

I try not to frown. If I frown, he'll suspect something. "I don't think Hudson would agree," is all I can think to say. "He was not happy about Mr. Jimenez pairing me up with Ivo instead."

"Wait, what? That should've never happened. You're ours. No one has the right to instruct another to—" Berkeley punches the coffee table. It cracks under the force of his strength and startles a screech out of me.

"Damn it, Berkeley," I snap, swatting him on the shoulder. "Chill out. The instructor had a good reason."

"You're under Hudson's care. This is his fault."

"Oh, no you don't." I snatch the back of Berkeley's shirt, forcing him to pull me up as he gets to his feet. It takes him two steps to realize I've attached myself to him before he reaches over his shoulder and yanks me into the air so fast I can't protest as I land in his arms.

"Fi, you've been through a lot today. As the King Coven leader, I will handle this. You will stay here and let Aspen entertain you." Berkeley tosses me to Aspen.

I scramble to get up, annoyed as hell that he throws me around. "You will not tell me what to do, Berkeley. This doesn't involve you, and I sure as hell don't need you to speak on my behalf. Mr. Jimenez ordered me to join the class to see the headmistress, so that's what I'll be doing. Got it? It's bad enough my peers think I get special treatment."

Berkeley gawks at me in surprise. I bet it's rare for someone other than Blood Life Corp and the headmistress to tell him what to do. I don't even think the vampire instructors do as much, considering the vampire students training here are more powerful than they are since they're being trained for high-power positions in the regions, and up until just yesterday, Berkeley was supposed to lead the entire Donor Division of a new region.

Berkeley flashes his fangs. "I can't tell if I should be pissed off or turned the hell on right now."

Aspen cracks up from the couch. "Our girl can hear you."

Berkeley swings his gaze to me and glares. "Fuck. Look at the shit you do to me, Fi."

I stick my tongue out at him. "I told you I was going to drive you crazy. Get used to it."

Groaning, he closes the space to me and holds out his arms. I allow him to lift me off my feet because I know I've won, and he's going to do what I asked.

"You look smug as hell," Aspen says, coming up next to me.

I grin wider. "I wasn't sure how often I'd get my way, but I think I might actually like being here with you. It's far more entertaining than my boring-ass life before."

"Maybe keep those thoughts between us, Fi," Berkeley says, lowering his voice. "And don't argue with the headmistress. We've already lost part of our good standing after..."

"After what?" I ask.

"Some of us, and I won't mention who, might have blown the hell up after our running for region head had been rescinded." Aspen tightens his jaw. "But it doesn't matter. We have time to show the board that we're still capable of the task."

Berkeley adjusts me in his arms. "So be good."

I sigh. "I'll do my best."

As Berkeley carries me from our suite, we nearly run into Rylie in the hall on her way in. It's far too early for her to be finished with her classes. She's as surprised as I am, and her gaze darts to both Berkeley and Aspen before dropping it to the floor.

"The human health practitioner excused me from the rest of my classes," Rylie says, hugging herself. "I'm not feeling that great."

"What's wrong? Maybe Berkeley can help," I say, pursing my lips.

"I'll see what I can do when we get back. I don't want

to miss much more of the meeting. Hudson can be a bit hotheaded. He might throw some blame on Mr. Nowak. While he wouldn't get severely punished—at least I don't think—I can tell you would prefer no one gets reprimanded on your account," Berkeley says.

Rylie's eyes widen. "Ivo's in trouble?"

"He stabbed a vampire protecting me," I say.

"Oh, shit." She waves her hand. "Hurry, go. You have to protect him. He's—he's the one I've chosen for a position on your staff."

"What?" we all ask her in unison.

"What about Patrick?" I ask. "I thought you liked him."

"He's applying to be a personal donor at the end of the term. He doesn't want another position. Supposedly that's the best place to be in a vampire household." She turns her gaze up to look at me. "Despite being under a vampire's fangs."

"If he is who you truly want, I'll need you to join us, Ms. Reynolds." Berkeley motions for her to come closer. He looks at me. "Would you mind if Aspen carried her. It's much faster if we don't have to keep her pace."

I raise an eyebrow. What a weird question to ask me. "It's fine with me if she's okay with it."

Rylie closes her eyes and nods. "Yes, it's fine."

It's not until Aspen picks her up that I realize something is utterly and completely wrong with me. I find myself frowning, a wave of jealousy rushing over me. If Rylie wasn't my best friend, I might even tell Aspen to put her down because I've changed my mind.

What the hell is up with me?

Sucking in a breath, I hide my face in the crook of Berkeley's neck. He tightens his fingers around me, his touch more desperate than before, and I can't stop from smiling. Teasing him helps me not focus on the strange feeling Rylie arose in me. I kiss his throat as the world blurs and only stop at the rumble of voices.

"You can't be serious," Hudson says, his voice echoing through the air louder than I've ever heard. "You're giving the region to them, even after this bullshit they pulled?"

"Calm down, Mr. King. It's not set in stone. Mr. Knightly was just trying to explain his reasoning for testing Ivo in class. It had nothing to do with you or Ms. King. It was all part of the process of lining up the right staff to offer entrance to the Donor Divide Competition to fill crucial positions in his household." Headmistress Rasmussen's voice rings through the air over Hudson's. "Now, please. Sit down. You've had your chance to speak."

The excuse I hear Headmistress Rasmussen give on behalf of the dickwad who attacked me is a load of shit and Hudson knows it. I'm sure everyone does. Berkeley doesn't wait for the receptionist to announce our arrival and strolls right into the room.

He tightens his hold on me under the scrutiny of the

group of vampires in the office—some sitting and some standing—and strolls right up to Headmistress Rasmussen and motions for Mr. Jimenez to give him his seat. The instructor does without complaint and moves to lean against the wall by Ivo and two other human students.

"Sorry to interrupt, Headmistress. I understand that Fiona's presence was required, but I'd like to keep it short." Berkeley turns me on his lap, so I have no choice but to face the headmistress. "I'd like to personally file a complaint against Mr. Jimenez for going against the personal donor rule that disallows others from touching Fiona without our consent."

Mr. Jimenez growls. "Mr. King allowed it." He's referring to Hudson.

"But I did not," Berkeley says, "and because our entire coven agreed to share her contract, you must gain permission from all of us. Or does that rule not apply in our case?" He looks at the headmistress.

"I have to agree with Mr. King," Headmistress Rasmussen says, tightening her jaw at his obvious revelation about what she allowed to happen with my contract. "Had you followed the guidelines, none of us would be here trying to stop a blood feud from occurring between two powerful covens." Sitting straighter, she glances at the rest of her silent audience. "And might I remind you that we do not tolerate such things on this campus. You are all here to learn to form alliances and build strong regions—together—so our territory thrives."

"Yes, Headmistress," a few voices say in unison.

"Now, if that's all, Mr. King, I'd like to excuse everyone back to class." The woman looks at me expectantly like she knows I have something on my mind.

But Rylie clears her throat from her spot next to Aspen by the door. "Actually, I'd like to have a word with you, Headmistress. I've made my decision on who I'd like to have the Kings offer a work contract to."

"I'm going to assume it's Mr. Nowak," she responds.

Rylie nods. "Yes, ma'am."

"Very well." Headmistress Rasmussen glances to the small group of jerks, two of whom I recognize to be part of the Knightly Coven. "My apologies, Mr. Knightly. I'm going to have to deny your early request to acquire Mr. Nowak's work contract. It'll be going to the Kings."

SIXTEEN

BONDS

STEAM CLINGS TO ME AS I exit Aspen's shower in only a towel. I freeze in my tracks at the sight of all the King brothers sitting on the couches in his room with a movie playing on the glowing projection screen.

Shit. That's a lot of intense gazes devouring me.

Gripping my towel tighter, I try not to react and show how much I enjoy their attention. It makes me feel incredibly sexy. Unlike back home, they don't want me to move up their status like a soldier would. They also obviously like me for more than my blood. I hope maybe even for more than their attraction to me. I guess I'll find out as I spend more time with them.

"Um, I need clothes," I say, focusing on Aspen.

He pauses the movie and gets to his feet. "I'm sorry, Fiona. Let me find something for you. I didn't expect you to be rooming with me today."

Disappearing into his closet, which is bigger than the dorm room I stayed in, Aspen returns with one of his T-shirts and a pair of his boxers. I stare at his offering for a moment and relent, taking them from him. Instead of returning to the bathroom, I stroll to the partition screen he brought in from Hudson's room in an attempt to divide a portion of his bedroom for me. He's crazy if he thinks I'm taking the small bed, though.

I drop my towel and listen to four distinctive breaths that come from them. They can't see me, but they have imaginations. I can't stop smiling and shaking my head to myself. Quickly shrugging into the too-big shirt and surprisingly comfortable boxers, I pad my way to where the four of them sit.

Aspen scoots over to make space for me, and I squeeze in between him and Torrance. I haven't seen Torrance all day, so I shift and smile at him, patting his knee. He graces me with a brilliant grin. He obviously enjoys that I give him attention.

Silence draws between the five of us. It's not exactly awkward, but I can tell they're all waiting for me to say something. I don't like that I can't look at all of them directly, so I get up and sit on the ottoman to face them. My movement makes them all sit straighter in anticipation.

"I'm just going to be blunt and say that today was a shit show, and I don't like not knowing what to expect or how to handle things," I say, linking my fingers together.

Berkeley leans closer and reaches for my hand. "We're sorry about that. This is all new to us, too. Things don't tend to change so quickly for vampires, so I have to warn you that things might take some time to adjust. Even for the rest of the head covens. What we're doing, splitting your contract, isn't normal."

"About that. I want to know more. No one has even let me read the damn thing," I say.

"It's not important," Berkeley says.

Torrance smacks him upside the head. "Don't be so oblivious. That contract affects more than our lives. It's her life too."

I bob my head. "Yeah, what he said. I need to know what is expected from me, so I can prepare myself if I need to fight it."

"If by fighting, you mean wrestling, and by wrestling, you mean cuddling, then I accept your challenge to fight with you over the terms of your contract." Hudson bites his lip with his smile. "But in all honesty, the contract is merely a guideline to assure your health and safety. Blood Life Corp frowns upon wasting blood sourc—hurting donors unnecessarily, especially women, so it basically binds us into properly caring for you. It's more of a contract for us than you. Everything else, like expectations, falls on us to figure out."

"And what kind of expectations do you have?" I ask, crossing and uncrossing my legs. I kind of know what they want but hearing them say it makes me a bit nervous. "There are four of you, so I hope you take that into consideration."

They all look at each other, various expressions crossing their faces. It's Aspen who says, "My only expectation is getting some time with you and having you fulfill some of my dietary needs. All of the other stuff, while I hope to partake in with you eventually, isn't something I expect. The majority of personal blood sources are not actually bed companions like your support group insinuated."

I release a relieved breath. "Okay, I think I can handle that. I'm sure I'll get used to being treated like an occasional meal."

"We don't consider you a meal, Fi." Berkeley squeezes my hand. "You are more of a caregiver in a sense, assuring our needs. You don't bond with your dinner, do you?"

"Have you seen me eat a cupcake? We're bonded for life." I laugh at the thought. He is right about that. "It's just the blood draw and shit. Back home, if I snuck blood to one of my bl—the vampires in our community, I'd just let them bite me. It was a lot more fun."

Torrance shifts to lean back on the couch and glances at the ceiling. "I love and hate imagining that."

Hudson grins at me. "I am perfectly fine with your desire for a little more fun with us."

"Same," Aspen says. They reach behind Berkeley and knock their fists together.

Berkeley combs his fingers through his brown hair before shaking his head. It's enough to stop me from whacking his brothers. "We can't do that, Fi. The school has a no-bite policy to protect you. Even personal donors outside of the academy don't get bitten all the time. You can't heal quickly enough."

"I healed just fine since my offerings were more of a blood exchange." I try not to react to the subtle groans humming from under their breaths. I realize that none of them like hearing about my past encounters with other vampires. "Nothing intimate or anything." Apart from occasionally kissing and some touching if I was really in the mood. But I don't need to tell them that.

The four of them shift to look at each other in consideration. They look like they want to agree with me, and I mean desperately to agree with me, but Berkeley tightens his jaw and shakes his head again.

"I'm sorry but no. It's not something we should risk, not only because of our new standing with the board but also your comfort. Very few people receive multiple bites from different vampires, and it's only permitted once a month in their line of work." Berkeley scoots to the edge of the couch so that my knees rest between his. "I really want this to work and don't want to do anything to jeopardize it. The only loophole to the no-bite rule is one given dur-ing...an intimate encounter."

I blush at the thought.

Hudson smirks at my reaction. "I don't know about my brothers, but if I'm going to get my way with you, it'll be far better than a five-pump chump and chomp."

I lose my shit at his words, my laughter echoing through the room. "I guess that's good to know."

"Satisfying your needs might have been your idea to in-clude in the contract, though I'm a bit offended that you think we needed such additions to assure it." Hudson grabs my hands and tugs me to him to wrap his arms around me. "I wish the rest of our day wasn't wasted so I could prove it."

I giggle and pat his chest. "Apparently you have the rest of my life to accomplish the task, so relax. I'm good."

He plants his lips to mine. "I want you to be more than good."

Tingles travel from between my legs and into the rest of me, and I release a small breath against his mouth and slowly ease off of him. The last thing I need is to get carried away. I'm far too hungry for blood to want to chance it. I haven't had any since the beginning of the day, and it feels like it has been weeks.

"Then let me make a few suggestions to help," I say, shivering as I suppress my oncoming lust. "If you want to make sure I'm better than good, how about you all start by assuring I have clothes in each of your rooms if I'm going to be sharing." I wave my hand. "As comfortable as this is, I need stuff like underwear and bras, more uniforms, stuff I can change into after class. Things I can work out in. I don't want to have to run from room to room to find shit."

"But you look so hot in my clothes," Aspen teases.

I stick my tongue out at him. "I must add that my undergarments better include more than the sexy lingerie you want to fantasize me wearing all day. I have boobs. They need support that isn't a band of lace."

"I think that's fair," Torrance says.

"What about sleeping arrangements, love?" Hudson asks. He turns to his brothers. "She will fight you for the bed."

I shrug. "Can you blame me? Look how big that thing is." I point at Aspen's giant bed, probably big enough for all of us. "I don't think I can sleep on something else just knowing how amazing that thing looks."

"You can't expect me to take the twin," Torrance says, raising his eyebrow at me. "I don't even fit on it."

I rest my elbows on my knees and think for a minute. How crazy would it be to suggest we co-sleep? Could I even sleep like that? Would I want to? Most definitely. "What if we share?"

"That's a terrible idea," Hudson says, grinning at me. "You're a bed hog."

I play-hit his knee. "Says the guy who can't even relax in his sleep. You toss and turn like crazy."

"That was only because I couldn't actually sleep," he says, rubbing his lips together.

I gawk at him. "So you let me pull you off the bed? You scared me."

"What? No..." He chuckles. "Maybe. Consider it a lesson."

"Mmmhmm."

Berkeley, Aspen, and Torrance all listen to us tease each other. Hudson's playfulness helps ease the tension that has been squeezing me since we left the headmistress's office. I hated seeing him beat up and angry and am relieved he healed quickly. I've never wanted to retaliate in the name of a vampire before, usually only for humans. But the thought of the Knightly asshole hurting Hudson again makes me feel...wild. Vampiric.

"Okay, so we'll try the bed sharing thing," Aspen says.

"And we'll attempt to give you space while you sleep," Berkeley adds. "You don't have to feel obligated to give us attention."

I turn my gaze to him. "You guys don't look that comfortable to cuddle anyways. I mean, all those hard-ass muscles."

Aspen laughs. "Now I feel like I must prove you

wrong."

Damn it, if I want him to do the same. The elders would flip their shit if they knew I was cohabitating with a coven of vampires, let alone sharing a sleeping space and teasing about snuggling. No sane rebel would dare risk lying with a predator. Lucky for me, I'm one myself.

"I'll consider it, but first you have to kick your brothers out. I don't want to make them jealous." And I mean it. I know by the way they reacted at knowing that Ivo even put his hand on me set them off. They undoubtedly also hate thinking about me and the blood sources from my past doing a blood exchange. I'd rather not push my luck and test their deep-seated nature, especially with each other.

"We'll be fine if you allow us to join," Hudson says, cocking his brow to see my reaction.

And boy do I give him one. I release a cross between an embarrassed laugh and a surprised gasp. He's out of his mind to even make such a suggestion. That would be awkward and weird, nerve-wracking...right? How would I even divide my attention like that without leaving someone out?

Torrance shoves him. "You're making her nervous."

"I was just letting her know that we're cool with whatever the hell she wants. I bet it's been chiseled into her brain that vampires are possessive." Hudson flicks his gaze to mine. "And we're not exactly that...at least with each other," he says to me. "I love my brothers, and I'd prefer to have a part of you rather than none of you."

I scrub my cheeks with my hands. "Okay, but still. This is new, and like Torrance so graciously pointed out, I'm nervous. I'm not sexually experienced despite what Berkeley originally thought." I stick my tongue out at him to show him I'm teasing. "And this—you all—" I can't even say what's on my mind. Or how nervous I am despite my vagina currently totally being on board to the idea of going to new levels. "I have another thing to talk about with you."

Hudson's smile fades. "Ah, hell. Here it goes."

I turn my glare to him. "Damn right, here it goes." Shifting, I meet Berkeley's gaze first. "Hudson commented this morning that one of you shared details from one of our moments together."

Berkeley shifts and motions to Aspen. "Don't look at me."

I groan. "Aspen."

"He already knew something happened between us, and technically, Hudson did most of the prying in his attempt to live vicariously through me," Aspen says.

Hudson releases a small growl. "Thanks, brother."

"Maybe next time learn to keep your comments to yourself or wait to find out exactly what it's like to spend time with Fiona instead of basing your expectations on my experiences with her." Aspen shoots his gaze to me. "And Fiona, I'm sorry. I should've just said that instead of blaming Hudson. It didn't dawn on me that sharing those kinds of details would bother you. You have nothing to hide or be embarrassed about."

"Thanks?" My voice hitches up in pitch. "So you know, I'm not exactly embarrassed, but yes to the part about you guys basing expectations on each other's experiences. That makes me feel..." I don't know how to put my feelings into words.

"Like you have to do the same things with all of us?" Torrance asks, filling in my silence.

"Yeah, sort of."

They all look at me with various expressions. Hudson's eyebrows shoot up on his forehead while Aspen puffs out his bottom lip slightly. Torrance scrunches his nose and looks at Berkeley like he wants him to be the one to speak for them.

Berkeley motions for me to come to him, and I sit right on his lap to face him. "I feel like we need to clear a few things up. We already told you our expectations—a little bit of your blood and time to share. That's it. What you build with each of us is up to you, okay? We don't have to rush into anything. You're our girl, and we would be furious with each other if you ever felt like you were in a position with us you don't want to be in."

"And as much as it makes me nervous to say, if you decide you don't want anything with me, I'll accept that." Hudson leans in and hugs me.

"The same goes for me," Torrance says, taking my hand.

"Us too," Aspen says for Berkeley. "I know this must be a lot to take in, and you hate the idea of being claimed, but we can learn to live otherwise."

I bob my head, the thought of not being with one of them strange to even think about. I've mostly enjoyed the time I've shared with each of them. "Thanks for saying that. I do feel a bit better," I say. "Especially about the sex stuff. I don't even know what I want. It's something I wanted to avoid before."

Hudson chuckles. "And what about now?"

I giggle, my cheeks burning at his question. "I'm not sure. I think you all are delicious. Hot."

"What about my charming personality? I'm more than a ruggedly handsome, self-proclaimed sex god who will treat you with respect and fulfill your every desire at the whisper of the word." Hudson licks his lips. "And if you allow me such an experience, I'll be gentle."

Ohmyfuck. I'm pretty sure my body will never recover from his words.

"I'm nearly certain you just cemented the fact that you won't be the one collecting her V-card," Torrance says, surprising the hell out of me.

Now, I'm really never going to recover.

Aspen covers his mouth, hiding his wide-ass grin at my reaction. Berkeley tightens his hands around me.

"This is why I don't want you sharing details," I tell Berkeley.

He bows his head toward me. "You're the one who declared yourself a virgin. I never told them. They probably had the same thought as me—that due to your upbringing and what we know of Blood Rebels that you wouldn't be."

I narrow my eyes. "So if that's the case, is it safe for me to assume you are all virgins? I mean, I've seen like three females total around here. I would totally understand and get it."

The looks they give me? Priceless.

Hudson nudges me. "I'll pretend to be if that gives me a better chance with you."

I tip my head back and laugh. "Okay, okay. That's enough. We're not going to talk anymore about this. All of you, except for Aspen, out. I need to get some sleep."

"And I need to take a cold shower before climbing into bed with you," Aspen says, making me laugh.

"No point. I'll just warm you up the second you're out. My curiosity about whether your muscles are as hard as they look won't let me actually sleep until I find out." I reach over and squeeze his bicep. "If they are, I'll be building a pillow wall between us."

Torrance gets to his feet and stretches his arms over his head, showing me a sliver of his abs in the process. "Good luck, brother."

"You're welcome for putting her in a better mood," Hudson says, whacking Aspen on the back before getting up.

Berkeley hugs me close as he stands. Setting me on my feet, he squeezes my hands between his. "Sleep well, Fi. We'll see you in the evening. Thank you for giving us this chance."

I stand on my tiptoes and brush my lips to his. "And thank you for listening to me. I wasn't exactly happy about this whole situation, but you guys have made it better than I expected. I just wish you didn't lose your region because of me. I'd be pissed off if I were you."

Torrance takes me from Berkeley to engulf me in a hug next. "Oh, I am pissed. Just not at you. At Culver."

"I think that maybe this was all for the best," Hudson says, patting Torrance on the back until he moves away from me so that Hudson can kiss me. "I can't imagine how he'd have led a region after seeing the way he acted with our girl."

"You forgot how easily she killed him. I gave him far too much credit, thinking he was powerful." Berkeley sighs. "But whatever. I fully intend to get us back in the running."

"I'll do anything I can to help," I say. "You guys are way better than those Knightly assholes."

The four of them nod but don't say anything.

I slide into Aspen's arms, and we watch his brothers leave, clicking the door closed behind them. A flurry of nerves swirls through my belly, and I shift on my feet. It was easy to tease Aspen, but now that we're alone...

He squeezes my hand. "Why don't you get comfortable

while I take a shower? You can watch TV, listen to music, or anything you want. Treat this like it's your room too."

Instead of answering him, I tilt my chin up and meet him for a sweet kiss. I can't help it. The King brothers treat me unlike anything I could've imagined. Tonight's conversation cemented the fact that I do want to stay. I don't need to risk my life out in the city, constantly worried about where my next blood source would come from or if I'd get caught. I no longer have this whole Blood Rebel fate set before me. And while I didn't get the choice about enrolling into this academy or getting claimed, I do get a choice in how I handle it and what I want. It's weird, but I feel freer than I ever have.

"I don't need to take a shower right away," Aspen murmurs, deepening our kiss. "I'd like to prove to you that no pillow wall is necessary."

I laugh against his mouth, and the world suddenly blurs as he lifts me off my feet and carries me at a vampire's speed to his bed. He doesn't push me back on it or lie on top of me. He sets me on my feet and pulls down the neatly made covers.

"Tell me if it's adequate," he says, nudging me to sit on his bed by guiding me by the hips.

I bounce on the comfortable mattress. "It's hard to tell without you."

Silver flashes in his eyes, and this time he does push me back, positioning his body between my legs to kiss me with a fervent passion that steals my breath away. I draw my fingers along the curves of his muscular stomach and to the small of his back. He scoots me higher until we're lying together, just tasting each other's lips. Savoring and familiarizing ourselves with each other. I link my fingers to the hem of his shirt and pull it over his head. I had no idea how much I wanted to check him out until my fingers caressed his skin.

"Fiona," he whispers, gliding his tongue against mine, exploring my mouth for a moment.

I ease away, sucking his bottom lip between my teeth to nip it just a bit. "Is this okay?"

"If it is to you." He presses his weight harder into me, framing my head with his elbows. "You can tell me to stop whenever. I just—I haven't been able to get you off my mind."

I break from his kiss and work my lips over his jaw and down his throat. The scent of him sets off my blood hunger, and I test him by grazing my teeth over his shoulder.

"Do you want to bite me?" I ask, shifting my neck so that my hair splays across the pillow. "Let me bite you back."

I regret the suggestion immediately, because Aspen pulls away from me to study my face. His fangs peek from under his lips, and I stretch up to him to pierce my tongue over his fang in hopes that he'll agree.

He flares his nostrils at the small streak of blood I coat

across his bottom lip. Instead of licking it away, he wipes his hand across his mouth and sits up. I freeze on his bed, my nerves and sudden annoyance quickening my breathing.

"Fiona, I can't bite you," he says, keeping his back to me.

"But Berkeley said that if it was during an act of intimacy..." Fuck, I sound whiny as hell. Desperate.

Aspen notices the change in my voice as well, and he swivels to look at me. His eyes widen for a split second, and I don't even have to know that my eyes flash silver at him. My stomach growls obnoxiously loud, his closeness and my blood hunger forcing me to lose control. It's like the second I'm not surrounded by the King brothers, my dhampir half wants to test its power when I have a better chance of survival while I'm alone.

"Aspen," I say, my voice cracking. "Please, don't hurt me."

He presses his lips together. "Why do you think I'll hurt you?"

"Because you look like you're scared. It's my eyes, isn't it?" I sit up on the bed and pull my knees to my chest. "I can see them reflecting in yours."

My stomach growls again, and Aspen raises his eyebrows at me, darting his gaze to my middle like he can see a growing monster in my stomach ready to devour anything that gets close enough.

"So it's been more than your super hearing that has lingered?" he asks, taking a deep breath. "This was something you should've told us. You sound hungry, making more noise than a usual donor makes. Are you in any pain?"

Like my body wants to prove him right, my stomach burns with ferocity, angry that Aspen didn't give in to my suggestion about a blood exchange. Now, I'm feeling bitey. Out of control. Sick, even. The feelings come on so suddenly that they scare me.

"Stay here. I'm going to get Berkeley," he says, getting up to stand.

Except I can't stay in place.

The second Aspen turns his back, my body takes control of me. I launch off the bed and tackle Aspen from behind. He growls and flips me over his shoulder. Instead of dropping me onto my back, he dangles me in front of him.

"Uh, brothers. Can you come here for a sec?" Aspen says, his voice remaining even despite his features twisting into hard lines. "Someone might want to bring some donor blood."

The door swings open and Hudson enters the room, gawking at me in Aspen's arms. "What the hell?"

Hudson reaches out and pulls up my top lip to inspect my teeth. I snap at him, catching the tip of his finger in my mouth hard enough to make him growl. He yanks himself free and hides his arms behind his back.

"Not the fingers, love. I need those," he says, lifting a brow.

"Whoa." Torrance's voice pulls my attention to him. "What did you do, Aspen?"

"I think she's stuck in a transitional state or something because of the venom." Aspen searches my face. "She asked me to do a blood exchange, and when I told her no—"

"Wait, what? You *denied* her?" Hudson asks.

Aspen growls. "Shut the hell up."

"I got the blo—" Berkeley stands in the doorway, a metal thermos in his hand. His wide, hazel eyes rove over me, taking me in inch-by-inch. He closes the space to me and shifts my hair off my shoulder, looking at the spot where Culver had bitten me. "Shit. This looks infected."

"Not infected," Hudson says, risking getting closer again. "That looks like the same reaction I get to venom bites."

Torrance gazes at the bite mark on my neck. "Because you're already a vampire. You can't change."

"But Fiona's not. I don't get it," Berkeley says, dropping my hair to rub his beard.

"Check her teeth again to make sure." Hudson twirls his finger at my mouth.

I snap my teeth at him in annoyance, making him jump. "I'm not a vampire," I say. "I don't drink human blood."

"Why does she sound like there's another type of blood she drinks?" Torrance asks his brothers like I'm not being dangled in front of them by Aspen.

Aspen releases the strangest noise from his throat, sending a chill down my back. "Oh, shit. That's because she does."

I thrash in his arms, my fear growing more intense as Aspen's face morphs from concern to surprise to something I can't decipher. I can see his thoughts spinning with realization. He knows what I am. There's no doubt about it. This is it. He's going to tell his brothers, and it'll all be over. They'll kill me or cage me. I'm far too dangerous to them otherwise.

"It's how she managed to kill Culver," he adds, his Adam's apple popping as he swallows.

"What the hell are you talking about, brother?" Torrance asks.

"Fiona is a d—"

Hudson roars, surprising Aspen enough that he loosens his hold on me. I hit the ground, but no one attempts to grab me. All their attention shifts to Hudson, and I stare in shock and panic as blood drips from a wound above his heart.

"Hurry, Fiona!" Rylie screams from behind him. "I can't get it out."

My head spins, shadows edging my vision. Something inside me snaps at the potent scent of Hudson's tantalizing blood. But I don't attack him. I can't get my feet to work. Rylie screams as Berkeley forces her to let go of Hudson without dislodging his heart.

Torrance grabs Rylie from Berkeley and shoves her back into the wall. She cries out again, her wide eyes meeting me as she yells my name.

Aspen locks his hands around my waist, spinning me toward him. "Don't hurt Ms. Reynolds. She's doing what she was trained to do if Fiona's life is jeopardized."

Torrance flashes his fangs. "She nearly took Hudson from us."

"Don't hurt her," Aspen demands again.

"Fiona, fight!" Rylie yells. "You have to fight! They know."

I struggle in Aspen's arms, but not in an attempt to fight him. My emotions run rampant, and I can't think straight. All I can smell is Hudson's blood. It sets me off like crazy.

Aspen relocates me to his bed and pins me down. Bringing his hand to my cheek, he caresses my skin, shifting my hair out of the way of my face. "You don't have to fight, Fiona. Just look at me. Take a deep breath. You can't drink from Hudson. He's too injured."

A shadow falls across us, and I grind my teeth, darting my attention to Berkeley.

Aspen growls at him. "Stay back, brother. She's scared."

"I'm not. I'm starving," I cry, my voice rising.

Leaning closer, Aspen blocks the view of the room from me so all I can see are his startling blue eyes. "I give you permission to bite me, Fiona. It's okay. You don't have to be scared. I just—I wish I knew sooner."

I release a shudder of a breath and bite Aspen just above the crook of his neck, filling my mouth with his blood. Tears burn my eyes as the weight of everyone's gazes lock onto us. A soft moan escapes Aspen's mouth, and he tightens his arms around me, lying on top of me like he needs to shield me from his brothers, from the world even.

"Oh, shit," Berkeley says. "Careful, Aspen. She looks like she wants to drain you."

He groans. "She might. She is a dhampir after all."

SEVENTEEN

DHAMPIRS 101

"DAMN IT. I WANT HER mouth all over me. Give her here, Aspen." Hudson waves his arms from the floor where he fell after Rylie tried to cut his heart out. "I don't give a fuck if I'm injured. She'll make me better. Her kiss will take my pain away."

I groan before a laugh escapes me, and I ease away from Aspen's neck. He's not quick to let me go, continuing to lie on top of me. Grabbing his discarded shirt, he runs the soft fabric across my mouth and kisses me so passionately that I lock my legs around him.

"Don't get carried away, brother," Berkeley says. "I need you to give me a short Dhampirs 101 course. I've heard a tiny bit about them, but nothing substantial has been included in my donor training, only that they're basically mythical."

"So our girl is a unicorn or some shit?" Hudson says. "Explains her choice in hair color."

Torrance kneels on the floor next to Hudson, checking out the wound on his back that cuts through to his chest, acting like his injury isn't a huge deal. "Well, she's not a mermaid. I don't think she can swim."

"Of course I can," I mumble against Aspen's mouth. "There was a lake near home."

"Fiona!" Rylie's voice cuts through the air, wiping the laughter from my lips. I had nearly forgotten she was still in the room, standing in shock against the wall. My blood hunger and lust plus the huge presences of the King brothers makes it impossible to focus on anything else.

Hudson growls from the floor, and I manage to nudge Aspen until he rolls off of me, though he stays super close, linking our fingers together before pulling me into his side in a half hug. I can't tell whether he's protective or possessive, but my bite obviously affected him. In what way? I'm sure to find out any minute now.

"Hudson, please. You have to calm down. Rylie didn't mean to hurt you," I say, forcing Aspen to close the space with me.

Rylie waves her hand, her face twisting in anger. "She's right. I meant to kill you." Rylie swings her attention to me. "You have to do it, Fiona. They know about you. It's not safe. They have to die like their brother."

Ah, hell.

I throw myself at Hudson, landing on top of him before he can get to his feet. It helps that his blood loss weakens him a bit. Flipping me off, he flashes his fangs, growling in annoyance that I dare tried to intervene.

Huge mistake.

Aspen grabs Hudson by the arm and throws him into the wall. "Don't you fucking growl at my girl."

"*Your* girl?" This comes from Torrance. "She is *our* girl. Get that straight. Just because she left her mark on you doesn't mean you get to personally claim her, Aspen."

The two of them start shoving each other, and Berkeley scoops me off my feet and spins me out of the way. I screech at the sudden movement, drawing everyone's attention to me. My fear instincts ignite as Torrance, Aspen, and Hudson close the space to us, their eyes flashing. They look ready to steal me away from Berkeley.

Berkeley growls. "Stop it with the bullshit and pull yourselves together. You're scaring our girl. She thinks you're going after her and not me."

A door slams, cutting through the silence. Hudson whips his head toward the living room. Everyone was so focused on me that they missed Rylie sneaking out.

"Go get her, Aspen," Berkeley says. "Lock her in her room until we can figure out what to do."

Aspen disappears without a word, and I hear Rylie's screech grow in volume as he carries her back into our suite like a child having a meltdown. Her interruption eases the tension between the guys, and my heart settles down, my body no longer expecting to get ripped apart at any second.

Berkeley rubs his big hand between my shoulder blades. "Fi, are you okay? Can we sit down?"

I bob my head, my throat tight with nerves. "Yeah," I manage to whisper.

Wrapping his arms around me, he engulfs me in a hug that pushes my trembles away. "I want you to know that you're safe, okay? We won't harm you. This is all a...surprise, but you obviously aren't a threat to us. We just need some answers. Did you know? I mean, about what you were?"

I rub my lips together. It's not like I can lie. I've been drinking vampire blood all my life, starting at maybe a couple of times a year as a kid and then more frequently as a teen. By the time I hit maturity as an adult, blood consumption had turned into a regular every other day occurrence or as often as I could sneak it. But ever since Culver bit me, I struggle if I go more than a few hours.

I don't want to spill a lifetime of secrets just yet, so I force my head to nod. "I did. It's what brought me here. I ran away from my home because the elders wanted me to produce an heir and then join the soldiers in their fight. It's what they did to my parents. I never even knew them. I was basically raised by other moms in the community."

Berkeley puffs out his bottom lip in an irresistible pout I can't help but kiss. He hugs me tighter, just breathing into my hair for a minute. "I had no idea, Fi."

"Of course you didn't. I've never talked about it. Haven't thought about it either." I ease away and glance at his brothers. "But it's fine. Just my life."

Aspen returns to my side and takes my free hand. "A fascinating life. I want to know everything about you."

Berkeley squeezes my other hand. "I think we all do."

Instead of strolling to the couch, I pull the two of them toward Aspen's bed and flop onto it face first. Hudson doesn't hesitate and climbs onto it next to me, tugging me by my hands until I lie on top of him. I lean up and tug his shirt up, unable to resist looking at his chest. A small cut already coagulates.

"You want to lick it, don't you?" Hudson asks, a chuckle lightening his words.

"I want to do more than lick you there." I try to keep my face straight. I draw my finger up his broad chest to his shoulder. "I want to lick you here, too."

"Damn," he breathes. "Look at her face. She wants to devour me."

I laugh and pat his cheek. "You have no idea."

"Can't possibly be more than how much I want to taste

every inch of you, love."

Aspen plops down next to Hudson and extends his arms to me. "My bed, my arms, brother. Give her here."

I raise my eyebrows.

"If that's okay with you," he adds with a smile that already has me stretching my arms out to him.

"That seems fair enough," I say, brushing my fingers along the killer bite mark I left on him. "I did ravage the hell out of you."

He shivers. "How often will you want to?"

And here comes the questions.

I take a breath and shrug. "Want to or need to? Because there's a huge difference."

Berkeley chuckles and climbs onto the bed and sits cross-legged between his brothers' legs. "This is—"

"Crazy?" I say, cutting him off.

"Interesting. Fascinating. Hot." He touches the top of my bare foot. "Do you know others like you?"

I shake my head. "Just me. I'm the first person born with a symptomatic dhampir mutation since my ancestor was bitten while pregnant during the uprising."

"Shit," Torrance says, finally joining us. "You drink vampire blood. You have traits like us but different weaknesses."

"Blood Rebels refer to me as a gift to humanity. They consider me a vampire's only real predator." I stare at my bare legs resting between Aspen's as I lean my back on his chest. I was partially right about the bed being big enough for the five of us, though only Hudson lies down with one hand behind his head and his other on my knee.

"But you don't hunt us," Hudson says. "Right?"

"Not actively, no. And some of these side effects are new."

I go on and explain everything that has changed since Culver bit me with venom. The four of them listen quietly, letting my words sink in. I've never in my life felt so comfortable talking to anyone, not even Rylie. I kept a part of myself from her, a huge part of myself, if I'm being honest, because she feared vampires. I feared the feral dickwads that wanted to murder me. Never the blood sources that fed me in the community, and especially not the four King brothers who all gaze at me and hold onto my every word like I'm the most amazing person in the universe.

"I know you think, or at least the Blood Rebels think, that you're some kind of salvation or weapon to use, but I question the hell out of that," Aspen says, hugging his arms around me. "While I've heard of the dhampir mutation and know how your existence is rare, that's about as much as I know. But now? Just being with you and knowing the truth? I couldn't explain the feelings I had before but now things are starting to make sense."

"Like the innate need to keep that cute ass of hers safe?" Hudson says, smiling at me.

"Or feed her," Berkeley adds. "And not just human

food. You're the first person I had ever given my blood to. Like I could sense that it's what you needed without realizing it."

I can't help smiling at him. "You know, one of the perks about me is that we can technically survive on each other."

Boy, does that elicit all sorts of sexy reactions from all of them. Aspen kisses the nape of my neck, his building arousal suddenly flexing against my lower back. I squirm under their delicious intensity, causing Aspen to tighten his hold on me so that I'll stop wiggling against him.

"Careful, love," Hudson murmurs. "I'm starving. Rylie really took it out of me with that shit she pulled."

Aspen extends his fangs. "I'm hungry myself."

The familiar clicking sound turns me on, and my vagina clenches, totally begging me to do something more than squeeze my legs together. Torrance licks his lips, noticing my reaction, but he doesn't point it out. All he does is shift a bit closer to rest his hand on my shin.

"I could give you a bit." I tilt my head so that my hair falls away from my shoulder.

"Gen. pop. blood will be fine for them," Berkeley says. He reaches over to where he left the thermos he grabbed earlier when Aspen thought I needed human blood.

Hudson groans. "It feels wrong to drink in front of her."

Berkeley points to the door. "Then leave the room. I

don't want to risk Fiona's health. I want to do a more thorough exam. If she is like us, maybe there is more to things."

I take the thermos from Berkeley and hand it to Hudson. "It's fine. Do you think I'll get jealous or something?"

He smirks at me. "Well, if you're half vampire..."

I roll my eyes and motion for him just to drink the damn blood already. He watches me watch him, bringing the cup to his lips to take a sip.

"Fuck," he mumbles, shifting to turn away. "I was right."

I flick his shoulder. "What are you talking about?"

He peeks at me from over his shoulder. "You are jealous. You're frowning at me."

"She is," Torrance says, agreeing.

I shake my head and fake glare. "Oh, shut up. I am not. I just...don't like knowing that you're drinking someone else's blood."

"Because you want to take care of him," Aspen says.

"And you." My eyes widen as my thought sounds from my mouth. "Ah, hell. Okay, maybe I am a bit jealous. But it's not a big deal. It's a damn cup."

"What if it were another donor?" Berkeley asks. "How would that make you feel?"

"Pissed the hell off. You better not. You're mine." I slap my hand over my mouth, surprised how much even the thought bothers me. And what the hell? There are four of them and one of me. I can't be jealous because I don't even know if I could provide enough blood for all of them. Berkeley won't even try.

Torrance releases a deep, sexy, throaty noise from his lips like the cross between a moan and a purr. His eyes flash silver, and he moves closer so that he can reach my face to touch my cheek and give me all his attention.

"I'm yours, huh?" he asks, his sultry voice doing all sorts of things to my body.

I scoot closer until our mouths are only an inch apart. "Do you have a problem with that?"

He tilts his head and waits for me to make the first move, obviously wanting me to kiss him. I give in to his need for affection and savor how soft his full lips feel against mine. "No problem at all."

"Good," I say with a smile. I ease away and look at Berkeley, Aspen, and Hudson. "What about you? Is that something you can agree on?"

"Hell yeah, you can claim me," Hudson says, grinning. "Bring that mouth over here. I'm ready to give you what you need right now."

I laugh. "And Mr. Jimenez thinks I'm the one who bonded with you."

He fake-glares at me. "You have. Don't deny it."

"I'm not," I say, hugging him. "I think I've kind of bonded with all of you. It's the strangest thing. Rylie's going to freak. She wants us to leave."

"Do you?" Berkeley asks. "It wasn't like you had a

choice in enrolling here. I couldn't blame you if you wanted to go."

"You're wrong. If I wanted to leave, I would've already. I chose to stay." I look at each one of them. "I wanted to see exactly what was in store for me with you. You guys are different."

"Maybe because we bonded with you as well," Aspen says softly. "I know I feel it. It's one of the reasons possessiveness can be a problem."

"But not with you," I say.

"Except for a few minutes after you bit him. And damn it do I want you to leave a mark like that on me," Hudson says.

Torrance shakes his head. "Of course you do, Hudson." Turning to me, he adds, "So do you like to bite like that all the time?"

"Shit, he's nervous," Aspen comments.

Torrance growls. "It was just a question."

Hudson leans in to look at Aspen's neck. "It is a bit savage, isn't it?"

Warmth blooms on my cheeks, and I flop between Aspen and Hudson to separate them and hide my head under a pillow.

The bed bounces and a thud sounds through the air. Berkeley tugs the pillow from my head, now sitting in Hudson's spot while he grins at me from his place on the floor.

"No shame, love. I wasn't teasing you. Just admiring

what you can do," Hudson says, winking at me. "No donor can bite like that. Neither can a vampire. The power of your mouth is exciting, like a surprise if you'll be gentle or a complete savage."

"I'm sorry, Fiona. I didn't mean for my question to turn my brother into an idiot." Torrance twists his lips.

"Don't worry about it. I don't want you to think you can't ask me something." I look at the rest of them, so they know that includes them.

"The same goes for us, Fi," Berkeley says.

I nod with a smile. "And to answer your question, no, I don't need to bite. I just sometimes...enjoy it. I mean, if it's something you like too."

"Like? I'm going to fucking love it. I can't wait," Hudson says.

I bite my lip. "Me either."

Silence draws between the five of us, the weight of the revelations of tonight sinking in. It feels like I've been underwater for so long and I finally reached the surface so I can breathe again. I nestle between Aspen and Berkeley, yawning like crazy.

Berkeley kisses my temple. "Why don't you get some sleep? We only have a few hours of the day left."

Torrance stands up. "What about Rylie? What do we do with her?"

They all look at me, like they want me to make a suggestion.

I hug the pillow to me. "Can you just leave her alone for a bit and let me talk to her in the evening?"

"What are you going to say? She's not going to be on board with any of this," Berkeley says. He rubs his fingers through his hair, his muscles flexing with his movements.

I press my lips together in thought. I already know what Rylie's probably thinking—that I'm either going to die at any moment or that I'm a traitor. And in either case, she probably feels all sorts of hopeless. But I can't go to her right now. She is too upset. She looked as if I betrayed her by not attacking the guys and making a run for it.

"Is there any way you can help me get her out of here so she can go home? It's what she wants." I glance at each of them in an attempt to read their thoughts.

Aspen slides his arms around me again. "And what about you? She doesn't seem like she wants you to stay."

"It's not her decision," I say, straightening my shoulders. It's not anyone's decision. None of the options before worked for me, including being Culver's personal donor. But this? I never thought I'd fall into a coven that doesn't see me as anything but who I am in front of them.

Hudson leans over and kisses me. "We'll see what we can do for her."

I bob my head. "Thanks. It'll help when I break the news to her."

Berkeley tightens his jaw. "About us?"

"Yeah," I say. "And how I want to stay."

If only I didn't think she'd blow up.
Or accuse me of being a traitor.
And maybe I am.
Maybe I always was.

EIGHTEEN

BETRAYAL

COOL LIPS CARESS MY SHOULDER, drawing me from my thoughts. I couldn't sleep for the life of me, even though I'm exhausted. After an hour of tossing and turning, I gave up on trying because Aspen wasn't going to fall asleep until I did, so I faked it until his breathing evened out.

"You didn't sleep," he murmurs, sliding his arm over my waist to curl completely against me. "Is something wrong with the bed? The pillows? My room in general?"

I smirk to myself as he goes through the list of things that would prevent me from sleeping apart from the obvious. "Everything is perfect." I pull his arm up to hug it against my chest. "Including your arms. I'm just wound up. Feel like someone gave me an energy boost for my mind but forgot my body."

"Do you think some more of my blood will help?" He shifts up a bit and sinks his fangs into his arm without waiting for my response.

My stomach growls louder than a room of angry vampires. Aspen chuckles and gets me to lift my head so that he can get his bleeding arm under me to continue spooning me. I don't say anything before I draw my tongue over his blood before it spills. His breathing quickens, his free hand digging into my hip. The fact that we lie in his bed, doing an act he finds intimate, doesn't get lost on me. I've never had a start to the day such as this one, and I savor every second of it.

"You're so beautiful," Aspen whispers against my neck, kissing my tingling skin.

He shifts against me until his raging morning wood rests between my legs. I hum in my throat, rolling my hips against him. Something about how turned on he is ignites my own lust, and I release his arm to roll over to face him. His lips crash into mine, desperate yet soft, and he slips his tongue into my mouth to kiss me with enough passion that I can't resist pulling him onto me.

I trail my fingers up his chest and to the tight muscles of his back, just mapping out his body as I familiarize myself with him. He presses his erection between my legs, rubbing it against me through our clothes, and I moan and kiss him again.

"Is this okay?" he asks, kissing my throat.

I nod my consent and arch up a bit to let him tug my shirt off me. He pauses to drink in the sight of my breasts, his eyes flashing silver with a desire that leaves my body buzzing. Running his finger across my throat, he pulls my hair out of the way and shimmies down a bit to glide his tongue over the curve of my boob until he takes my nipple into his mouth and sucks it just hard enough to drag an embarrassingly loud moan from my mouth.

"Your skin tastes as good as your blood," he murmurs, before showing my other breast his attention.

I can't stop myself from grinding against him, my body craving more. I don't know if it's because he accepted who I am, something I never expected, or because he let me put my own claim on him, but something shifts between Aspen and me, awakened by our deep-seated natures that both want each other.

"Can I taste more of you?" He tilts his head up to look at me, his handsome features sharp with desire.

I comb my fingers through his blond hair and nod, expecting him to pull himself up higher to kiss my throat, but he moves lower to lick down the length of my stomach. A dozen thoughts swirl through my mind as I realize he doesn't want to bite me, his fangs never extending. He brushes his lips along my hips, memorizing my body with his mouth.

His fingers curl around the hem of the boxers he gave me to wear, and I inhale a sharp breath at the torturously slow pace he eases them off me. His eyes flick to mine to watch my reaction, and I suck my bottom lip into my mouth and arch my back to let him undress me completely.

I rub my legs together, nerves tingling through me at the way his eyes rove over me as I lie bare before him. I've never been so exposed in front of anyone, but he makes me feel so hot and sexy, desired.

He smiles at me, guiding my body until I bend my knees and ease my legs open. I lean back and close my eyes, panting hard in anticipation for what's about to happen. He lies down between my legs, his broad shoulders pressing into my thighs and ass cheeks as he eases my body up a bit. His lips start slow, trailing across my inner thigh, his kiss just a whisper against my heated skin.

My muscles tense the second he kisses between my legs, a burst of sensations yanking a gasp from my mouth. Aspen moans deep in his throat at my reaction and tightens his fingers to my hips to hold me in place.

I grip the blankets as a wave of pleasure crashes through me. Aspen starts slow, just tracing his tongue over my clit while familiarizing himself with my body. Pressure builds between my legs, his mouth working over me in a way that I lose myself to my desire. Every sensation he creates with his tongue and lips grows more intense until I'm gasping and moaning, squirming to grab onto anything I can hold on to.

My body tingles and buzzes, my toes curling. It takes everything in me to stop from screaming out in pleasure as he takes me to my point of release.

I lose control of my rebel mouth, my body tensing, my muscles pulsing. I trap Aspen with my thighs and arch my back until he slows down and laces his fingers through mine, watching me catch my breath.

"That was better than I imagined. Incredible. I find everything about you intoxicating, Fiona." Aspen eases up and hugs me, kissing my neck.

I meet his gaze, still feeling his hardness press against me. I know he doesn't expect more from me, but I want to take care of him as well. My body still hums, my desire playing and mingling with his.

"Will you let me find out what you like?" I ask, chewing my lip in a teasing smile.

He raises his eyebrows, his eyes flashing silver with his lust. He nods and eases off of me to lie on his back. I trail my gaze over his bare chest and down the hard planes of his abs. I rub my fingers over his boxers, feeling his hard-on through the thin cotton fabric. He sucks in a shuddering breath as he tenses and relaxes his muscles.

"Fiona..." I love the way he says my name, a small breath of desire surrounding the whisper of his voice.

Hooking my fingers to the hem of his boxers, I tug them down until his incredibly intimidating erection frees for me to see. I can't stop myself from staring at him a moment, my mind just needing to take in the sight of him. He helps me undress him completely, and I kneel next to him, my heart racing at the fact that we're both completely naked.

"Don't feel like you have to do anything," he murmurs, twisting the strands of my dark purple hair between his fingers.

Heat blooms across my cheeks. "I don't feel like I have to do anything. I want to. I just...your body is amazing."

He grins at my words. "I love that you think so. Because I find every part of you lickable. Kissable. So sexy and beautiful. Leaving this room might be the hardest thing I've ever faced in my existence."

"I hope so," I tease, lacing my fingers around his boner. He flexes it with his moan, keeping his eyes trained on me like he wants to imprint this moment in his mind to hold onto forever.

"I can guarantee it."

He releases a soft moan with his comment, reaching out to touch my shoulder as I draw my tongue up the length of his shaft, just testing and tasting his body. His sweet skin tantalizes me, and I get more comfortable and curl my legs under me to suck him as far as I can into my mouth.

And damn does he like it. My nerves over my lack of experience disappear, and I listen to him to see what he likes and what makes him moan louder. His hand shifts from my shoulder, and he sits up, massaging his hand over my back. He continues lower, digging his fingers into my ass cheek as I pick up speed, sucking him in and out.

My body hums with the exploration of his hand, his finger gently rubbing between my legs until he slips it inside me, wanting to continue to pleasure me while I pleasure him. I stop for a moment to enjoy the sensation of good pressure.

"Aspen," I say, kissing his tip.

"Is this good?"

I don't think anyone has asked me that before, definitely not the blood sources back home. "Mmmhmm," I respond, working him over with my mouth again.

Silence falls between us with only our panting and moaning to fill the air. I focus on Aspen and every good emotion and sensation he arouses in me. He's all I want to think about in this moment despite the soft muffle of voices sounding through the air. No one comes to the door, giving us privacy.

Aspen's breathing turns harder, his muscles tightening and relaxing. He digs his fingers into my shoulder. "Fiona, I'm going to cum."

I don't stop what I'm doing and continue to pleasure him until he arches his hips and orgasms, the intensely sweet taste of him surprising me.

Pulling back, I wipe my mouth with my discarded shirt and blush crazy hard at the way he looks at me, his fangs showing off with his brilliant smile.

"I don't think we're going to class today," he murmurs, combing my hair from my face before opening his arms for me to slide into. "I don't want to be away from you for even a minute."

"I won't be far," I say, tracing a circle on his chest. "Plus, I can hear Rylie. She's getting restless."

He chuckles. "I think that's Hudson."

I squeeze my eyes shut, trying not to groan. "They could hear us, huh?" Of course they can.

"Don't worry. They're masters of selective hearing and pretend privacy." A smirk plays on his lips, and I'm sure that while his brothers might be that, they might not be able to control themselves in regards to me yet.

I shake my head with a smile. "I'll give you all a bit of time to practice. I understand how hard this might be."

"So, so hard," Hudson says, his voice sounding through the door. "Mostly me hard for you."

Aspen throws a pillow at the door, and the force of it sends feathers flying through the room. I crack up, not as embarrassed as I thought I'd be, and grab the sheet to pull around me. I let it fall open in the back, giving Aspen a bit of a view. He shifts up in bed to watch me head to the door. I smile over my shoulder before opening his door a crack to see Hudson only a foot away, waiting for me to come.

He sweeps his gaze over me with the best smile. "Have you come to offer me a peek?"

I roll my eyes and flick him. "Maybe if you find me a clean uniform and get my necessities from your bathroom, so I can get ready."

Narrowing his eyes, he says, "Asking me to dress you wasn't the greeting I was hoping for."

I stick my tongue out at him and turn my back to give him the same view I gave Aspen. "It'll just have to do."

Hudson play-growls at me and disappears.

Aspen tips his head back and laughs. "You forgot to close the door, brother."

"He knows," Berkeley says from behind me.

I swivel and see him and Torrance grinning at me in the doorway. I wag my finger at the two of them and disappear into the bathroom. I half expect Aspen to ask to join me, but he gives me some privacy, probably needing a moment to get himself together.

When I exit the bathroom in my towel, I find a crisp uniform with the tie already tied in place with it only needing to be tightened. A matching pair of cotton and lace undergarments lay on top of the clothes, and I stare at Hudson's choice of the boy-shorts cut of the panties. The bra is also a perfect fit, accentuating my cleavage though no one could glimpse it through my button-up shirt.

I stop at the door and listen to the soft voices coming

in from the living room. I hadn't expected to find myself alone.

"Fiona? You dressed?" Aspen asks me, probably hearing my failure to eavesdrop.

"Yeah. I'm coming out now."

I take a deep breath and exit the room to find the four of them sitting together on the couch. Only Aspen isn't dressed, wearing just his boxers. They all notice me checking him out, and I bare my bottom teeth.

"The shower is all yours," I tell Aspen, hugging him from behind.

He spins to face me and lifts me off my feet to kiss me. Dangling me in front of him, he says, "Someone grab her before I take her back to my room. I think I'm addicted to her."

I swing my body and catch him with my legs. "One more kiss."

He releases a sexy noise and kisses me. "I have to go. Right now."

"I hope it's hard."

He sets me down and groans. "Torture."

An annoyed breath before a slew of swear words comes through the door of Rylie's room. I cringe, realizing she's been so quiet because she was listening and not sleeping. I turn to the King brothers with wide eyes. I don't even know how to handle this.

"She's going to try to murder us all," I whisper, wring-ing my hands together.

Torrance focuses on her closed door. "Probably just us."

"Not if she thinks I'm a traitor to humanity. Don't you know anything about Blood Rebels?" I hate to even think about the possibility, but I'd be naïve if I didn't take how she was raised into account. I've seen families turn on each other over such things. If you don't fully believe in the resistance, you're an enemy, plain and simple.

"But she's your friend," Hudson argues, draping his arm over my shoulder. He obviously doesn't know much, which is exactly what Blood Rebels want. Soldiers will even take their own lives to assure vampires can't use them against their people.

I pout. "I ruined her life." The answer is far simpler an explanation. I'm not sure I'm ready to give much away about my colony. While I didn't agree with their plans for my future, I still care about many of the people—even Ms. Maggie and Elder Newberry, the more dominant people in my life apart from Rylie.

Berkeley links his fingers on the back of his head. "We'll fix it. You can tell her that right now. We only have a little bit of time to head to class and would prefer to settle things before we do. We don't have permission to follow her like we do you."

I bob my head. "Okay, but give me a few minutes alone with her first."

"No," Torrance says, surprising me.

Hudson tightens his arm around me. "He means no fucking way. Absolutely not. She stabbed me. We're not giving her the chance to do the same to you."

"Brothers, she needs to do this. If we go, Rylie will assume we're forcing her," Berkeley says, keeping his voice even. "Blood Rebels trust no one who chooses to stay around vampires, and Rylie saw us all together."

Both Torrance and Hudson growl.

"I'm with Berkeley," Aspen says, cracking his door open to peek out in only a towel. He smirks at my gaze devouring him. "If Fiona can handle Culver, she sure as hell can handle her friend. Rylie might even surprise you."

"Or make us kill her," Hudson mutters.

Torrance elbows him. "Not the time to joke."

Hudson flashes his fangs. "Who says I am?"

His scowl softens with one look at my face, but he doesn't apologize. I can't exactly blame him for his comment. I'd be pretty pissed off if someone literally stabbed me in the back. No one says anything as we stare at each other, waiting to see who breaks first.

I do, and say, "Please try not to do something that'll get you kicked out of this place before our next day together."

"What do I get for being good?" he asks, looking at me expectantly.

I tap my finger to my chin. "What do you want?"

"To take your virginity." His teasing smile says he

knows I'll say no but that he won't pass up the opportunity to make me blush.

I deadpan and place my hands on my hips, my face hotter than the gates of hell. "Hudson, really?"

He leans over and kisses my heated cheek. "You asked, love. I promise romance and biting and everything you want to make sure it's the perfect cherry poppin' experience for you."

"I don't think there is a cherry to pop," Berkeley says oh so matter-of-factly.

Fuck. Me. I'm dead, dead, dead. They are ridiculously just...nonchalant...about sex and my body. "Are you kidding me? You guys need to stop right now. Do I even want to know why you think that?"

"Uh-oh," Hudson says, glancing at Berkeley and then to me. "Brace yourself, Fiona. Your question just triggered Berkeley's health keeper mode, and our playful little game of who can make you blush more might turn into the unsexiest learning experience of your life."

Oh, boy. I glance at Berkeley. Hudson is totally right. I can see him already thinking about how to start a conversation I seriously don't want to have with all of them. It's not like I haven't been informed about intercourse. Elder Newberry back in Mount Light Haven assured I was informed and ready to fulfill my supposed duty to pass on my dhampir mutation.

I giggle and pat Berkeley's cheek. "Later, okay? I could

do without Hudson's commentary, and I'm a better learner if I get hands-on experience instead of a lecture."

"Damn," Aspen says, coming into the room dressed and ready in his perfectly tailored uniform. "We can still ditch, Fiona. I'll submit the form that we're taking the day for some home-studies."

Hudson waves his arms. "Wait a minute. This is between me and Fiona. She was going to reward me for good behavior."

I crinkle my nose, bobbing my head. "He is kind of right. Even if it wasn't good behavior, Rylie did stab him on my behalf."

"Don't take too much pity on him," Torrance says, grabbing Hudson by the tie to pull him into a choke hold. "He gets stabbed on a regular basis and was just being dramatic because he wanted you to kiss his wounds."

"I nearly died," Hudson says.

Berkeley laughs. "The knife was inches from your heart."

The soft sound of the alarm rings through the air, alerting us to start getting a move on it. I wonder if they're always up early or if it's because of me. Pounding on Rylie's door forces me to acknowledge the fact that she's still locked in her room, probably furious because she knows I'm out here, using the Kings to distract me from a moment that will change our friendship forever.

"You guys can't leave me in here all day," Rylie says,

hitting something to the door in an attempt to break it open.

"Uh, I'm pretty fucking sure we can, you backstabber," Hudson says, releasing a growl.

I whack him on the arm and finally gather my nerve to face her. Holding up my finger, I motion for the four of them to wait where they are. The last thing I need is for her to think that they're the ones coaxing me to tell her what my plan is.

Padding to her room, I take a breath and touch my palm to the lock to open the door. It swings inward, and Rylie stands off to the side with a chair in her hands, ready to swing it to hit whoever enters.

"Rylie, it's just me," I say. "I know you're scared and angry, but please don't do anything that could get yourself killed. You know the risk you face if you threaten me in front of a whole coven of vampires."

Her eyes widen and glass over. "Hurt you? I'd never hurt you, Fiona. I'm scared for you."

Glancing over my shoulder, I peek at the guys one more time before entering the room and closing the door behind me. "You don't need to be scared. I'm fine. *We're* fine. The Kings aren't going to hurt us."

Taking my hand, she tugs me farther from the door and across the room to the corner. She leans in close to press her lips to my ear, trying to stay quiet so that no one but me can hear her whisper.

"What you're doing...Fiona, you're going to get yourself killed," she says, her voice hitching, struggling to whisper. "You can't trust them with your secret. They're manipulating you."

I pull back and frown at her. "They're not in my head."

She purses her lips. "That's not what I'm talking about. There is no way that they're okay with this. You drink their blood. It not only gives them a disadvantage in controlling you, but they know what you're capable of."

"They promised they wouldn't hurt me," I say, trying not to get angry.

I understand where her thoughts are coming from. I get why she's scared. She can't see them like I do. She doesn't know them for the protective, incredibly sexy, and totally bonded to me vampires they are.

It was something I had been warned about—the elders never wanted me near the blood sources because of a vampire's nature to be possessive. The longer I'm around the Kings, the more I realize that the reason might not exactly be possessiveness and more of a bond based on our deep-seated nature to survive on each other. It's hard to explain it to even myself, so I know Rylie could never grasp it. It was like the universe knew if I was going to survive outside the colony that I'd need a coven, and not just one that claimed me. One that allowed me to claim them as well.

"You can't honestly believe them, Fiona." Rylie waves her hand around the room. "Look at this place. Look at how things are run here. They are training these bastards how to properly keep the human population placated. They refer to all of us as donors—even the Kings. You'd have never just accepted being called a donor back home. You'd have requested the asshole be thrown in the cages."

I blink at her words, trying not to react. I'd never, and I mean never, ask the elders to put a vampire into one of the sun cages. The one time I saw them put a former blood source into the cage to burn all day in the sun as punishment for a consensual bite, I let the guy go. I nearly asked him to take me with him. I was starved for over two weeks at the time as punishment, which is how I knew my previous breaking point.

"I don't know what changed with you, Fiona, but you're different now. I was hoping you'd see how bad things were outside the city and then willingly come home with the city soldiers, but—I don't know you anymore. And now you've doomed me." Tears pool in Rylie's eyes, and she turns away to stare at the wall. Her words poke at me, sending a flurry of questions through my mind.

"What exactly do you mean about me willingly coming home with the city soldiers?" I ask, hugging my arms over my chest.

"Don't be so naïve. Do you really think it would have been so easy for us to leave home? That I could steal a car from a soldier and drive you away without anyone trying to stop us?" She swings her gaze to me.

Her admission tightens my chest, and I step away from her. "You told the elders that I was planning to run away."

She clenches her fingers into fists. "I had to! You were going to get yourself killed, Fiona. You're my best friend and like a sister to me. I didn't want to lose you all because you couldn't see what was best. I knew you'd eventually change your mind about everything."

"How could you do this to me, Rylie? This wasn't your decision to make. You're not a dhampir. You don't understand what it's like. You think I was going to get myself killed out here, but they were assuring I was going to die regardless." Grief and betrayal run through me. I can barely see straight.

"Oh, stop acting like you were sentenced to death. You were going to get a fulfilling life. But none of that matters now. It's over. Everything is ruined. You're going to make sure I die in this miserable place."

I cross the room, needing to put as much space between us before I blow up at her. "I'm not. I'm getting you out of here. The Kings will help me. They promised."

She releases a strangled laugh. "For what in return?"

"Nothing," I say.

"Yeah-fucking-right. I don't believe you."

I dig my nails into my palms. "It's true. We're getting you out of here."

"And what about you?"

"I'm staying."

"So getting me out of here is pointless. The elders will never allow me to go home without you." She shakes her head, drooping her shoulders. "You're their concern. Not me."

"Rylie..."

"Just leave me alone, Fiona. I've heard enough from you. You're too selfish to care about anyone other than yourself. Maybe you deserve whatever fate awaits you here. Just don't ask for my help. I'm done trying to help you."

And like that, I feel our friendship smash to pieces.

I feel a part of me die, the part that kept me connected to humanity. I feel as if my past is gone forever. If only I could see the future in front of me.

Rylie's words get to me.

What if I don't have a future at all?

NINETEEN

DHAMPIR NEEDS

I SIT IN THE DONOR dining hall at a corner table with the King brothers. Aspen holds my hand, sitting so close that it's like he's resisting the urge to pull me onto his lap while Torrance practices his skills in feeding me with a fork. I didn't even protest to them treating me like I can't take care of myself only because I know it isn't about that. It's more about the idea of showing that they can take care of me. It's a bit silly, but I could use the distraction from the soft gossip swirling through the room.

Berkeley nudges my foot with his, drawing my attention from Torrance cutting off a small piece of chicken like he's afraid I'll choke. "This is a good time to practice your selective hearing, Fi."

I peek up at him, my eyes flitting past to stare at Rylie sitting at a table across the room with Patrick and Ivo. The three of them glare in our direction but only the other tables speak about us. After a short argument between Hudson and the rest of his brothers, they agreed that the best thing to do was pretend nothing happened. I doubt Rylie would open her mouth to anyone, and she most definitely won't try to murder the Kings in front of a room full of people, but I'm still on edge.

I don't like that she's hanging with Ivo or that Berkeley had to offer him a formal work contract to join the Kings' staff upon completion of his daylight security training program.

"Are you sure we can't just go eat in our suite?" I ask for the third time. "I think I'd even prefer to sit with you in the vampire dining hall. Anything is better than this."

Hudson waves his glass of gen. pop. blood at me. It sloshes around because I'm nearly certain he's waiting for me to turn my back to drink it. He's taking the possibility of me becoming jealous seriously. It's almost silly. "We're required to mingle for meals with very few exceptions, and right now, I prefer to hear a bunch of people complain about us being here than deal with a bunch of covens trying to get your attention. The Powers are completely obsessed with you since Berkeley announced our claim."

"They can't comprehend how we willingly chose to share you," Torrance adds.

I sigh. "So, they also think I'm a unicorn." The more attention I get, the harder my secret will be to keep.

Hudson smirks at me. "No, they just imagine you being fucking delicious."

"Which is absolutely true." Aspen pulls my hand out from under the table to kiss the back. "Then we also have the Saints betting that we'll annihilate each other before the end of the term."

Hudson bares his fangs and waves his hand. "Don't even get me started on the Regals."

"I can deal with all that," I say, turning to them. A bunch of intrigued vampires is the least of my worries. At least they would whisper low enough to talk behind my back.

"Yeah, sure. You will unintentionally stab the beasts. We were instructed not to rub you in anyone's faces." Hudson thunks his head on the table. "Which is impossible. I want everyone to die of jealousy."

"We also want to keep an eye on Rylie," Berkeley admits, shifting in his chair to purposely stare at her. She and Patrick drop their gazes to their plates, but Ivo braves staring right back, even daring to turn his focus to me.

Lifting his hand, Ivo waves. Rylie grabs his fingers and yanks his arm down. I can hear her hiss his name all the way over here. The action reminds me how the elders promote fearlessness instead of common sense. They find it important to show vampires that they can try to make them submit with fear but they're far from cowardly.

"That guy is obnoxious as fuck," Hudson mutters, the silver flash in his eyes turning the green color turquoise. "He might show great potential as the head of daylight security, but I'm going to lose my shit if I have to work with him. I don't like how he looks at our girl."

"I'm sitting right here," I remind him, reaching out to push his shoulder.

Hudson twists his lips, crinkling his nose. "I don't like how he looks at you," he repeats. "And sorry, love. I'm not ignoring you. Since I can't whisper to my brothers things I don't necessarily want you to hear, you're just going to have to pretend you don't."

I grin at him. "Never. But you should know that I like how unfiltered you are. I'm still learning to read you, so you make it easy to know what's on your mind."

"You'll probably change your mind soon," Aspen whispers.

Hudson growls. "Look at him. He is testing us, knowing he has the contract. I'm going to go over there and—"

Aspen chucks a carrot at Hudson, getting it right in his mouth to shut him up. Hudson spits it out into his hand and puts it into a napkin. Scooting closer, Hudson searches the table for something to retaliate with, but I smack his hand as he tries to grab a grape from my plate.

Torrance stabs at Hudson's hand when he tries again, missing his finger. "I think you've misplaced your annoyance, brother." He offers me another bite of broccoli while talking to Hudson. "Mr. Nowak went over and beyond to protect Fiona. I think you're mad that Mr. Jimenez put you both in a bad position in the first place."

"And that the board gave the region to the damn Knightly brothers," Aspen adds.

"Don't fucking remind me." Hudson stands from his seat and gulps his cup of blood so quickly that I don't realize it until he sets the empty glass on the table. Strolling around, he bends over my shoulder and silently asks for a kiss with his eyes.

I tilt my head without giving in. "If it makes you feel any better, I don't like Ivo either. Maybe you can stick him in an outpost or some shit. That's what the elders used to do with the soldiers they found...inadequate to be around the females."

He groans. "You did not just make me think that the elders did something right."

I smile and kiss him. "Pretend it was all my idea."

"My brilliant love," he murmurs, kissing me again. "I can't wait to be done with the training program so that we can enjoy you without the bullshit of everything else here."

"How much longer do we have, anyway?" I ask, staring into his green eyes.

"Eternity."

I raise my eyebrows.

He sighs. "Well, it feels like it, especially now that we had to swap our training focus from regional head to city head. There's an adjustment from knowing you're running it all to having to answer to some other asshole."

Aspen pats his back. "Could be worse, brother. They could've removed us from the program completely."

"Don't remind me." Kissing me once more, Hudson straightens up. "I expect you to take good care of our girl the rest of the day, Aspen." He rests his hands on my shoulders. "See you later, Fiona."

Torrance kisses my cheek and gets to his feet next. "Try not to get into any trouble. I look forward to getting the day with you."

Berkeley fills Torrance's suddenly empty seat and drapes his arm over my shoulder. "Don't forget. I've requested some private time in the lab after your Personal Donors Support Group. We can run some tests on you then."

"You sure that's a good idea?" Aspen asks.

Berkeley tightens his jaw. "I will not leave evidence anywhere. I need to see a few things to make sure Fiona's okay and compare her bloodwork from when she was enrolled until now."

Aspen releases a small growl. "As long as you know she's not a fun, new subject to experiment on."

I squeeze his hand. "Aspen, relax. I asked Berkeley to do this for me. I want to see if things have changed since the you-know-what." Now that the guys know about my dhampir mutation, they can help me out. I don't enjoy feeling like I have no control. I need to know exactly what changed and if things are permanent.

"Okay," Aspen says quietly. "If it's what you want."

"I do. It's important in helping me fit in. I get out of control in certain situations worse than ever." I say the words like I do just in case. They both know what I'm talking about. "During our time—"

"You don't have to worry about that. I'm okay. You're fine. It was quite the experience I'd like to happen again." Aspen rubs the spot on his neck where I bit him, which is now completely healed.

His words trigger my blood hunger, and I shiver. Berkeley leans in close and touches my chin until I look at him. He kisses me sweetly, letting me enjoy the softness of his lips. Aspen sandwiches me between his brother, also giving me attention by kissing my neck.

I blush at the utter silence falling through the dining hall. "Everyone's watching."

"Let me get you out of here," Aspen says. "I know somewhere we can sneak to before your next class."

I bob my head and smile. "You sure you can handle it again?"

"I'll gladly assist," Berkeley says with a grin.

"Actually, that might be a good idea. You're quite insatiable." Aspen's whispered breath gets to me in a good way.

The two of them stand at the same time and pull me to my feet. Everyone's gazes follow us as we stroll together through the dining hall hand-in-hand. Rylie's face turns from annoyance to full-blown disgust. I try to remain expressionless. The other donors stare at us in more awe and fascination, some with a look of what I can only describe as jealousy. One guy near the door frowns in pity.

"Good time to practice selective vision, Fi," Berkeley says, sliding his arm around my back. "It'll come in handy."

I focus on the floor, watching how our steps remain in perfect sync. "I don't know if I'll ever be good at any of that."

"Start by looking at something you like," Aspen says.

I sweep my head to look at each of them a few times. "I'm going to get a neck ache keeping this up."

Berkeley chuckles. "But you managed."

He's right. I got right past Rylie and Ivo without wanting to scream. I probably looked ridiculous doing it, but I'd rather feel lame than out of control with my anger. Every time I think about Rylie and what she had planned with the elders makes me so upset. I thought she was my best friend. I never imagined she'd do that.

"Quick, Berkeley," Aspen says, speeding ahead of us to open a door at the end of the hall.

Berkeley lifts me off my feet, kissing me to steal any

possible noise from escaping my mouth. My back hits a wall, and he continues to kiss me, slipping his tongue into my mouth, turning my hunger into lust in the process.

"Don't bite him," Aspen whispers, standing ultra-close. "Let him bite himself."

I ease away from Berkeley. "Don't let me drink more than you can handle."

Berkeley smirks at me. "I don't think you realize how impossible that task is."

"It's a good thing there are four of us," Aspen teases, "but why don't you let me hold her? I kind of like having you around, brother."

Berkeley laughs as I jokingly squeeze his waist between my thighs, making it harder for him to detach me. Aspen hooks his arms around me and nudges my hair from my neck, extending his fangs, knowing how my body reacts to the thought of taking things somewhere we're not supposed to under the academy rules. But I hate rules and laws and being told what to do. I was raised as a rebel after all.

"Careful or I'll ask you to bite me," I whisper.

"I think we could get away with it. If that's what you want." Aspen flips me around to kiss me. "Just a taste."

"Just a taste," I repeat.

Berkeley loosens my tie to unfasten a few buttons on my shirt. Shifting behind me, he eases my top from my shoulder for Aspen. Aspen uses his teeth to pull my bra strap down to kiss my tingling skin. Shifting me up higher, he brushes his lips to the top of my breast showing from my bra. I gasp a small breath at the sensation Aspen creates while listening as Berkeley extends his fangs. He bites his arm, and the scent of his blood trickles through the air.

Pressing his chest into my back, Berkeley assures no space between the three of us as he offers his arm to me, caging my head a bit. His other hand glides around my stomach, taking over holding me in place. Aspen meets my gaze with Berkeley's arm between us. His eyes flash his hunger and desire, sending my heart racing.

"You sure about this?" he asks, his voice deep and breathy with lust.

Just the thought turns me on, and I moan my consent, savoring the taste of Berkeley while yearning for Aspen to savor the taste of me. Tipping my head back, I rest it on Berkeley's shoulder, stretching my neck a bit to give him a choice of biting me anywhere from my neck and shoulder to the top of my breast.

Berkeley breathes softly near my ear, his heart thumping against my back in an attempt to race mine. "Take a breath and relax."

I don't even feel the prick of Aspen's fangs and only a bit of good pressure as his mouth takes over to suck my blood from a spot on the front of my shoulder. I moan against Berkeley's skin, the sensation better than any bite I've received before.

I break my mouth from Berkeley's arm and stretch my

neck to kiss him. He shifts to stand next to us, watching my face as his brother drinks. From his obvious lust-filled eyes, Berkeley doesn't care who bites me as long as I enjoy it. Meeting my lips again, he kisses me more passionately than the tease of a kiss he gave me when they brought me into this empty office.

Aspen eases his mouth from his bite. "That was indescribable, Fiona. You're so—"

"Mister and Mister King," a familiar voice says.

The door to the small office swings open, and Headmistress Rasmussen stands in the doorway with her hands on her hips. Berkeley pulls from our kiss before I realize what the headmistress caught us doing and rushes to the door. He rolls down the sleeve of his shirt and wipes his mouth. A second later, he disappears from the room with the headmistress.

"Just bring out Ms. King," she snaps.

"The three of you have some explaining to do."

TWENTY

REBEL DESTINY

"WE'RE IN SO MUCH TROUBLE, right?" I ask, keeping my voice low.

"We'll be okay. Don't freak out." Aspen's quick to staunch the bleeding of his bite to button my shirt. He sets me on my feet and takes my hand, guiding me to the door. Voices murmur through the wood, and I hear the headmistress call out Aspen's name for him to hurry.

Aspen gives me a once-over and rubs the pad of his thumb over the corner of my mouth to assure not a drop of Berkeley's blood is present. Nerves bunch my stomach at the whisper of my name as Berkeley and Headmistress Rasmussen discuss me.

Aspen straightens his shoulders and opens the door, stepping out first. "Forgive us, Headmistress. Ms. King...wanted us to fulfill part of her contract without an audience, and we didn't have time to head back to our suite."

I nearly die at his words and how they can be misconstrued. "He means kiss. I wanted to kiss him."

"No need to share such details, Ms. King," Headmistress Rasmussen says, tightening her mouth. "Your relationship with the Kings is none of my business unless you have a complaint or they break one of the rules such as the no-bite policy tied to your contract. Was Mr. King feeding on you or was it something else?"

I drop my gaze to the floor, wishing it would open up so I can get away from her. I don't know if I'll ever get used to vampire customs. They are far less modest about things than humans. With the way some of the humans looked at me in the dining hall while I was letting Aspen feed me, I had to keep checking to make sure I wasn't suddenly naked or some shit.

I lick my lips. "Something else."

"I apologize for making you state the obvious, but it must be done to assure you aren't being mistreated. I hope you understand." Headmistress Rasmussen's words surprise the hell out of me. She almost sounds as if she cares about the donors here. Maybe she does. I don't know her well enough to be certain.

"I do," I say.

"Very good. Now, if you will excuse us, I need a moment of the King Coven's time. You may head to your next class. You are no longer on probation for being a flight risk." Headmistress Rasmussen waves in the direction of the wing where most of the donor classes are.

"Allow me to walk her, headmistress," Aspen says. "I'll be fast."

"I don't think that's necessary, Mr. King. One of the biggest obstacles personal donors face is getting space outside of their keepers. You don't want to smother her." She waves at me again to get moving. "It also helps to teach you control, so you don't fall into a habit of wanting total isolation. You can't manage a city if that becomes the case."

I squeeze his hand. "I'll be fine."

The soft mumble of voices from the dining hall grows louder as the donor students disperse. Headmistress Rasmussen turns to look at the group of people. "If you'd feel more comfortable after yesterday's unfortunate occurrence, Mr. Nowak can walk Ms. King where she needs to go."

Ah, hell.

Before I can tell the headmistress that I'm fine on my own, she motions for Ivo to come in our direction. He doesn't hesitate, his eyes already on us like he's been looking for me, and picks up his pace, leaving Rylie with Patrick.

Neither of them waits, and they disappear into the crowd. I wonder how much she's told the future personal donor about me. Hopefully nothing.

"Mr. Nowak, will you please escort Ms. King to her next class? It's Donor Sex Education with Dr. Abernathy."

"What?" I ask, turning to Berkeley. "When did this happen? I thought I was taking strength training next."

"Your misters have the right to change your courses to anything they feel necessary at any time, Ms. King. Expect to bounce around quite a bit this term as your coven figures things out and decides what programs are most beneficial. Now, go along."

Ivo stiffens, curling his fingers into fists. "Right this way, Ms. King."

I groan and hug Berkeley, silently swearing into his ear that he's in so much trouble for changing my classes without telling me first.

"Wasn't me," he murmurs. "It's Aspen's night. He tailored your schedule."

Aspen spins me from his brother. "I'll accept all punishment you find necessary, but I think learning from a lecture before you get your hands on experience will—"

"Shhh," I say, covering his mouth with my hand. "No excuses."

"You'll thank me later," he says into my fingers. "I saw Berkeley putting together a lesson plan for your time together."

I scrunch my nose and glare, turning away from them before my mind wanders to anything sexual that could happen between us. Straightening my back, I steel myself to Ivo's gaze and stride past him. I don't exactly want to turn my back on him, but I also don't want to walk beside him. I glance over my shoulder at the now empty hallway, trying my best not to freak out at Berkeley and Aspen's sudden absence as they disappear with Headmistress Rasmussen.

Ivo picks up his pace to stroll next to me anyway, purposefully getting into my personal space now that the guys aren't watching. "You okay, Ms. Flamme? Rylie mentioned having a rough day, but she wouldn't say why."

"We had a fight," I say.

"They didn't hurt you, did they?" Ivo rushes to cut me off to give me a once-over.

His eyes rove from my face to the front of my shirt, and I cringe, realizing I have two noticeable blood spots blossoming on the fabric from Aspen's bite. Reaching up, Ivo attempts to tug at my collar for a better look. I swing out and smack him across the face, my whole body screaming to kick him in the balls next for trying to touch me without my permission.

"I didn't fight with my misters. I fought with Rylie," I say. "And try to touch me like that again, and I'll break your hand. The blood isn't mine."

He knows I'm lying since vampire blood is darker than human blood, but it's none of his business. "What was your fight about? Maybe I can say something that can help." I'm glad he doesn't accuse me of lying or persist to ask questions.

"It was nothing," I say. "We'll get over it."

He steps a bit ahead of me to gaze at me directly again. "Sorry to hear that."

"Wait, what? You don't want us to get over it? But you said—"

"I meant I wanted to say something to help you make the right decision to leave her here. You don't belong here. You're better off back home. But Rylie? She scored us both positions in an elite household. She *is* better off here. Maybe the elders wouldn't hoard so many women then. The elders don't understand the benefit of creating family bonds in a vampire household. Work contracts pass down to children. We're talking about growing an army behind enemy lines with people these blood suckers trust."

Holy shit.

"Plus, Rylie's perfect. She's hot, not one of those anti-expand the donor population people, and she can handle herself. I can't wait for my formal union to her. I know she likes that Patrick douche, but she'll come around with me."

This. Guy.

I might be pissed off at Rylie, but there is no way in hell that I'm going to stand listening to another second of Ivo talking about Rylie like the soldiers talk about me. He doesn't want a partner that comes with a union. He wants to use her to advance his status and secure a future that dooms all of his future heirs.

"She won't come around to you, because she won't be here," I snap, shoving past him to pick up my pace. "I'm getting her out of here."

"The only one leaving is you," he says, raising his voice enough to get me to stop in my tracks. "It's time you stop resisting. You don't want me to declare you a traitor to the elders now, do you, dhampir?"

I hiss and rush him, slamming into his broad chest to knock him off his feet and onto his ass. Swinging my arm, I punch him in the nose. "Never, and I mean never, call me that again. Are you crazy? Do you want to get me caught and killed?"

Ivo twists his face and spits out blood on the floor next to us. "That would get you to run, wouldn't it? We have soldiers waiting in the city to take you home. Isn't that what you'd prefer? Go home instead of getting caged and drained over and over again until some asshole takes it too far and finishes you off."

Anger rushes over me, and I slap him across the face. "You wouldn't dare. I don't even know this place well enough to get out of here."

"That's what I'm here for, dhampir!" Ivo shouts, locking his hands to my wrists before I can punch him again. "No one will suspect it's me to show you. You just ran away. You managed to overpower the guards. You beat the hell out of me when I stopped you. You are a dhampir. You can take on these asshole vampires. That's what you were born to do!" The narrative he creates could work on a number of people. I'm not exactly docile.

Fear erupts in my heart, tightening my chest. I break free of his tight hold on my arms and swing at his face over and over again, trying to get him to stop yelling my secret.

"You better run, dhampir. I think I hear a guard coming. If they catch you, you'll be dead."

I grind my teeth and sock him so hard that his head jerks sideways, but still, he doesn't stop laughing and yelling like a psycho.

"Run, dhampir! Run!"

I can't believe this is happening. The last thing I expected was for Ivo to resort to forcing me to leave the academy by giving away my secret. And my burst of fear proves him right. I can't stay here, not if more people discover who I am. Being considered a donor is bad enough. But a dhampir? They'll treat me worse than a donor. They'll treat me like an animal. A mythical creature. But not in the way the Kings treat me. I don't know what it is about them, but they're different. They claimed me before they even knew about me. That claim led to a bond, one I can't imagine breaking.

"Run, dhampir!" Ivo yells again.

Scrambling off him, I get to my feet and stare around the hallway. Voices murmur from all different directions, but they all sound like they're coming toward me. I dash a few feet away from Ivo and try to open the door to one of the offices. If I hide, one of the Kings will surely find me. They'll help me. I know they will.

While Ivo might be right about me choosing to run instead of risking staying here to be caged, he's utterly wrong to think I'd dare run to Blood Rebels. I find both options utter shit and will create a third plan. I did choose the Kings and life with them after all. I intend to see it through.

"What are you doing, dhampir? You can't hide. You must run!" Ivo pushes me from behind, forcing me to stumble in the direction that leads to the lobby of the donor education wing.

"Hudson!" I yell, hoping that he's connected to one of the security feeds I know are capturing every one of my moves.

"I put the cameras on a loop, dhampir. The only ones coming for you will be those who hear your yells. They're probably fighting each other now to get to you first." Ivo tries to grab the back of my shirt to slow me down.

"Hudson!" I yell again.

"Are you stupid? You don't think I wouldn't assure those blood suckers who've claimed you would be around to fight in your name."

Icy dread drips down my back. It's probably why the headmistress called Berkeley and Aspen away. Ivo knew that they'd hesitate leaving me, so he happened to be there. He knew that since he got a contract, she'd ask him to walk me.

I spin out of his reach and hit my ass on the floor, only to jerk my foot up to kick him in the balls. He drops to his knees like I expect, clutching what I hope is a bruised as hell cock. I kick him again in the solar plexus, making him heave and spit out more blood.

Catapulting to my feet, I dash away from Ivo. All I need to do is reach the reception counter. I can force the receptionist to call one of the guys, and they'll help me. They'll protect me against people I might not be able to protect myself from.

I only make it twenty feet away before an alarm blares so loudly that my head spins, my brain feeling like it'll explode at any second. I cover my ears and bow forward. Something collides into my back, sending me sprawling.

Ivo drags me from the floor, pinning me against his chest. I flail and buck, trying my best to knock him off balance. "You've taken too long, dhampir. You might not make it out now. The alarm should give us a few extra minutes."

The alarms cut off. My ears ring and my head pounds. I can barely focus on the world around me.

"Fiona?" Rylie's voice cuts through the incessant ringing in my ears. "Ivo, what are you doing?"

"Get the door," Ivo snaps. "Hurry. Security's coming."

"No! Rylie, don't. He's psychotic. He won't stop yelling that I'm a dhampir." I kick my legs up, stopping Ivo from forcing me through the door Rylie holds open.

Rylie blocks Ivo from trying again. "Are you kidding me? You're going to get her killed."

"Only if she stays. This way she has to go," Ivo says, spinning and running backward, not giving Rylie a choice but to move unless she wants to get knocked over. "Now, go run ahead. Get the next door. We have minutes."

Rylie hesitates.

"I have a job. *We* have a job. The elders gave her a rebel destiny. You don't want her to get captured and caged, do you? She'll take us with her. She'll tell them what we've done. It's bigger than her." Ivo tightens one arm around me to grab the next door.

"Please, Rylie. He'll guarantee you never go home. He wants to knock you up and force a lifetime service contract on your heirs. He thinks you deserve to be here," I say. "Don't help him. Get the Kings. They won't kill me."

"They'll just cage her once they find out."

Rylie surprises Ivo by grabbing a dagger off his belt. She aims it at him, forcing him to stop. "They already know about her."

"What?" Ivo asks.

"They've bonded. I've seen it myself." Her soft voice grows stronger. "They let her claim them."

"Come on, Rylie. You're not going to stab me. Just move before they find us." Ivo tries to dodge past her, and she jerks out the dagger, catching it on his jacket.

"No. Let her go," Rylie demands.

"I can't. We have a job."

"She's not a job. She's my best friend, even if I don't understand any of her decisions." Rylie jabs the dagger again. "Now let her go. If she wants to stay and put her life into the hands of the Kings, then let her."

Ivo grunts in my ear. "No, you fucking traitor. This isn't your choice to make. She belongs to the elders, not a bunch of elitist monsters who want her to drop to her knees and bow down to their every desire."

Ivo spins and rushes Rylie with me between them. Fire explodes through me, the dagger sinking into my side. I scream out in pain and thrash hard enough to break free. I clutch my side, pushing through the pain to run in the direction we came from.

"Fiona, wait up. Come this way," Rylie says from behind me.

I spin to see her standing at another door that I thought was an office but it's a stairwell going up. Ivo gets to his feet, drawing my attention to him. He yells out in anger and yanks a gun from under his jacket in a hidden holster.

"Rylie, get down," I say, pushing my legs to move.

Ivo fires the weapon, hitting the door. Something dark inside me snaps. I charge forward, the pain in my side triggering my dhampir mutation instead of weakening me. Ivo points the gun at me next, but he doesn't shoot. He hesitates, frozen in the fear I elicit inside him. I launch at him and knock him onto his back. Wrapping my hands around his throat, I squeeze as hard as I can.

"Fiona, hurry. We have to go," Rylie says.

I clench my teeth. "I can't leave him."

"You're not a killer."

"I'm not the fucking gift to humanity either!"

"Fiona, behind you!"

I don't get a chance to move before two strong hands rip me away from Ivo. I thrash and buck, kicking my legs and flailing my arms, doing everything I can to break free of the vampire restraining me.

"Dhampir! She's a dhampir," Ivo says from the ground. "She's a fucking dhampir here to destroy everything the academy stands for."

"You asshole!" I yell. "He's the rebel. He's trying to kidnap me from the Kings. Get my misters."

"Right away, Ms. King," the familiar voice of Mr. Jimenez sounds in my ear. "But please, you have to stop fighting."

I relax in my combat instructor's arms until he sets me on my feet. I clutch my side. "I've been stabbed. Please, call Berkeley."

"Mr. Knightly, please take Ms. King. Be sure to apply pressure to her wound. It would be a shame to waste any more of her blood," Mr. Jimenez says. "Ms. Reynolds, please come closer and let Dawson pick you up and relocate you to the headmistress's office. I'll assist Mr. Nowak."

The sudden sharpness of his voice ignites fear inside me. "Please, let Rylie go. She had nothing to do with this."

A figure blurs in front of me, and the dickwad who tried to bite me in the middle of class materializes in front of me. "Ms. King, don't fight. Don't scream."

This fucker. He's trying to manipulate my mind.

I jab my fist up and clock him in the nose.

He snarls.

ETERNAL BLOOD SOURCE

THE KNIGHTLY ASSHOLE SHOVES ME against the wall and digs his fingers into my side. I scream out in pain and anger. It takes everything in me not to black out, the edges of my vision shadowing.

"You little bitch," the vampire says, bringing his bloody hand to his mouth. He sucks my blood off each of his fingers. "She's consumed blood."

"Because she's a dhampir!" Ivo shouts.

"Shut him the hell up and sit his ass down," Mr. Knightly says to Mr. Jimenez. "Prove to me your worth if you want to be the head of security in Orion Falls."

"Yes, Monterey," Mr. Jimenez says. The combat instructor grabs Ivo by the collar and locks him in his gaze.

"Please, you can't believe anything he says. He was trying to kidnap me," I say, purposely softening my voice. "He doesn't think the Kings should get to claim me."

The corner of Monterey's lips pulls up into a whisper of a smile, his eyes flashing silver at me. Something dark flashes in his grayish-blue eyes that lack any definition, giving him an eerie look. They glow against the deep brown, nearly black color of his long hair hanging loosely over his shoulders. The vampire's not exactly handsome, more beautiful maybe, ageless to a point that I can't tell how old he might've been when he transitioned.

"I never thought I'd agree with a donor, but here I am. The remaining King brothers lucked out inheriting your contract like they did. One might think they planned to betray Culver to strip him of his position to take over. The bastard wasn't exactly one I'd want to serve." Monterey's fangs extend past his lip the longer he holds my gaze.

"Please, I need a health keeper. I'm bleeding out." I don't know what else to say to get him to do something other than memorizing every inch of my face with a leer that scratches at my nature. I hate being under his scrutiny.

"Hmm, I have some medical experience, Fiona. Allow me to take a look."

I don't get a chance to protest as Monterey tugs the

hem of my untucked shirt up to expose my middle to him. His cool fingers brush my side around the accidental stab wound. My heart races, my body stiffening under his unwanted touch.

"What a surprise. The wound coagulates already. Her body's regenerating unlike anything I've seen on a donor," Monterey says, bending down a little to get a better look. He shocks me by jamming his finger into my side once more, opening the wound all over again to spill my blood.

I scream and jerk my knee too fast for him to avoid, smacking him hard in the chin. His jaw cracks under the force. Monterey releases a guttural, scary-ass sound and locks his fingers into my hair, yanking me off my feet. My body stretches with the movement, the pain so intense I black out.

A deep growl yanks me from a void in my mind, and I flail, pressing my hands into...not the floor. I gawk down at Monterey beneath me, both of my hands crushing his bones in his chest. He can't even scream out as I squish everything inside him with my movement. Someone locks their hands around me to drag me off him.

"Stop her," Dawson yells.

"Run, Fiona!" Rylie pulls me with her, the shock of everything sending my mind whirling.

I clutch onto two handfuls of guts and shattered bones, the force of my punches so strong that I broke through Monterey's sternum and everything with my bare hands.

I ripped out his heart.

I rub my mouth on my white sleeve, turning it red. Shit. I drank his blood. I have never been able to do this before, but it was like my injuries and anger, everything terrible about this situation, released the wild beast inside me.

"Don't let them escape," Dawson says, abandoning his brother's body to get to his feet.

Mr. Jimenez materializes behind me. "I will drain Ms. Reynolds if you resist."

"Run, Fiona," Rylie says, pushing me away from her. "I'll hold them off."

None of us has time to react when the school alarm blasts through the air again. I bend forward and cover my ears, trying to muffle the ear piercing noise. Dawson hooks his hands around me and lifts me to my feet. Rylie yells, trying to fight off Mr. Jimenez. Neither vampire reacts to the noise.

"They're on their way," Mr. Jimenez says. "Won't be long until they fix the problems Mr. Nowak caused."

"Then come on. We just need to get them out of here," Dawson says near my ear. "We can claim they ran."

Panic explodes through me, and I kick and thrash, trying once again to break free. Dawson locks his arms around me, keeping me facing away from him so that I can't try to punch his heart out like I did with Monterey.

These fuckers are going to take me instead of turning me into the headmistress. What they plan to do with me? I have no idea, but there is no way in hell I want to find out. The lighting shifts with the change in the air, and I automatically gasp in a breath of the cool night. It's been a while since I've been outside, and I had no idea how much I'd miss it. How much it makes me want to fight even harder.

"Take them around to the guest cottages," Mr. Jimenez says. "We'll lock them up until we get them on the move outside of the premises."

"I'll call the rest of my brothers. They'll want to be here when I drain her," Dawson says.

"It would be a shame to kill her. You saw how quickly she heals. I've heard stories during The Divide about dhampirs. They're apparently eternal blood sources. A gift that will give us blood forever without having to rely on the shit show that is left of humanity." Mr. Jimenez closes the space. "Isn't that right, Ms. Flamme?"

I snap my teeth at him and yell, "Help!"

"Didn't I warn you what would happen to Ms. Reynolds?" Mr. Jimenez adjusts Rylie off his shoulder and dangles her placid body in front of him. She doesn't move or scream, trapped in the awful hold of Mr. Jimenez's mind manipulation.

"Rylie," I say. "Rylie, fight. Fight. You can break out of it. Please, you have to fight."

She remains unmoving in Mr. Jimenez's arms, her head lolling to the side to expose the skin of her neck. I jerk my head back and head-butt Dawson in the nose, catching him off guard. He drops me to the ground, sending pain exploding in my knees. Instead of rushing to pick me up again, he yanks Rylie from Mr. Jimenez.

"Mr. Knightly, let Ms. Reynolds go." Headmistress Rasmussen's voice cuts through the air, drawing everyone's attention to her. "If you do not, you'll face a meeting in front of the board."

Dawson ignores the headmistress and extends his fangs. "It'll be worth it. They'll praise me for taking care of the rebel problem you let grow within the academy."

"Mr. Jimenez, would you like to test your luck as well? Last I checked, you should have already left the premises for purposely breaking a rule the board has set in place for everyone's safety."

Mr. Jimenez growls and rushes me, snatching me from the ground. He throws me over his shoulder, spinning to look for a way out. Dozens of shadows move and shift through the manicured hedges and sleepy gardens of a grand courtyard.

"To the left," Dawson tells Mr. Jimenez. "My brothers will meet us."

Mr. Jimenez chooses to go right instead, and Dawson growls and releases Rylie. I reach down and grab at the vampire's belt, trying to find a weapon while his attention focuses on evading Dawson.

"King brothers, you may now intervene. Remember protocol," Headmistress Rasmussen says, her sharp voice whipping through the night. "Let this be a test."

Figures blur, and I spot Hudson running in our direction with a scary-ass sword ready to fight. He doesn't get to close the space. Another vampire darts in front of him, knocking him out of the way.

The world spins out of control, and we hit the ground rolling. I yell out in pain before my voice cuts off at the escape of my breath. I think I pass out again because one second I'm scraping my back on the pavement and in the next I'm hanging over Mr. Jimenez's shoulder with the world blurring around us. Annoyance and anger blend with my slight panic. A game of keep away with me leaves me anxious. If these assholes wouldn't move so utterly fast, I could attack.

I stay frozen, pretending to be unconscious, using everything I know about Mr. Jimenez and the Knightlys to strategize a plan. It takes me a few seconds to get my shit together, my human fear instincts begging my dhampir side to show this asshole who I really am.

Obviously Mr. Jimenez, while an instructor for security and combat, lacks the same power as the vampires he trains. If he didn't, he'd be running a city or region or whatever instead. But, he knows his shit, so he has the advantage of strategizing and knowing what his students are capable of and what they lack. He's fleeing with me to better his chances of survival.

Peeking through my eyelashes, I tilt my head slightly

and glance at Mr. Jimenez's weaponry belt. My options are less than stellar. I don't have training in using the gun, and the one locked on his belt doesn't look like the ones the rebels use from the back-world. I think Mr. Jimenez might have explosives as well. Not exactly something I want to pull free and hope for the best.

The last weapon available looks to be some sort of utility knife. I silently count to three and snatch it, fumbling to spring the blade up. Bunching the fabric of his dress shirt, I yank it free from his pants and jam the blade into his lower back. He arches and flips me off of him, but I force him to the ground with me, my fingers refusing to let his shirt go.

A deep, guttural snarl cuts through the night, and I shove Mr. Jimenez off me and scramble to get to my feet. My sluggish movements can't keep up with my brain, screaming that I need to hurry my ass up or die.

Dawson materializes next to Mr. Jimenez and kicks him hard in the gut, sending him rolling. He crashes into the cement base of the tall, wrought iron fence sectioning off the massive academy property from the dark, wild landscape of who-knows-where.

I stumble away, using the fence to help support my awkward footing. The best I can hope for is for Mr. Jimenez to put up a fight to keep Dawson away from me long enough to get back near the center of the academy. I want to yell for help, but I also don't want to risk some other asshole taking advantage of the situation.

"Fi-i-i-o-o-ona-a-a," Dawson calls from behind me. "Stop running from me. I won't hurt you if you comply. This was all a misunderstanding. I don't want to end your life. I want to make you mine. I'm far more powerful than any of the King rejects. They can't even get past my brothers. You need someone far more powerful for you to take care of."

I slow down, knowing that running is pointless. He only lets me get this far ahead because he can catch up.

"*Me* take care of *you*?" I say, crossing my arms over my chest. "You know what I am, right?"

"An eternal blood source," he says, flashing his fangs.

I glare. "Who survives on vampire blood. A lot of it."

"Is that all it'll take? You want some of my blood?" He raises his eyebrows, his eyes trailing from my face and down the rest of me. Now that I'm not fighting, he's no longer trying to scare the shit out of me. I guess that's why Blood Rebels end up hurt or killed. If you comply, you survive. If you fight, you die.

But I'm not doing either.

I lick my lips, trying to remain calm as he closes the space to me, creeping me the hell out. Instead of letting him touch me, I press my hand to his chest and touch his face to push his messy blond tresses off his shoulder.

"I wouldn't mind a taste," I say, lowering my voice.

"Me, first." Dawson locks his hand around my waist and yanks me to him. Pausing, he grabs a handful of my hair and shifts it from my shoulder. "You will always take care of me first."

My breathing quickens as he slowly leans into me. I link my fingers to his shoulders, standing on my tiptoes. My heartbeat pounds in my head, and I focus on the dark night behind him.

That's where I see him.

I try not to react as Torrance stalks through the shadows of the row of trees that decorate the outskirts of the property. His eyes flash so quickly that they nearly look solid silver. Just the sight of him gives me the courage to do something crazy. To risk my life.

Taking a deep breath, I jerk my head forward and sink my teeth into Dawson's shoulder, biting him hard enough through his shirt to still make him bleed. He hollers but doesn't shove me away like I had hoped. Instead, he smashes my back into the wrought iron fence, lifting me off my feet high enough to catch my shirt on the decorative spikes lining the top.

Reaching for his back, he unsheathes a long sword and aims it at my chest. "Come any closer, and I will cut out her heart."

Torrance stops. "It's over, Mr. Knightly. Your brothers have surrendered. If you hurt Ms. King, it'll be an act of war against my coven. I'll have the right to take your head under the Blood Life Corp authority."

"I think I'm willing to risk it," Dawson says, ripping

the front of my shirt with the tip of the blade.

Torrance releases the scariest, deepest growl in all of existence. "Is she worth your death?"

"You say that like such a thing is possible." Dawson lowers the sword and stabs it an inch into my torso.

I scream and swear, reaching up to try to free my shirt from the fence. Dawson tips his head back and laughs. Torrance rushes closer, unable to control his instincts to try to save me. Spinning, Dawson swings his sword, slicing it through the air. Torrance barely stops in time, taking the blade across his chest.

Dawson rushes Torrance, and the two of them blur in a fight. I take advantage of the distraction and swing myself as hard as I can to free myself from the fence. The fence shakes at the force of something—no, someone—smashing into it. I gasp at the sight of Torrance trying to pull himself free of the wreckage.

"Don't you see, Fiona? This asshole isn't worthy of your servitude. Your blood." Bringing his arm back, Dawson aims his sword at Torrance. He jams it into Torrance's chest faster than I can scream.

Torrance grunts at the force, attempting to dislodge the weapon. Twisting the hilt, Dawson slowly carves the blade up higher to try and cut Torrance's heart free.

"Wait. Wait!" I yell. "Don't kill him. Please."

"You want me to show mercy?" Dawson says, his mouth widening in a smile.

I flick my gaze to Torrance, who shakes his head at me. "Please," I say. "I'll do whatever you want."

"You will anyway." Dawson jerks his arm again, impaling Torrance with the sword.

Another deep growl sounds through the air, and I catch sight of Hudson standing in the middle of the walkway, his shirt torn and stained with blood. Dawson snarls at Torrance and jams the sword so far into Torrance's chest that it stakes into the concrete wall.

Dawson rips one of the broken wrought iron bars and closes the space to me. He doesn't hesitate and shoves it so hard into my stomach that my vision blurs. Something snaps inside me, my need to survive taking me over, and I rip the front buttons off my shirt and thrust myself forward too fast for Dawson to react.

Someone grabs me from behind, dragging me away from Dawson. Bright lights flash through the air, and I buck and twist, my body so filled with adrenaline that I can't feel or hear or barely even see. My eyes focus solely on Dawson as Hudson yanks him to his feet.

"Fiona, it's me. It's okay. I got you," Aspen says, whispering into my ear.

Berkeley kneels in front of me, his eyes darting over every inch of my exposed torso, assessing the damage. He probes at the rod impaling me with his fingers, his face twisting in rage, his fangs extending longer than I've ever seen them.

"Give her blood, Aspen," Berkeley commands.

"But the headmistress is—"

Berkeley snarls. "Do it, now."

Aspen bites his arm and holds it to my lips, the scent of his blood prodding at my very nature. I latch my fingers to him, sucking harder, making him moan in the process.

"Surrender, brother," a masculine voice calls through the air, distracting me from Berkeley lacing his fingers around the rod. "If you surrender, we can salvage our standing."

"We won't need to. I know something that'll change everything," Dawson says, grinning from Hudson's arms. "Just look at her. Look at Fiona. See it for yourself."

Panic tightens my chest. This is exactly what Ivo wanted. He wanted everyone to know what I was so that I'd have to fight. There is no way in hell that I'll just accept a fate other than one of my choosing.

Hudson unsheathes a blade and holds it to Dawson's throat. "Shut up."

"You'll have to kill me," Dawson says with a growl.

A figure materializes behind Hudson. "Mr. King, release Mr. Knightly to me. His indiscretions will be heard of in front of the board. As leading coven of the Academy of Vampire Heirs, the Knightlys have given me word that they will do what is necessary to maintain their status. I will take over from here."

Dawson snaps his head back and releases a loud laugh

at the same time Berkeley pushes the rod completely through me. My screech draws everyone's attention my way, and I squeeze my eyes shut in case my dhampir side decides to reveal itself.

Hudson shoves Dawson away to help Torrance from his place on the ground. More vampires materialize out of nowhere, surrounding us in a small circle, mostly security personnel. I heave a breath, fury pulsing through me at the sound of Dawson chuckling again.

"See, Fiona. Look how many it took to save you." Dawson's mocking voice digs into me. "Come on, now. Open your eyes."

Aspen doesn't have the chance to tighten his grip before I break free. I move faster than I have ever before, the movements enough to stop anyone from reacting. Hudson tries to intercept me, but Dawson thrusts the headmistress out of his way to beat him to me. I crash into Dawson, sending him back, but he flips over and crushes me to the ground.

"Fi!" Berkeley yells.

Dawson grabs my hair, yanking my neck to the side. His fangs extend, and he jerks down to bite my throat. Swinging up, I punch him in the face so hard that one of his fangs lodges in my knuckles, and I break it free, causing him to scream. I shove him off, only to launch on top of him. I pin him to the ground, catching my eyes flashing silver in his wide gaze.

Warmth engulfs my hand, and the scent of Dawson's blood leaves me gasping. Silence falls over the world around us.

"Fiona, please," Berkeley says, coming closer. "You can't kill him. It can't be you."

"Control Ms. King, Mr. King. It seems Mr. Knightly and his coven have a lot of explaining to do." The taps of heels click across the pavement. "Now, which one of you was it? Who transitioned Fiona?"

Transitioned me? Shit. She doesn't know what I am. She's assuming like the Kings first did that I'm a vampire.

No one says anything to her.

"Who transitioned her?" Headmistress Rasmussen repeats.

"No one. Now get her off me, and I'll explain," Dawson says, locking his fingers around my wrist.

Headmistress Rasmussen inches closer to me. "Ms. King. Let him go. If you do not, you'll face some consequences that I'm sure you'd rather die than experience."

"Fiona, please," Hudson says, helping Torrance move closer. "We will take care of him. We have laws. His coven surrendered. If you do this, we might not be able to protect you."

Except I can't just let Dawson go. He knows too much. The Kings have too much faith in their laws, laws I never expected to follow. This is more than about me and them. This is about the future everyone wants to use me against. I can't let that happen. I won't. I don't need protecting. I need someone to stand with me. And I'd like for it to be the Kings. I want it to be them.

I shake my head. "I'm sorry. I can't."

"Ms. King!"

Sinking my hand deeper into Dawson's chest, I lace my fingers around the squishy organ lodged with bone fragments. Dawson's eyes widen, fear stealing away his cocky smile. The Kings surround me, not letting anyone come near. They don't stop me either.

It's in this moment that I realize that they're truly on my side. They know the repercussions of my actions. They know what can happen. Yet still, here they are, backing me up.

I remove Dawson's heart and squeeze it between my fingers, my strength pulverizing it into mush. The weight of my actions catches up to me at the sound of cacophonous growls reverberating through the air, sinking into my body to vibrate deep in my bones.

I fall over into Hudson's arms, and he cradles me against him, automatically biting his arm to give me some of his blood. No one moves near, but I feel the burning stares scorching across my skin.

"Mr. King, that will not work," Headmistress Rasmussen says to Hudson, her voice piquing with curiosity. "She needs donor blood, though I'm not sure I should allow it."

"Allow me to explain, Headmistress." The tenor of Mr.

Jimenez's voice cuts through the air, setting me off. "Fiona is not a vampire. She's a dhampir, and more lethal than I have ever imagined. She has killed three of our best students on this campus, and according to Mr. Nowak, she was sent here to destroy the academy."

"What?" I say, breaking away from Hudson's arm.

Mr. Jimenez flashes his fangs at me. "You have to kill her. If you don't, I will."

NOT A DONOR

BERKELEY, TORRANCE, AND ASPEN RUSH Mr. Jimenez. He doesn't even have the chance to react before Berkeley holds him by the hair and Torrance severs the instructor's head with the discarded sword. Blood splashes over me, and I stare in shock. Hudson catapults us to our feet, and his brothers return to surround us.

"Head to the west wall," Hudson whispers. "We'll leave through the tunnel."

Headmistress Rasmussen appears in front of us, flashing her fangs. She places her hands on her hips instead of unsheathing a hidden weapon. Despite her small frame, the Kings don't try to attack her.

"If you leave, you'll be expelled from the academy. Blood Life Corp will outcast you from the territory," she says. "All inherited assets will be given to the school, including Ms. King's contract."

"We won't let you hurt our girl," Aspens says, releasing a growl.

"If you try to take her, I won't be given a choice." She meets my gaze. "But if you stay, perhaps we can work things out."

"How?" Berkeley asks.

"Return to your suite and wait for my call."

The headmistress disappears with the guards and the rest of the Knightly brothers, leaving us alone with the two vampires we killed. The four of them quickly engulf me in the best hug of my life, sandwiching me between their arms. My muscles loosen, my breath finally slowing. While I'm confused as hell, I can't help but feel relief.

The four of them finally let me go after a quiet few minutes, the night air making me shiver as it cools my clammy, sticky skin. Hudson unbuttons his dirty shirt and drapes it over my shoulders while Torrance helps me stick my aching arms through the long sleeves. Berkeley hunches down in front of me, doing his best to wipe away the blood staining my skin to get a better look at my beaten, bruised, and wounded body.

"This is incredible," he says, touching the small hole from the wrought iron bar. "She's healing faster than a donor given blood does."

"I still think she should drink more," Hudson says, shifting closer. "Now. From me." Opening his arms, he meets my gaze like if I don't hurry, he might die from anticipation.

I wobble a bit, my injuries and exhaustion catching up with me. The adrenaline coursing through my veins dissipates, leaving me feeling weak and utterly human despite the burning swirling through my stomach, begging me to throw myself at Hudson.

I don't have to because he scoops me off my feet and picks me up. Our bodies meet, our bare stomachs touching together as he adjusts my legs around him. He brings his lips to mine and kisses me softly, combing his fingers gently into my hair to hold me to him for a moment longer.

"If that asshole wasn't already dead, I'd murder him for his blood coating your chin. I need to get you cleaned up immediately," he says, wiping his hand across the smear of blood my kiss left on his face.

"I'll kiss her. I don't fucking care if she bathes in our enemies' blood. I just want her close," Torrance says, stepping behind Hudson. He leans over his shoulder and sees if I'll meet him halfway for a kiss. I do.

"Are you okay? I'm sorry I couldn't stop him sooner," I murmur against his mouth.

He groans. "You're not apologizing to me for my failure to protect you."

I smile. "No, I'm apologizing for not saving your ass like I should've."

Chuckling, he kisses me again. "Let's not make a habit out of this. What happened to staying out of trouble so that I could enjoy my time with you?"

I shake my head and roll my eyes. "You can't ask such impossible tasks of me...which leaves me wondering. What now? Why didn't they force us to go with them?"

"It's a test," Berkeley says.

"A test? How can we be tested on something with tasks that force us to fail no matter the answer we pick? She said if you leave, our lives are basically over. But if you stay...I can't. I can't stay. She knows what I am." I rest my head on Hudson's shoulder so that I don't have to look at any of them. "I have to go."

"Fiona," Aspen says softly. "We have to talk about this."

"I'm not letting you leave and ruin everything you guys have worked for. I've ruined enough of your lives." I close my eyes, my heart clenching with my words. It screams at me for saying such things out loud. For daring to put it through something I don't want to happen.

"Come on, love. Don't make me get all sentimental on you," Hudson says. "You didn't ruin...much."

Laughter bubbles in my throat. "Back at you, Hudson."

He hugs me closer. "And you can't expect us just to let you go. We already planned a future together. I'm pretty set on you giving me your virginity."

I lean away and pat his cheek. "How much time do you think we have now?"

He play-growls at me. "Don't tease me."

Four chimes ring through the air as their com devices go off. Berkeley pulls his out of his pocket and looks at the screen. His face twists with his worry, and he glances from his brothers to me and then to the broken fence behind us.

"Fiona," he says, touching his hand to the small of my back. "I'm sorry for this."

I puff out my bottom lip. "It wasn't your fault. I'm healing. I'll be okay."

He swallows, his Adam's apple bouncing with his nerves. "That's not what I'm apologizing for."

Cool dread runs down my spine as his unsaid words ignite panic inside me. I press my hands into Hudson's chest, but he only shifts me to grip me tighter.

"Hudson, please. Put me down," I say.

He buries his face in the crook of my neck. "I'm sorry, love. I can't do that."

I wiggle in his arms, not wanting to full-on fight him. "I need to go. Please. Please. I can't stay here."

"We'll figure this out," Aspen says. "The headmistress—"

My heart falls into my stomach at his words. "She'll kill me."

"We don't know that," Torrance says. "All we know is that if we go, it'll be worse."

"And you're our girl." Berkeley takes me from Hudson. "We're not letting you leave without us. I'm sorry, Fi. You have to stay."

⸺ 👑 ⸺

The second my feet touch the floor, I shove Berkeley to get him away from me. He doesn't even budge an inch while I nearly eat shit, ricocheting off him. Torrance grabs me before my ass hits the floor and hugs me to him, restraining my arms in the process.

"If you don't put me down, I will bite you," I say, my nose pressing into his sweet skin.

"Then bite me," he says. "Whatever you need to do to calm the hell down, do it."

I groan and graze my teeth to his shoulder. I don't actually want to bite him to punish him or anything, but I'm fucking upset. "That makes me not want to bite you."

He relaxes a bit. "Good, because I'm injured as hell and don't know what to expect."

"Give her here. She can bite me," Hudson says, extending his arms out. "I need to make up this bullshit to her."

I swing my attention at him and glare. "Biting you isn't going to make much of a difference if I get killed or caged."

"We won't let that happen," he says.

I struggle in Torrance's arms until he relents and puts me on my feet. "And what do you plan to do? That asshole Ivo ruined my life. The elders ruined my life. I don't think you understand the extent of this. Mr. Jimenez knew things I didn't. So did the Knightlys. They called me an eternal blood source."

"What are you talking about? Ivo? What did he do?" Berkeley says.

It's now that I realize we're not alone in our suite. Rylie sits in utter silence, watching us from the couch. Ivo lays face-first on the floor in front of her like someone mind manipulated him to sleep and just tossed him inside.

Rylie pales at Berkeley's question, at the fact that she falls under the Kings' scrutiny.

"If I tell you, you four better stay in control," I say, sucking my bottom lip into my mouth. "I mean it. If you think I'm mad at you now..."

"Mad? Mad at what? Us saving your life? Us not wanting to see you do something insane? Us refusing to let you break our bond? What kind of mates could we possibly be to let you go so easily?" Torrance's anger surprises me. It's not the first time he's called me out.

"Knock it off, Torrance," Hudson says.

"I have every right to be angry at her too," he snaps.

Hudson flashes his fangs. "Well, save that shit for later. We have more important things to deal with than your hurt feelings."

"Hudson," I warn. "You need to chill too."

Berkeley growls. "Everyone, my room. Now."

One second I'm in the living room and in the next, my back hits Berkeley's bed as Hudson tosses me onto it. I chuck a pillow at him, and he lets it hit him in the face and glares at me like I'm the one in the wrong. The tension between the five of us nears peak level, and I'm afraid something will happen or they'll say something that will bring out the worst inside me.

Berkeley hands me a glass of his blood, the scent so fragrant that my stomach complains that I better hurry and gulp it. "As hot as you are feisty and bitey, I need you to stay in control. It's one thing to attack in self-defense, but to act out in anger is another. You need to be as least threatening as possible, Fi. If the Blood Life Corp board and the academy think otherwise, we're going to face things we're unprepared for."

I chug the glass of his blood, swallowing it so quickly that I don't even enjoy it. Holding out the empty glass, I say, "I need more."

"I got it," Hudson says, biting his arm.

"No, she can have more of mine." Berkeley fills up my glass. "You're acting far too...desperate to take care of Fiona that I worry you might do something stupid."

"Stupid like what exactly?" Hudson presses his hand over his arm to stop the bleeding.

Aspen looks at him. "Run away with her."

"Try to murder the headmistress," Torrance adds.

Berkeley gives up on the glass when I hold it out again and joins me on the bed to pull me onto his lap. "Possibly blow up the academy."

"Don't think this will distract me," I mumble, sucking hard enough that I turn him on in the process. "And I want Hudson next."

Hudson releases the sexiest noise. "See, look what you guys did. Now she wants to test me."

I pull my mouth away and smile. "I'm ready for you."

He flares his nostrils. "Damn it. She's even sexy with your blood all over her face."

I can't stop thinking about what Hudson's brothers accuse him of. They're afraid he'll let our bond get to him. He obviously thinks I'm his weakness, despite knowing that I'll do whatever I can to get them all on my side.

"If you can convince your brothers, I'll let you give me blood in the shower."

"No," Berkeley, Aspen, and Torrance say in unison.

Hudson fake-glowers at me. "So, so naughty. You better save that thought for later."

I sigh and flip off Berkeley to land face-first on his bed. "You guys are pissing me off. You know there probably won't be a later."

"If you keep wasting time trying to use Hudson's horny-ass in your favor, then you're probably right, Fiona." Torrance turns his back on me.

"Someone's moody," I mutter under my breath.

"Because you can't get that this isn't just about you. You think you're the only one in jeopardy, but so are we. We need you to stop thinking like all is lost and remember what you are and what you're capable of, especially with the four of us here with you." Torrance growls under his breath. "You might not be a vampire, but you're also not a donor. If we strategize things right, we might be able to persuade the headmistress into ignoring Mr. Jimenez's declaration about why you were supposedly here. We just need proof."

I roll over and get up, feeling like crap for not just hearing them out and assuming the worst. But it's hard for me to think any other way than the way I was raised. I've been told hundreds of times that if my secret got out, it was over.

"You can give me to the headmistress." Rylie's soft voice draws my attention from Torrance and to the doorway where she hovers. "I will tell her the truth. She can get it from me."

I crinkle my nose. "No, Rylie. You don't have to do that."

"Yes, I do. It's my fault that you're in this position. I should've told you what the elders had planned. I should've stood up to Ivo. Tried harder. I should've been a better friend." She rubs her palms across her cheeks, smearing her tears. "I just want to help, Fiona. It's the least I can do."

"But the elders might find out. They'll consider you a traitor," I say. "You have your own plans."

She braves coming into the room. "I don't care. They've already sentenced me to a life I never wanted. I finally understand why you asked me to help you leave. I can't believe I was sentencing you to the same. I'm really sorry."

I close the space to her and wrap her in my arms. "I'm sorry too. I let everything get into my head and got caught up with...my needs. I didn't consider how awful this must be for you. I don't want to make it worse. I can't ask you to do this."

"Then we'll make Mr. Nowak," Aspen says, standing near the door.

"They'll kill him," both Rylie and I say in unison.

The four of them look at us, but it's Berkeley who says, "Actually, he already has a work contract with us. So does Rylie. It's our responsibility to punish as we see fit. The crimes aren't as intolerable as..." He lets his voice trail off as he looks at me, and I don't even have to hear his thought to know he's silently thinking about the fact that I've killed vampires. "Blood Life Corp doesn't like to waste blood sources if they don't have to. That's what separates us from other territories."

"Other territories? You mean Blood Life Corp doesn't control all donors?" I can't stop my curiosity from getting the best of me.

No one gets the chance to answer because a loud alarm rings through the air, unlike anything I've ever heard. It's loud enough even to send the guys to their knees. Figures blur through our suite, and someone pushes my head to the floor, binding my arms and legs so I can't fight. Berkeley yells for me to stay calm and not to resist.

The last thing I see is the headmistress's heels step inches from my face before she covers my head in a black bag.

"Don't worry, Ms. King," Headmistress Rasmussen says. "I have a few ideas about what to do with you."

With how sharp her voice sounds, I doubt I'll like any of them.

TWENTY-THREE

QUEEN

MY KNEES HIT THE SOFT carpet before I fall forward and land on my stomach. Without the use of my arms or legs, I struggle to roll onto my side. Someone yanks the bag off my head, ripping out some strands of my hair in the process.

"Damn it," I say, stretching my neck up to glare at an unfamiliar vampire that disappears.

Soft voices mumble through the room. It sounds like the whole vampire student population hangs around, waiting to see this shit show unfold. Rolling again, I squish my arms under my back but manage to kick my legs and use my core strength to catapult to my feet. The movement silences the room. I wobble, trying to balance on my bound legs. The task seems impossible, and I fall forward, squeezing my eyes shut as the floor sneaks up on me.

"Got you, love," Hudson says, swiping a knife through the ropes on my ankles.

Torrance takes care of the bindings on my wrists, and I automatically swing my arms and engulf Hudson in a hug. He chuckles into my hair, far less worried about the fact that the headmistress and the security personnel stormed our room to capture us and bring us to stand in front of...not the entire vampire student body. Only a few guys from different covens including some I recognize like the Saints, Powers, and annoyingly one of the remaining Knightly brothers. The three other vampires, including a female, are from covens I haven't had the displeasure of meeting.

All of them stare at me as if I'm the most fascinating thing in the world—and I hate it. It doesn't elicit the good feelings the King brothers do. I feel more like an abomination than the extraordinary being Berkeley, Aspen, Hudson, and Torrance swear I am.

I shift on my feet. "What's this about? This better not be some freaky-ass group feeding. I'll ki—"

Berkeley covers my rebel mouth with his hand. "It's a gathering of city heads that were supposed to belong to the

King—and then Knightly—Region. Anytime there is a shift in power, we're supposed to meet. Usually it would be in front of the board, but the region we were forming hasn't been created, so we keep things under the headmistress's supervision."

Headmistress Rasmussen slaps a wooden rod on her desk, drawing our attention from each other to her. "As you all know, we've lost two powerful, potential region heads in less than two weeks."

All gazes fall on me. I straighten my back, tightening my jaw. If these vampires wanted to intimidate me, they're completely succeeding, but I won't give them the satisfaction of knowing that.

"Outmatched by someone we suspected was a Blood Rebel," the headmistress continues.

"Is she not?" the female vampire asks, studying me from my dirty mouth to my disheveled clothes.

Headmistress Rasmussen locks her eyes on me, daring me to try to deny what she's about to say. "No, she is not. It seems we've unknowingly enrolled a dhampir into our academy."

"A dhampir?" another guy, the leader of the Powers Coven, asks. "What the hell is that? She looks and smells human."

"She basically is." This comes from the Saint leader. "I've heard of the dhampir mutation, and I know that most carriers do not show symptoms. And there aren't many carriers at that. Not anymore. Not since The Divide."

The female places her hands on her hips. "Symptoms?"

The Saint guy looks at me, his brows pinching together. "Those who are symptomatic to the dhampir mutation feed on vampires."

The various expressions crossing everyone's faces cause blush to burn across my cheeks. Only Hudson's big-ass grin helps ease the weird scrutiny—like no one actually believes the truth of my existence. He kisses my temple and whispers that he's glad the fuckers don't look at me like they want my teeth anywhere near them. That he's mine.

"So that's why she killed Culver and Dawson?" the Powers guy asks.

"And Monterey," one of the remaining Knightly brothers says.

"Fuck," someone else whispers.

The female vampire flashes her fangs at me, silver lighting her eyes in fury. She takes a step closer, but Berkeley cuts her off, puffing his chest to make himself even bigger to block her view of me. Torrance and Aspen surround me and Hudson, the wall of muscle helping calm the anxiety triggered by my human half.

"I demand she be punished in accordance to Blood Life Corp law," the Powers guy says.

Torrance growls. "If you actually knew Blood Life Corp law, you would know that females are protected from final donations. Also, as a student of this academy, she has the right to defend herself from attacks by elitist assholes who think they can do whatever the hell they want because of the positions they train for."

The Saint leader cracks his knuckles. "Those laws only apply to blood donors."

"Which she is," Aspen says. "We have her contract that says as much."

"Human blood donors," the female says.

"Enough!" Headmistress Rasmussen interrupts the start of a fight, materializing in between the Kings and the rest of the room. She flashes some impressively long fangs and unsheathes a weapon for the first time ever. "I did not gather you to act as jury and judge to Ms. King's discrepancies. I only gathered you to make a formal announcement. My decision in regards to Ms. King has been made."

Shit. Shit. Shit.

I wish more would argue to prolong what I can't help fearing might be an awful fate for me. They obviously want me dead. They want supposed justice for a bunch of dickwads who never deserved mercy.

"I've decided to allow Ms. King to remain enrolled at the academy," Headmistress Rasmussen says, shocking me. "You all, as the heads of your covens, will be responsible in ensuring that you keep your covens in line at this announcement. Any act against Ms. King will lead to automatic expulsion from the academy."

"What, really?" I ask.

She finally turns her attention to me. "Would you prefer if I brought you in front of the board, Ms. King?"

I shake my head. "No, it's just—I don't understand your reasoning."

Her lips quirk up in a smile. "You don't have to, Ms. King. But if you must know, I took it upon myself to interrogate Ms. Reynolds and Mr. Nowak before I returned them to your suite. Under carefully handled mind manipulation, I extracted some rather interesting information about you and what was planned of you."

I open and close my mouth, a wave of anger rushing through me, hearing that she manipulated Rylie's mind and made her forget. I know Rylie wanted to do what she could to help me, but it could've been handled differently.

I must make a face, because the headmistress takes a step back.

"You're angry," she says.

I consider denying it, but my mouth can't help from agreeing. "Of course I'm angry. I don't agree with getting into people's heads like that. It's invasive."

Obviously, most of the room doesn't agree.

"And how would you suggest we get answers?" She looks at me expectantly.

I shrug. "I don't know. You could've asked me for them. Or at least asked for Rylie's permission."

"And Mr. Nowak?"

"I don't give a damn about that asshole. He tried to

force me to leave," I say.

"Which you didn't want." Headmistress Rasmussen tries to fill in what's going through my mind, but not like she needs the answers, only confirmation for what she suspects.

I throw my hands up. "Of course I don't want to leave, but I also like living. Not being caged."

"Having every one of your needs satiated," Hudson whispers.

I elbow him. "Now's not the time."

He chuckles.

"Indeed, Mr. King. It is not the time. Save your fascinating bond for some other time. I'd like to carry on and excuse you before we lose the entire day for rest." Headmistress Rasmussen links her fingers together. "So, as I was saying, I discovered some interesting information in regards to you, Ms. King. And while my decision might be a bit unconventional, I'd like to see where this goes."

I shift in Hudson's arms and glance at Berkeley, Torrance, and Aspen. "I'm still not sure I understand."

"Of course you don't, but you will. I've decided that you will not only be enrolled as a personal blood donor to the King Coven but also enrolled as the next region head of the King Region."

What the fuck?

The room bursts into growls and yells, all the city heads ready to rush and fight me. The headmistress saunters to her desk and hits something on her computer, setting off an alarm through the room. Everyone drops to the ground, covering their ears at the shock alarm she set off. She returns to me and offers her hand out, helping me from the floor.

Headmistress Rasmussen holds out a glittering dagger to me, leaning in close. "If you feel any of these city heads are not suitable to serve beneath you, now is your chance to eliminate the problem. I'll turn away."

I blink a few times, staring at the heavy dagger in my hand and to the King brothers, already pulling themselves from the ground before anyone else. They disappear from around me and hover over the other vampires, weapons drawn, fangs flashing. They prepare to cut all their hearts out without even a second thought. All for me.

"Wait," I say. "Don't. If you kill them, it could jeopardize the humans who expect to gain contracts in their households."

The shock alarms snap off, and the coven leaders pull themselves together to get back to their feet.

"Remarkable," Headmistress Rasmussen says. "Your decision to spare them due to what you believe would or wouldn't happen to the donors was rather...interesting." She turns to the coven heads. "Let this be a lesson. Running a city goes beyond the power you hold and to what that power can do. Now, return to your suites. Alert your covens of my decision and handle their reactions appropriately. You will tell them she accepted a Blood Vow and will train for the transition. Do not speak of Ms. King's dhampir mutation to anyone outside this room. Consider it confidential until a formal announcement gets made. Everyone apart from the Kings is excused."

Everyone disappears, leaving us with the headmistress. Confusion whirls a dozen thoughts through my mind. What the hell just happened? Is this some kind of joke? She can't be serious about me, a dhampir, enrolling as a region leader. A region-fucking-leader. No one's ever just going to let that happen.

"Are you crazy, Ravenna?" Berkeley says, running his hand through his brown hair. His hazel eyes flash silver. I don't think I've heard anyone ever refer to the headmistress by her first name. "Every vampire in Blood Life Corp will come after Fiona."

"Maybe even other territories," she says, flicking her gaze to mine. "Which means you four must prove your worth to your new coven leader."

"New coven leader?" Berkeley tightens his jaw. "I'm head of our coven."

"Not anymore. Your brothers' loyalty grows stronger for Ms. King. Do you not see it? Do you not feel it yourself? I expect you to continue to fill the King's position of first in line and also as Fiona's health keeper." The headmistress looks at Torrance, Hudson, and Aspen. "The rest of you will act as her advisors and personal trainers. I also expect you to join her in the Personal Donors Support Group on occasion."

"What?" they all ask in unison.

She smirks. "You should understand the dynamics in providing blood, since fulfilling her every need is in her contract."

I blush so crazy hard and try my best to push my nerves away. Because I still have one question, one I won't leave this office until I get the answer to. "What do you get in return? You can't say you've chosen to go through all this trouble because you find me fascinating."

"You're quite perceptive," she says, tilting her head toward me.

"Tell me." My. Mouth. It's already gotten me into so much trouble. I wish it would learn.

"You're a dhampir, Fiona. Someone donors call a predator to vampires or what some vampires call an eternal blood source. But you're neither. You're stronger than I imagined. Different than what I've known. I want to study you. Help guide you. You have not been blinded by the purpose others have given you in life." Reaching out, she pats my shoulder. "You are exactly what our territory needs. You will assist me to gain better control of our future. The board won't be able to deny us the power we deserve."

"This is about power."

"It's always been about power." She turns to the guys. "Now, if you'll excuse me, I have work to do. Take a few days to get everything situated. Possibly celebrate your ascension into the position you deserve."

I don't get a chance to say anything or argue with her before Hudson relocates me into the hallway. The four of them surround me, leaning in close. I take a few deep breaths. My shot nerves leave me trembling.

"Power," I whisper. "She's using me for power."

No one responds, allowing me to process things without pushing their thoughts onto me.

"Doesn't she know it's more than that?" I snuggle my face into Hudson's chest.

"We'll show her," Aspen murmurs, hugging me close.

I purse my lips and look at each of them. "If I can even survive. You saw everyone's reactions. When the world finds out..."

Berkeley laces his fingers through mine. "They'll realize how amazing you are."

"Or deadly," Hudson says with a smirk.

I sigh. "What about being your coven leader? I saw the face you made, Berkeley. Can you handle me telling you what to do?"

Torrance chuckles and whacks him on the back. "We'll guarantee it."

"As long as you don't make me bow," Berkeley says, his voice as light as the silver flashing through his eyes. We hold each other's gazes, his handsome face softening under my scrutiny. I consider teasing him, but he leans in and kisses me.

Aspen shakes his brother's shoulders, pulling me back a bit. "What about if she makes you get on your knees?"

Hudson tips his head back and laughs. "I'd gladly. Maybe she'll do the same."

My mouth drops open, and I scrunch my nose. "Seriously, Hudson?"

Leaning in, he laughs as I nip his lip when he tries to kiss me. "What? I thought you'd like things to be fair."

"What are we getting ourselves into?" I ask, mostly to myself.

Berkeley steals me away from Hudson and envelops me in his arms. "Nothing we can't handle. Not with you by our sides."

Hudson sandwiches me to Berkeley. "Would it be cheesy if I said that I'm happy us Kings found our queen?"

I laugh, my muscles finally relaxing under their touch, their attention, and their confidence that we'll get through this. "Incredibly cheesy."

He fake glares at me. "Whatever, my queen. My thoughts still stand."

I grin and cup his cheeks. "It's a good thing I agree."

DHAMPIR HEIR

"FIONA, WHERE ARE YOU GOING?" Torrance lets me pull him away from the Personal Donors Support Group and toward the elevator that'll take us back to our suite. "We only have a couple of minutes to get to Donor Management."

I smirk and pick up my pace. "A couple of minutes is plenty of time to complete the assignment for class."

"We'll have plenty of time later." He tightens his mouth, tugging my hand to slow me down without forcing me to stop even though he can. "You don't want to be late to your first official region leader class."

"But I can't stop thinking about..." The second the elevator opens, I nudge him on, cornering him against the mirrored wall. He releases a breath through his lips and glances from me to the door sliding closed. "You don't like breaking any of the rules, do you?" I ask him, touching his cheek. "I'm kind of jealous how longingly you just looked at the hallway."

Torrance hits his head on the wall with a laugh, his whole face lighting up. "I break plenty of rules for you, Fiona. And I was not looking at the hallway with anything other than caution. I prefer the stairs."

I stand up on my tiptoes to close the space a few more inches. "You're afraid of being trapped in a box with me."

"When you look at me like that...maybe." He slides his hand around my waist. "But not because of what you think."

"And what exactly do I think?"

Torrance avoids my question by brushing his lips to mine. The elevator dings, and he lifts me up to carry me into the hallway leading to our suite.

"You think I don't want you to bite me," he murmurs.

"That doesn't matter to me." I snap my teeth at him. "I'd be afraid too. I know I can be a savage."

"Far from it," he says, setting me on my feet outside our door. "But I won't lie to you. I might be a bit of a so-called savage myself. I just want to be careful with you. I struggle with my restraint."

I graze my teeth over his bottom lip. "You're not the only one. We can practice our restraint together."

He moans, deepening our kiss. "You drive me crazy."

I ease back a little to meet his dark eyes. "In a good or bad way."

"Both. You infuriate me when you insist on unintentionally testing my capabilities...like at breakfast."

"Gilroy Powers deserved that face full of yogurt," I say with a laugh.

He smirks, nodding. "I know, which is why I appreciate that you do push me to be better. Stronger. Worthy of you. I had never pinned that asshole like that before."

I swing his arm with mine. "I don't believe that. You look like you can handle anyone."

"You make me feel like it, too."

"Which is why it won't be a big deal if we're a little late to Donor Management. We're each other's donors, and we have things we need to manage."

Torrance laughs again and slaps his palm against the digital pad to unlock the door to our suite. A strange scent trickles through the air, stopping both of us in place.

I swing my gaze from Torrance and cover my mouth with my hand. In the middle of our living room, bleeding on the floor, lies a guy I never thought I'd see again in my life.

"Oh, shit," I say, breaking away from Torrance to rush

forward. Dropping to my knees, I push over the familiar Blood Rebel from Mount Light Haven. "Alder? Alder? Can you hear me?"

"Fiona," Torrance says softly, trying to pull me away.

I jerk my head to look at Torrance. "Give him your blood. Quick. He's been badly bitten. You don't think—"

A growl sounds through the air, and I turn my attention to the door to see Berkeley, Hudson, and Aspen hovering around Rylie.

She gasps and runs to me, joining me on the floor to take Alder's hand.

"Oh, my God. What happened?" she asks me. "Did Torrance...?"

"Who the hell is this guy, and how did he get in our room?" Hudson asks, closing the space.

I look up. "We just found him like this. You guys didn't—no, never mind."

"Of course we didn't do this," Berkeley says like he must confirm. "We'd never."

I purse my lips. "I know. I'm sorry. I didn't mean— never mind. Help him, Berkeley. He lost a lot of blood."

"Fiona," Torrance says, squeezing my hand. "He's dead."

Rylie releases a small cry and covers her face with her hands. "Why is he even here? I don't understand. Do you think Ivo got a message out?"

I glance up to look at Hudson with the same silent

question.

Hudson shakes his head. "It would take some serious mind power to break the lock that the headmistress put on his mind. He doesn't even know he was ever a rebel."

"Then who?" I ask. "Alder is from my colony. The elders were training him to be my handler."

That gets all sorts of gruff, growly responses.

A soft knock sounds from the doorway, and a vampire leans on the doorframe, wiping blood from his mouth with a handkerchief. His gaze lands immediately on me, and he offers me a smile, showing off his white, straight teeth without fangs.

"Is this the Kings' residence?" he asks, his melodious voice speeding up my heartbeat.

Berkeley closes the space to him and blocks his way. "Yes." He doesn't say anything else but looks at the vampire like he's preparing for an attack.

"I'm looking for Ms. Fiona Flamme. I heard that she was a personal donor at this residence." The vampire stands taller, glancing at me over Berkeley's tall frame. He smiles again, showing off a dimple on his clean-shaven cheek. His light brown eyes match the golden brown of his hair, shining in the glow of the overhead lights.

"There is no one by that surname here," I say, shifting to get to my feet. "But if you're looking for Fiona King, you have found her."

The man raises his eyebrows. "Fiona King, is it? That's

an interesting change. I think I'd prefer if the academy would recognize your true heritage."

A blip of fear trickles down my back. "I'm sorry? You must be mistaken. I am the leader of the King Coven. If you have a problem with my last name, you can fuck the hell off."

"Ms. Flamme, that is not the appropriate way to greet such a prestigious guest." Headmistress Rasmussen appears in the hallway behind the vampire. "Mr. Flamme, my apologies to have kept you waiting. I had expected Ms. Flamme to be in class."

"I suppose I should've expected she'd take after me, always breaking the rules and whatnot." The man forces Berkeley to move out of the way to enter our suite.

I squeeze Torrance's hand tighter, shifting slightly to get behind him. "Am I supposed to know you?"

He peeks around Torrance. "Actually, yes, dear Fiona. I've been searching for you for a rather long time...well, I've been searching for the Flamme dhampir line. I had lost track of your great-great-grandfather shortly after his birth after the uprising due to Blood Rebels. They took your ancestor and hid him away. Hid you away."

"I don't think I'm following."

He reaches into his pocket and pulls out a weathered piece of paper. "I've come to put my claim on you as my descendant. The power you hold is not meant for such covens as the Kings'. You were born for a far better purpose."

I still, my blood turning cold. "I know my purpose."

"Of course you do. You are my dhampir heir, after all."

To be continued...

Thank you so much for reading *Dhampirs 101*! Check out *Blood Sources 102*, book two of the Academy of Vampire Heirs.

If you love the Vampire Heirs World, don't forget to check out these other Reverse Harem series that take place in the same universe.

The Divine Vampire Heirs
and
The Royale Vampire Heirs

OTHER BOOKS

REVERSE HAREM
The Divine Vampire Heirs Series
The Royale Vampire Heirs Series
Academy of Vampire Heirs Series

YOUNG ADULT PARANORMAL
Call of the Ocean Series
Demon Watcher Series
Demon Within Series
Destined for Dreams Series
Finding Nate Series
Going Ghostly Series
Spark of Life Series
The Merman's Spark Series
When Souls Collide Series

YOUNG ADULT CONTEMPORARY
Falling into Fame Series
Life After Lila

ABOUT GINNA MORAN

GINNA MORAN IS a writer from sunny Southern California. She started writing poetry as a teenager in a spiral notebook that she still has tucked away on her desk today. Her love of writing grew after she graduated high school, and she completed her first unpublished manuscript at age eighteen.

When she realized her love of writing was her life's passion, she studied literature at Mira Costa College in Northern San Diego. Besides writing novels, she was senior editor, content manager, and image coordinator for Crescent House Publishing Inc. for four years.

Aside from Ginna's professional life, she enjoys binge watching television shows, playing pretend with her daughter, and cuddling with her dogs. Some of her favorite things include chocolate, anything that glitters, cheesy jokes, and organizing her bookshelf.

Ginna Moran loves to hear from her readers so visit her

online at www.GinnaMoran.com. You can also find her on Facebook, Twitter, and Instagram. To stay up-to-date on new releases, sign up to her newsletter. You'll not only get exclusive access to extra stories, but you'll be able to participate in monthly giveaways!